Dear Reader,

In the opening scene of *The Safekeep*, Isabel is working in her garden when she finds a broken piece of ceramic under the roots of a dead gourd—"the shard nicked through her glove, pierced a little hole." She brings it inside and places it on the mantle, eyeing it with suspicion, puzzling over its provenance.

I was instantly seduced by the ominous simplicity in these first pages. I cannot tell you how lucky I felt when I learned that Avid Reader Press had prevailed in a nail-biting ten-way auction to be Yael van der Wouden's American publisher. *The Safekeep* is one of the most assured debuts I've ever read—a tale of twisted desire, histories and homes, and the unexpected shape of revenge—and it is a privilege to be sharing it with you now.

It is 1961, and Isabel lives alone in a stately old house in the Dutch countryside; having grown up there with her mother and brothers during the lean years of the war, she prides herself on being the house's truest and most steadfast steward now that the other members of her family have either passed on or moved away. She guards the house and its contents with forensic vigilance, so when her brother brings his vivacious girlfriend Eva to the house and insists that Isabel let her stay for a stretch of time, the two women do not fall into a natural, easy rapport. Isabel is fiercely resistant to Eva's charms and gestures. But over time her suspicion evolves into an infatuation that will bring both women closer to truths they've long ago buried.

This is a deftly plotted page-turner with a great many points of entry—it's for readers interested in World War II and its aftermath, who enjoy forbidden romance (be warned that things get spicy . . .), suspense, and mystery. It is a triumph of character, of language, of pacing, of breadcrumbs being dropped at just the right time. While at first there's a cool detachment to these characters, this story, the heat builds and builds, until the pages start turning themselves.

Though she's Dutch-Israeli, Yael writes in English, and we see this as a novel that's in conversation with modern classics such as *The Paying Guests* by Sarah Waters, *The Reader* by Bernhard Schlink, *The Price of Salt* by Patricia Highsmith, and *Atonement* by Ian McEwan.

As with some of these classics, the ending of *The Safekeep* has made for some particularly passionate and insightful debates among early readers, and I truly cannot wait to hear what you think!

Yours,

Lauren Wein

Lauren Wein | Vice President and Editorial Director
lauren.wein@simonandschuster.com

THE
SAFEKEEP

A Novel

YAEL
VAN DER
WOUDEN

Avid Reader Press

NEW YORK LONDON TORONTO
SYDNEY NEW DELHI

AVID READER PRESS
An Imprint of Simon & Schuster, Inc.
1230 Avenue of the Americas
New York, NY 10020

This book is a work of fiction. Any references to historical events, real people, or real places are used fictitiously. Other names, characters, places, and events are products of the author's imagination, and any resemblance to actual events or places or persons, living or dead, is entirely coincidental.

First Avid Reader Press hardcover edition May 2024

AVID READER PRESS and colophon are trademarks of Simon & Schuster, Inc.

Simon & Schuster: Celebrating 100 Years of Publishing in 2024

For information about special discounts for bulk purchases, please contact Simon & Schuster Special Sales at 1-866-506-1949 or business@simonandschuster.com.

The Simon & Schuster Speakers Bureau can bring authors to your live event. For more information or to book an event contact the Simon & Schuster Speakers Bureau at 1-866-248-3049 or visit our website at www.simonspeakers.com.

Manufactured in the United States of America

1   3   5   7   9   10   8   6   4   2

Library of Congress Cataloging-in-Publication Data

ISBN 978-1-6680-3434-7
ISBN 978-1-6680-3436-1 (ebook)

To Mr. Nijstad, as promised

PART I

The Netherlands, 1961

1

ISABEL FOUND A BROKEN PIECE OF CERAMIC UNDER the roots of a dead gourd. Spring had brought a shock of frost, a week of wet snow, and now—at the lip of summer—the vegetable garden was shrinking into itself. The beans, the radishes, the cauliflower: browned and rotting. Isabel was on her knees, gloved hands and a stringed hat, removing the dying things. The shard nicked through her glove, pierced a little hole.

It wasn't a wound and it didn't bleed. Isabel took off her glove and stretched the skin of her palm tight, looking for a puncture. There was none, only a sting of pain that left quickly.

Back at the house she washed the piece and held it in watery hands. Blue flowers along the inch of a rim, the suggestion of a hare's leg where the crockery had broken. It had once been a plate, which was part of a set—her mother's favorite: the good chinaware, for holidays, for guests. When Mother was alive the set was kept in a glass vitrine in the dining room and no one was allowed to handle it. It had been years since her passing and the plates were still kept behind the closed doors, unused. On the rare occasion when Isabel's brothers visited, Isabel would set the table using everyday plates and Hendrik would try to pry open the vitrine and say, "Isa, Isa, come now, what's the point of having good things if you can't touch them?" And Isabel would answer: "They are not for touching. They are for keeping."

3

There was no explanation for the broken piece, for where it had come from and why it had been buried. None of Mother's plates had ever gone missing. Isabel knew this and still she checked now. The set was as it had been left: a deck of plates, bowls, a little milk jug. In the middle of each one—three hares, chasing one another in a circle.

She took the piece with her on the train to Scheveningen the next day, wrapped in brown paper. Hendrik's car was parked outside the restaurant when she arrived, and he was at the wheel: windows down, smoking. Rubbing a thumb into his eye, looking like he was having a conversation with himself over something, a disagreement. His hair was longer than she liked it. She bent down and said, "Hello," and he startled and knocked his elbow and said, "Jesus Christ, Isa."

She got in the car next to him and kept her purse in her lap. He sighed out smoke and leaned over, kissed her three times— once on each cheek, and one more for good measure.

"You're early," she said.

He said, "That's a nice hat."

She touched it. "Yes." She'd worried over it, leaving the house. It was bigger than what she usually wore. It had a bright-green ribbon. "How are you, then?"

"Oh, you know." He ashed his cigarette out the window, leaned back. "Sebastian's been talking about going home."

Isabel touched her hat once more, her nape. She pushed a bobby pin further into place. Hendrik had called recently to tell her as much: Sebastian's mother's health taking a turn for the worse, Sebastian wanting to visit her. Sebastian wanting Hendrik to come with him. Isabel had not known what to say of it, and so she said nothing. And so she ignored the information and instead updated him about the state of the garden, about Neelke the maid and how she might be stealing things, about Johan's

4

disruptive visits that left her nonplussed, and about a recent car bill. Hendrik hung up quickly after that.

"I think I will have to go with him," he continued, not looking at her. "I can't let him go alone, I can't—"

"I found this," she interrupted, and took the wrapped package from her purse. Opened it for him, still in her palm. "Buried in the garden. Under one of the gourds."

He considered her for a moment, confused. Then, with a quick blink, a breath, took the piece and inspected it. Turned it over. "One of Mother's plates?"

"It is, isn't it?"

"All right," he said cautiously, and gave it back. On the other side of the street, a couple argued while they walked. The woman tried to hush the conversation, the man only raised his voice in response.

Isabel continued on a held breath: "I think Neelke—"

"Isabel." Hendrik turned to face her now, cigarette still in hand. The space between them clouded with smoke. "There's not going to be any maids left in the province if you keep on firing all of them with some imaginary ideas of—"

"Imaginary! I have been *stolen* from. They have—"

"Once," he said. "That happened *once*, and she was so young, Isa, come on. Haven't you been young?" She'd looked away from him and he ducked to catch her eye. He was putting on his funny voice. "Haven't I, once?"

They were not old now. She was nearly thirty, and he was younger still. The youngest of them all. She wrapped the piece back into the paper and put it back in her purse.

"And besides," he said. "It could've been in that ground a long time. Maybe Louis accidentally broke a plate once and panicked and—"

"Mother would've noticed," Isabel said.

Hendrik wasn't taking her seriously. "Well, I mean, who knows how the house was kept before we moved in."

"What do you mean, before?"

"Before we moved in. Someone else might've broken a plate. There were always only five of them, no? What happened to the sixth?"

"Those are—Hendrik. Those are Mother's plates."

"No no. The house came with the . . ." He gestured vaguely. "Crockery. Chairs."

She had been eleven when they moved to the east of the country, and Louis—the oldest—thirteen. Hendrik was small for his age at ten, a hollow-cheeked and melancholy boy. Isabel hadn't thought he remembered much of those early days in the house. They mostly spoke of what came before: their childhood in Amsterdam, Father before he got sick, the smell of the city in December, a toy train that went round and round.

But he was right somehow. An odd angle of a thought that hadn't struck her before—they'd moved into a finished house, a full house. Nearly everything laid out: the sheets, the pots, the vases in the windowsills.

"But it was Mother's . . ." Isabel trailed off. Their mother had loved the hare's pattern. The house was full of it: hare figurines on sills, hares on the tiled back of the hearth.

Hendrik said, "We used to have—Oh, you remember, in Amsterdam, we had the plates with the bluebells. No, I think it belonged to—that woman Uncle Karel was married to back then, no? Didn't she get the house ready for us?"

"Uncle Karel was never married," Isabel said.

"Oh, briefly. Tall. Birthmark on her cheek. Would say hello with a yodel."

"No."

"She was with us for a while, before Mother joined. You really don't remember?"

She didn't remember a woman. She didn't remember the day of their arrival, or anyone showing them around, telling them where to go, where to sleep, why the beds were already made, already—

"Don't obsess over this," Hendrik said. "Isa? Don't do that."

She was pinching the skin on the back of her hand. She stopped. Cleared her throat, touched her hat a third time. "Well, maybe Louis knows."

"Right," Hendrik said, like the thought of Louis knowing anything was entertaining. "He's bringing a girl, did he tell you?"

Louis usually brought girls to their dinners. The last time they'd had a meal with just the three of them had been accidental: Louis's date stood him up. Isabel had thought, *Good riddance*, and then found that Louis—when not in the company of relative strangers—in fact had little to say to his siblings. It was a long and stilted evening. Hendrik got very drunk, first loud and then very quiet. She and Louis had had to deliver him home: Hendrik lolling in the back of Louis's car, throwing up in the gutter outside his building. Sebastian had leaned out the window in a dressing gown and called down, *Jesus, what have you two done to him?*

"I reserved for three," she told Hendrik. It was the principle of the thing, the fact that Louis yet again hadn't told her he'd be bringing a girl. Hadn't called her. He never called her.

"I know you did."

"It's bad manners."

"Hmm," Hendrik agreed.

"Is it the same one as last time? I didn't like her. Her neck was too wide."

Hendrik laughed at this. Isa hadn't meant it as a joke. He told her, "No. He's bringing a new one," and Isabel *tsk*'d and Hendrik smiled, closed-mouthed. "The love of his life this time, I'm told."

"Really."

"Really." The cigarette was finished. People were coming in and out of the restaurant, guided by a server in a buttoned suit. Hendrik said, "Shall we?"

"He's not inside yet."

"I know." Hendrik rolled up the window. "But shall we?"

They went. It still took another half hour before Louis showed up, during which Hendrik smoked three more cigarettes, drank two beers, chattered idly, and then started up again about whether or not he should join Sebastian on his trip to Paris, to see the ill mother. It would be an indefinite stay. The doctors weren't overly confident. He said this and kept eyeing Isabel in a way that felt like he knew she didn't want to hear it and still he wanted her to tell him: to either go or not go, to give him some sort of blessing. Isabel could not. Isabel said, "You must do what you want to do." She had a glass of water. She drank from it.

Hendrik said, "Would you be all right? If I were gone for a while?"

"Is that how you think I live? Breathlessly awaiting your next visit?"

"Isabel."

"You're gone now, too. You don't live at home, might as well be in Paris, really. Might as well—" Isabel wanted to say more but stopped herself. She had never been to Paris. She knew it was far. She knew that when *their* mother was sick, all Hendrik had had to do was take a single train home, and that he rarely did.

Hendrik touched her arm. "Never mind," he said. Then he picked up a new thread, a cheerful "So never mind that for now,

8

anyway tell me something new, something exciting. Tell me how's your man, Isa, tell me about that."

It brought her up short. "My—what?"

"Oh, you know. Old neighbor Johan."

A terrible kick of a feeling—as though she'd been caught in embarrassment: showing too much skin, speaking out of turn. She ignored the heat at the base of her neck and answered with a "Johan is certainly *not* my—"

Hendrik's gaze drifted, refocused on the entrance: Louis had arrived. He was having a stern conversation with the maître d', leaning too far over the front desk, gesturing his argument. His new girl stood to the side, looking embarrassed and nervous, a shaky smile stuck on tightly. She had a violently peroxided bob, a badly made dress—the bodice had been sewn too tight and the hems were messy. Her face was very red. She was pretty in a way men thought women ought to be pretty.

"Good lord," Isabel said, and Hendrik snorted. Louis looked up just then, to nod at them in indication to the manager. Hendrik waved good-naturedly. The couple made their way over, a fourth chair in tow, and the first thing Louis said was, "They said they didn't have enough *chairs*, can you believe how—"

"I reserved for three," Isabel said. Louis sat down in a huff, arranging his dinner jacket, and his girl hovered awkwardly—did an uneasy dance with the waiter who'd come with the extra chair, his trying to get the seat pushed under her, her not understanding, fumbling.

"They're a restaurant," Louis said. "They should have spare chairs."

"Hello, Louis, welcome," Hendrik said. The table stilled a moment. Then Louis answered with a sound, a short and frustrated sound, and got back out of his chair: leaned over to kiss Isabel, shake Hendrik's hand. He smelled strongly of cologne. His hair was slicked back. His tie done tightly against the apple of his throat.

He said, "Hello. This is Eva."

The girl rose to shake hands. She tipped over the flower piece with her chest, said "Oh no," and tried to right it, accidentally pulled at the tablecloth when she sat back down. All the cutlery gave a shake.

Hendrik said: "Lovely to meet you."

"Oh, it's so good to meet you, both of you. I've heard so much, and I've been telling Louis how I've been wanting to meet you, haven't I, Louis? Haven't I been saying how much I—"

"She has," Louis confirmed. He was inspecting the menu.

"So you two have known each other for—" Hendrik started, and Eva jumped back in with an "Oh, a little while but it feels like forever, doesn't it, Louis? I always say, I always say how it's only been a few months but I'm sure we must've known each other in a past life because I'm so certain we're—"

"Shall we order?" Isabel said, waving down a passing waiter. Louis had kept them waiting. She wasn't used to eating so late in the evening, was hungry, all the more irritated for it.

Eva, caught midbreath, kept her smile intact. She turned even redder. "All the same," she said, and then trailed off, didn't finish her thought. When it was her turn to order she fussed and said she'd never heard of half the words on the menu, and leaned into Louis and said, "Oh, but you order, darling. You're always so smart about these things anyway."

They went with the scallops. When the food arrived Eva asked what scallops were, and Louis meant to answer just as Hendrik jumped in and said, "Oh, but guess."

Eva seemed caught out but then guessed, quietly: a potato of some sort?

No one said anything a moment, and then Hendrik jostled as though he'd been kicked under the table. He put his elbows on the table and asked Eva what it was that she did—if she studied, or worked, or lounged happily about all day—and Eva, in reply, cycled through a new flush, took her time in answering: putting down her cutlery, wiping her hands on her napkin, draining the last of her glass. It was her second, Isabel noted, or third. "Well," Eva said. And, "Well, you see—" And then a tumble of words: "Oh, must we talk work? So boring."

Isabel looked away, out the window. It was only the reflection of the restaurant, echoed back at them in muted shadows. She said, "You don't seem the type who can afford to be bored of it."

Louis said her name once, a dagger: "*Isabel.*"

Isabel met his gaze and offered no apology.

Louis said, "Eva is being humble. Aren't you?" He didn't wait for Eva to reply, answered for her: "Eva was a typist for Van Dongen. She stopped, recently, when ah, an . . . ah—"

"An aunt," Eva supplied.

"An aunt, yes, you see, passed on a sum of money—"

"Yes," said Eva, breathless.

"So this clever girl here is quite self-sufficient, Isabel. I don't care to think about what you were implying."

Isabel retreated into a sharp silence. The conversation continued—stopped and stuttered. Hendrik pushed at the tension, teased in a way that went over Eva's head. Louis clearly noted it, then ignored it: with every irritation he turned to Eva and immediately went soft with a wet-eyed look, an easing of the mouth. Isabel thought the expression made him look stupid. Louis had also brought a girl to their mother's funeral, years ago. She was in all the pictures now, and no one remembered her name. Not even Louis, the one time Isabel asked him. She'd been making an album.

When they were leaving the restaurant, Isabel excused herself to the bathroom. She hadn't had much wine—it always made her heavy-headed, mean—but the little bit she'd had, in the humid evening, settled over her like a fever. She wet a paper towel, pressed it to her neck.

Eva came in right then. Isabel threw away the towel. Eva didn't go into any of the cubicles: she leaned back against the counter, clumsy. She was drunker than Isabel. The crooked hemming of her dress showed even more like this. The lights gleaned brightly off the yolky shine of her hair. Isabel thought she could almost smell the peroxide.

"Tonight was lovely," Eva said.

"Mm," Isabel said, washing her hands.

"I really *have* been wanting to meet you, you know. You most of all. Louis has told me so much. You live in the old family home, right? In the house where you three grew—"

"I did not invite you here tonight."

Eva was caught in a breath, mouth moving a moment. There was a sheen of sweat under the line of her collar. Isabel was annoyed by the very act of looking at her right then. Annoyed by the tight seams of her dress, the dark roots of her hair, the painted eyebrows. How humiliating, she thought, to have a bad performance show so plainly.

Then Eva laughed. A single, humorless laugh. "Well!" she said. "Don't you speak your mind!"

Isabel dried her hands. "I don't mean to be rude." This was a lie. "But you will be gone soon." She made sure it came through clearly: "He will be bored of you, and I'll never hear of you again."

It didn't have the desired effect. "Oh," Eva said. She tilted her head. "We'll see." It wasn't the same voice she'd used before, not the same voice that laughed nervously over every exchange, not the same voice that apologized—*oh sorry, oh I'm so silly I'm sorry*—when knocking over a glass, scraping a knife too loudly on the plate.

Isabel looked at her and caught a flash of something in her expression—a fissure, something, but it was gone very quickly and immediately Isabel couldn't say whether she'd imagined it. If it had been there at all.

Isabel made to leave. Eva didn't move from her perch, watched her go, gaze steady. Keen. Outside on the street it was hot and wet all at once, a misty drizzle in the air. The sea pushed into the streets, the smell of salt. Louis asked, "Where is Eva?" And Isabel said, "Am I responsible for her now?"

Hendrik hooked his arm into hers. She held on. Louis said, "You were terrible tonight. You were terrible to her."

"Oh, pooh," Hendrik said.

Louis took a step closer, trying not to raise his voice. "What will it *take* to *get* you two to—"

But then Eva joined them again. She was fixing her hat. It was very red. Her lipstick had been redone. It was noticeable now, how short she was in comparison: the three of them were all tall, all narrow. "What did I miss?" she said, and the voice was back again: higher than before, lilting. She seemed to think it made her softer. It didn't, Isabel thought. It didn't at all.

Louis sweetened at her presence and turned from them. "Nothing," he said. "What could possibly happen without you around?"

She liked that. Went peach-cheeked, leaned into him, then quickly insisted the night could not yet be over—it couldn't possibly be over! "Come over for drinks, oh please, oh, you must!"

"To—Louis's?" Hendrik asked. Louis had a sparse, small room in a second-floor apartment near his work. It was old and badly kept, a moldy shower, and he shared the house with a suspicious little man with a heavy brow and rimmed glasses. But the rent was covered by his engineering company, and Louis was often abroad. Isabel never came by for anything other than to pick him up, drop him off.

"Oh, it was a dreary place, wasn't it? But I've helped him re-decorate, haven't I, darling? And it's really very lovely now, oh, you *should* come by, if only to see."

"You've helped Louis *redecorate*." Hendrik said it like a punch line. Eva didn't notice, only confirmed enthusiastically. Isabel didn't want to go. The night had gone on for long enough. She said as much, claiming train times, and how dark it was getting, but then Hendrik leaned in and whispered a wry *Oh come on don't you want to see her decorations?*

It was decided: they would go. One drink, only the one. "Oh, of course only one," Hendrik said.

It was a short walk down the boulevard. Louis lived nearby. There was no reason for him and his girl to have been late to the restaurant, no reason other than not having left the house on time, and why would they not leave on time? An answer came to Isabel, a sharp, unpleasant answer—a flash of an image, of a bed. The things people did alone in rooms together. She looked away from it physically: turned her face to the sea. The setting sun was a distant spill of light behind a blanket of gray. The sea pushed in and in, roiling and then pulling away, roiling.

Then Eva paused, fell into step beside her, said she needed a moment away from "the boys"—some sort of conspiratorial word. Isabel scowled at it. They walked into Louis's street. The wind calmed here. Taller buildings, little gardens. Eva began a soft prattle, Isabel's speech back at the restaurant seemingly forgotten. She was not saying anything much, just commenting on the gardens, posing her statements as questions: Weren't the begonias blooming nicely? And shouldn't she just love a garden of her own? It seemed like this was a question for Isabel, but it wasn't, immediately followed up with a quick and distracted sigh of: "Oh, but I would just be terrible at it, wouldn't I? I would just be terrible at having a garden, I'd kill just about anything I'd try to grow, I just know it."

"Then don't get a garden," Isabel said. Eva pursed her lips into a hard line.

Upstairs, when they entered Louis's room, Hendrik squeezed Isabel's arm harshly—a message. Out loud he only said, a creak in his voice, "Oh, how lovely!"

It was gaudy. Eva had hung red gauzy fabrics from the ceiling to drape over the bed like a canopy, pulled them through to the rest of the room: over the cabinet, over the chair. There were too many carpets on the floor, overlapping. On the wall she'd installed several clumsy paintings of abstracted faces.

"Aren't they nice?" she said. "A friend of mine painted them. A secret genius, wouldn't you say?"

"Oh," Hendrik said, nodded excitedly, squeezed Isabel harder. "Oh, absolutely. Absolutely."

There was not really anywhere to sit. Louis took the armchair. Hendrik and Isabel sat on the edge of the bed. Eva brought a stool from the kitchen, and then drinks, all poured in assorted glasses. They all stayed in their tightly stretched silence. Eva's furious blush was back. Louis was flipping through a book he'd left by the chair's leg. Then Eva said, "Music!" and went to put on a record. Too loud at first, she had to go back to lower the volume. Then, reinstalled, she began with a—

"So Louis tells me all three of you grew up in—"

"Do you live here now?" Hendrik interrupted, looking around him. "In this room? With Louis?"

"Oh, I," she started, and Louis said, "We're looking for a new place." And Hendrik said, "*Together?*" And Louis said, "What of it, together? Of all people who are you to—"

Hendrik turned sharp. "'Of all people,' what does *that* mean?"

"Not so loud," Isabel said, looking at the wall, and Louis huffed and said, "Maurice is not home, Isa, you are saved from social embarrassment," and Isabel, not wanting to reply to the comment but still wanting to push back, said, "I don't *like* that man," at which point Eva jumped in with an "Oh really?"

They all looked at her. Isabel said, "I don't."

"Oh? Why not?"

"I just don't." Isabel wasn't often asked to explain her likes, her dislikes. Isabel was not often asked anything at all, between the house and the shops and weekly calls with Hendrik. Who was there, to ask her anything? She said, "He acts—suspicious."

Something glimmered in the way Eva considered her now. That flash: there it was. She was sitting up straighter, just a fraction. She said, "Suspicious how?"

"He skulks." One time Isabel had waited for Louis in the hallway, and Maurice had stood there with her the whole time: eyes blank on a bit of the wall just above her shoulder.

"*Skulks?*" Eva said it like she had never heard the word before.

"Oh, who cares about Maurice," Louis said, louder than the both of them, and Isabel blinked. Took a breath, looked away. Sat up straighter now, too. Eva went to fiddle with the music again. Her blush was gone. The back of her neck looked brown against the yellow of her hair.

When Hendrik and Isabel left, she was small and saccharine again: standing by the door, short and leaned into Louis, arm around his waist, waving, waving. Saying, "So lovely! *So* lovely! We'll see you soon!"

When she'd leaned in to say goodbye to Isabel earlier, she'd briefly steadied herself with a hand to Isabel's waist. Squeezed, quick but sure. Isabel felt the weight of that touch as they walked back down the boulevard—pressed her own hand to it. To Hendrik she said, "I don't like her."

Hendrik laughed very loudly. "Didn't you, now? I hadn't a clue."

"No, I mean," she began, reordered her thoughts. "No, I mean, I think—there's something, I don't think she's—"

"God, the gauze," Hendrik said, lips tight around a cigarette, trying to light it against the sea wind. Night had fallen in full. The sea hissed on the beach below. "I thought I was going to *cry*, oh my God, and Louis just let her—the carpets! I can't believe it. He is never going to live this down, he is *never* going to—"

"Wait," Isabel said, but it was very quiet, and carried away by the wind. Hendrik didn't hear it. He continued on, listing moments: when she—! And did Isabel see when she—!

Isabel thought of the quick widening of Eva's eyes when she said, *Oh really?* The flare of her nostrils. The line of her spine. That pinch of goodbye at Isabel's waist. How Louis went a little slack when Eva touched him. *Don't obsess over this*, Hendrik had said earlier that night. He said it at least once every time they met. Over the phone, too, in his letters: to not obsess over money, to not obsess over the way the maid cleans the windows, to not obsess over Johan and his intentions, the way he stared, the way he put his hand to Isabel's waist—fingers fanned out.

Isabel worried the skin on the back of her hand. Hendrik noticed, midspeech, pulled her hand away, took it in his instead. He wavered in his walk, unsteady. They were nearing his car.

"I'll drive you," she said.

"Noooo." He leaned his head into her shoulder. "I'm fine!"

"I'm driving you."

"*Isa*," he said. "Your train! Your train times!"

"I'll take the tram to the station."

"Sister," he said now, trying to wrap his arms around her, locking her at the elbows. She didn't like this kind of touch, the kind that restricted, and he knew it, did it with all the purpose in the world: too heavy, too tight. Drunk. "Och, sister sister sister!" She struggled against him. He laughed some more, let her go.

She drove him home. He tried to get her to come up with him, to come say hello to Sebastian, come have a last drink to end the night. It had been so long since she'd seen Sebastian. He said this with shiny-wet eyes, said it quietly, seriously. His hold on her wrist was harsh. The light was on upstairs: Sebastian had waited up for him.

She said she would go home. Hendrik nodded and nodded and bared his teeth in an almost-smile. He promised to call. Promised to come by with Sebas at some point this summer, before they maybe left for Paris: they could stay for a few days. Swim somewhere. Take a trip somewhere. It had been so long, he repeated himself, since Isabel had seen Sebastian.

On the train back to Zwolle she took out the small packet, unwrapped it. Considered the found piece. The china was thin. Blue, white, blue. The train lights flickered with each bump in the rails. Home, when she arrived, welcomed her with relief. *There you are*, said the dim light in the kitchen, left on for comfort. *I've waited up for you*, said the rattle of key in the door. The hallway had kept within it a chill, but upstairs Neelke had left a few embers to burn in Isabel's hearth. Isabel crouched and held out her hands to the heat.

She tried to recall her first night at the house, young and scared and sirens wailing at a dark distance. She tried to recall what had been there already—what things, what shapes, what vases and paintings and embroidery to the edges of which sheets. She recalled nothing. She recalled the thump of a knock and Hendrik's cold little foot under the blankets and a feeling like a fist on the inside of her throat.

A window slammed shut across the hallway. Isabel startled and rushed toward the sound. It had come from her mother's old room—she had aired out the room earlier in the day. She had left the window open. Nothing was the matter, nothing had been broken, only a picture frame had been blown face down on the bedside table.

The photograph had been taken that first summer after the war. Her mother, reedy in a long skirt, sitting on the bench out in the garden, the two firs rising proud behind her. She sat neatly, looked straight into the lens.

Isabel put the picture back in its place and righted it.

2

SUNDAY MORNING WAS SPENT AT CHURCH, THE smell of varnish and old curtains. Sunday afternoon had the sun beating down broadly, open-armed, and Isabel went to work on the garden. The lilac shrubs needed pruning and the roses needed tying in, and Isabel rooted around in the ground for other sharp objects that might be found. There was nothing but earth. Monday she paid a visit to the solicitor about her allowance, Tuesday she had an appointment with the upholsterer about the chair, on Wednesday she did the groceries she didn't trust Neelke to do, and on Thursday she had tea at the Van den Berg household because Johan was in town—and if Isabel went to him then he would not come to her, which was how she liked it: parking by his mother's home, saying her neat hellos, being invited for coffee before dinner. If she did not do this, Johan would take matters into his own hands. He would show up unannounced at her front door, walk himself inside with his keen eyes, and linger in the room, touching things, asking about her life. He would press close in doorways.

She did not know what to do when he did this. It made her dizzy, a little nauseated, all of it, but she had been told by Hendrik these were only nerves, and perfectly normal. At his mother's dinner table Johan put his hot hand over Isabel's under the table, under the fall of the tablecloth. He kept it on her knee, while his mother went on about *Did Isabel hear what happened with the Huijers?* The weekly help had been caught stealing, things had been disappearing for a while, but "Oh, just small things, a spoon, a plate, and then of course one morning Mother Huijers wakes up and where is her best necklace? Well, they caught the girl eventually. Tipped out her bag before she left. What do you think? A whole drawer of silver came falling out: knives and forks and—"

Johan pushed his hand up Isabel's thigh. The fabric of her dress bunched, slid. She excused herself to the bathroom. The house was once a farm and still smelled of straw. Johan's mother didn't grow anything on the land but kept a lovely rose garden in the back. Isabel rearranged her dress, pinched her stockings into order. When she returned to the table, her breath was even, her hands steady.

She stayed for dinner and then the weather turned: a rumble of fast-moving clouds, wind, a young tree near the end of the pasture bending deeply. Isabel said she must get back before the rain would start. Johan's mother didn't approve, worried, insisted that Isabel stay longer, or stay the night—they had plenty of rooms. Johan agreed eagerly. He licked his bottom lip.

Isabel said she *must* get back.

The rain started when she was in the car. The wipers whipped fast over the window and still she could barely see the path ahead. The debris of the storm ticked against the car. The road was muddy, and the tires slipped occasionally, but home was close. Between the trees the horizon had darkened fully.

At the house, Louis's car was parked up the gravel path. The living room lights were on. Isabel found a newspaper in the glove compartment and used it as an umbrella. She ran and was still miserably soaked by the time she was inside. Two coats on the rack, one of which was Louis's. A bright red hat hanging from a hook.

"Louis!" Isabel called into the house. The stairwell was dark, the hallway was dark. One hum of light came from under a closed door—through the sitting room, the dining room. The two of them were sitting at her mother's table, Eva with a glass of sweet port, Louis gesturing around the room at the various paintings of old family members—making fun of them. Making Eva laugh.

Isabel still had the wet newspaper in hand. She was dripping on the floor. She said, "Louis." They both noticed her then, a skipping pause—Eva's laughter quieting, Louis's hand still in midmotion—and then Louis was up, walking, saying:

"Ah, you're back, great, wonderful, we've been waiting, see—"

"What are you doing?" Isabel asked, by which she meant, *Why are you here?*

Louis's good humor faltered. He put his hand on the back of a chair. He seemed as though he'd hoped to find her in a better mood, and now had to rethink his approach. Louis only ever came to the house twice a year: Easter, and to visit their mother's grave on the day of her passing. The cemetery was on the outskirts of Zwolle, a twenty-minute drive from the house.

Their mother died in November. It was now the end of May.

Eva said, "You have a lovely home, Isabel." Her mouth was port-stained. The bleach made her hair frizz out of its pins. She was wearing a different dress today, just as badly made. The fabric looked like it had once been a quilt. Isabel wanted her out of the house.

"The thing is," Louis started, and then Eva jumped in with "Darling, should I—" And Louis stilled her with a gesture, said, "No, no, just—"

"What are you talking about?" Isabel looked between the two of them. The rain clattered loudly against the windows. Louis took her by her elbow, tried to steer her toward the kitchen, and Isabel pulled away from him with an eye on Eva and said, "Don't—just tell me what—"

"Please," Louis said, and nodded to the kitchen door. "A moment, Isabel, just . . ."

She went, but wouldn't let him touch her when he tried again. The rain cooled quickly on her skin, fabric heavy, and Louis and his girl hadn't got any of the fireplaces going. The kitchen was colder than the rest of the house. It was several steps down, had a high ceiling for hanging game. No one hung game these days, but the rack was still in place, metal slats and a series of ropes, levers.

An old round table and a painting of the house itself over the mantelpiece. Isabel threw away the wet newspaper, went to wring out her braid over the sink. Louis gently closed the door behind them.

"So I have to go for a while, Isabel," was how he started, hand still on the door handle. "Nelis was supposed to oversee the Brighton conference, but his wife just gave birth, he asked if anyone could go in his place and it's a—an opportunity, you see, a big one, I don't know how long before something like this could—"

"Fine," she said. She didn't care for the buildup. "Why are you here?"

"Eva," he said, lowering his voice now. Trying to whisper.

Isabel leaned back against the sink. "No," she said.

"She can't stay alone in my room for all that time, can she? Sharing with Maurice? And—"

"Let her stay with friends. Let her stay with her own family."

"She doesn't have any."

"No friends?" Isabel said it in the way she meant it: that Eva seemed like the kind of person to have plenty of friends, and that this, in Isabel's view, spoke badly of her. Friendship had always seemed a distrustful thing to Isabel.

"No family," Louis said. He was still whispering. Isabel wasn't. "Not my concern."

"It'll only be, what, a few weeks, a month at most, and you're all alone here, Isa, all these rooms for what? All this space, for what? Why can't she stay? And who knows, it might be good for you, no, for once, to have someone to—to get to—"

"It's *my* house," she said, and it was out and she knew she had misspoken, and Louis knew it as well, barely letting her finish the phrase to cut in with an "Is it, Isabel?" He took a step forward. "Yours?"

Isabel's heart gave a dull thud. She looked away. Uncle Karel had promised the house to Louis, should he ever want it. The unspoken caveat was: should he ever want it for a family of his own. Isabel never had reason to worry: Louis never *did* seem to want for a family, never did seem to want the house at all. Had kept himself so far away from it. Isabel had developed a thought over the years and the thought was: They would allow her to stay here, her brothers. Her uncle. They had to, where else could she go? She had nothing else in this world. Nothing but these clean floors and neatly made beds. It was enough. If she could keep it, it would be enough.

She made herself stand taller. "Well, I'm the one who actually lives here, Louis, the one who keeps it in order, who cleans, who—So I get, I'm the one who gets to . . ." Her breath didn't sound as steady as she intended.

Louis softened, sat down at the table. "Listen. The thing is, she really likes you, Isa. She barely stopped speaking about you since you met. You made an impression, you know. Actually, she was the one who suggested—"

"Oh, *she* did?"

"Don't be like that." He glanced at the door, went back to a whisper: "She's very shy, you know. Don't embarrass her about it. She's not happy to be in this position, to have to, to . . . to be so *reliant* on—"

"She's tricking you," Isabel said. She hadn't even thought the thought to herself yet. The words were out and then she had no choice but to own them as her own belief.

"Pardon?" Louis said, and Isabel started with a quick:

"Who is she, Louis? Who is she, where did she come from, do you even know her, how long have you known her, who's to say she is who she says she is, that she's not trying to—"

"Keep your voice down!" Then: "Trying to what?" He looked at her, bewildered. She didn't know how to finish that thought, now that it had been cut off. She breathed high in her chest, and he just looked at her. The silence stretched. Then he said, "You've been alone for too long. You've not been around people for too long."

"I'm *not* alone."

"The maid doesn't count," he said. "Saying hello to the baker twice a week doesn't count."

She could feel a flush rising. There was no reply she could give that wouldn't confirm the awful way he saw her: sometimes she went for tea at the Van den Bergs. Sometimes called with Hendrik. Small moments, too small for someone who lived with others; who went to work, who went to bars, who had girlfriends who decorated his apartment for him. Hung up gauzes for him.

"So what now?" she said. "I'm to play hotel for every girl you bring home, just because you think I'm in need of—"

"Not every girl," he said, adding an emphasis like it meant something. Isabel looked at him, hoped he wouldn't elaborate. He did all the same: "I like her, Isa. A lot. I think I . . ."

"Oh, God," she said, and turned away, pressed the heel of her hand between her eyes. The swirling dredge of a headache. They were quiet for a while. Then Louis said:

"It won't be that long."

"How long?"

"Look, I have to go ahead, arrange some—It doesn't matter. I'll be a little while is the thing, if I do well enough and they want me to finalize the negotiations; they've—they've put an awful lot of trust in me, Isabel. A promotion could be, it could mean—"

"When," Isabel said. "Will you be back?"

He swallowed. "July."

"July first."

"Isabel."

"July first."

"The first week of July, let's say, yes."

"God," Isabel said again. A month. Even Hendrik, when he visited, never stayed longer than a few days.

Louis rose, scraped the chair back into place. The wind pushed wildly against the windows. Louis said, "You will be nice to her."

"I will be nothing to her," Isabel said, and when she cast him a glance he seemed tired with her. Seemed to have tired of the conversation, and her company, and then he left her. He would be staying, for the night, and would leave in the morning, make for the coast, be on the ferry before the day's end.

Isabel stayed in the kitchen for a while longer. She lit a small fire, pulled a chair near, and sat there to dry. There were low voices in the dining room, then a giggle, then a playful hushing. Footsteps up and down the stairs. Once she had dried, Isabel went through the cupboards and the drawers and the cabinets and made sure there were no missing things. She thought, perhaps, one teaspoon had gone, but wasn't sure anymore how many they had in the first place. She counted them: twelve. Laid all the spoons out on the table from biggest to smallest.

That's when Eva leaned into the room, hand on the doorpost, and said:

"I just wanted to say thank you. I appreciate it so much that I can stay here. You really have no idea."

She had put on the voice again. Isabel looked up at her with an even gaze. "It wasn't my suggestion," she said.

"No, I know," Eva said, and smiled like that was a good thing. A kind thing. Like she was having a conversation with a different person, someone who was nice to her. "It's so warm in here! Lovely. What are you doing? Are you polishing the spoons, in the middle of the night?"

"No," Isabel said, and offered no other explanation.

"Well," Eva said. "Well. Well, good night then, Isabel. Can I call you Isa? Louis does. Like we're sisters. We almost are, no?"

Isabel didn't answer. She collected her spoons and put them back in the drawer, kept her back to the door. Eventually, Eva left. Did so with a soft "Well, good night," and sounded less sure now. *We'll see about that,* Eva had said at the restaurant, and she had been someone else in that moment. Someone whom Isabel could only think of indirectly, vaguely. A pinprick of a person.

She waited for the shuffling upstairs to die down, then went up herself. The corridor was shadowed, lights off, but a strip of light shone from under one door: her mother's old room. Inside, the two lovers were talking, laughing quietly.

Isabel showered in stilted movements, had to rebraid her hair several times, got into bed, and seethed. The chimney breast from downstairs ran through her room and warmed the space just enough. Still she shook under her sheets. She stayed awake for a long time, listening to the sounds from down the hall. Once, she thought she heard a hum. Once, a gasp. She ran hot, and then cold. Eventually, the house quieted, and there was nothing to listen to but the slowing of the storm.

She woke up early, exhausted, the back of her hand pinched red.

It was Uncle Karel who had found the house for them in the winter of '44. It was the tail end of war and a famine tore through the west of the Netherlands. The three siblings were sent ahead: on a boat heading east, huddled with other children their age—strange children, children who coughed like it was a secret, behind the lapels of their jacket. One girl showed Isabel what was in her suitcase: a doll and a pair of shoes and a fork, a plate. The foster family would feed her, she said, but they did not have enough forks. Isabel had thought it was a made-up story, and she disliked made-up stories. She had gotten angry, said, "Nonsense, who doesn't have enough forks?" and didn't speak to the girl for the rest of the trip.

Uncle Karel came to collect Louis, Isabel, and Hendrik at the harbor. It was freezing. They stood there a long time, outside of the car, while a German soldier held their papers in rough-gloved grip and asked many questions. Uncle answered them all jovially, smiling, nodding.

Mother remained in Amsterdam, could not come—only children were allowed to cross. A week into their stay, Isabel, eleven years old, wrote her mother a letter:

Dear Mother,

Louis wrote to you this week but I saw his letter and it was only just a few lines of very bad penmanship and I am worried you could not read it and it was boring. House is bigger __much__ bigger than ours in Amsterdam and we all like it very much it has three floors and we are three, which means each of us can have a floor (Hendrik says he won't

28

mind sleeping in the kitchen where it's warm. It gets very cold upstairs in the night yesterday they said on the radio the temperature was –1.3). Will you be here for Christmas? Louis says I shouldn't tell you to come because it is not allowed yet but it would be very nice if you were here for Christmas. We have found a chest of toys in the attic and Uncle Karel says it was left there by Saint Nicholas for us to have. One of the toys is a stuffed toy of a hare, which I am allowed to keep. Someone has drawn a horse on the wall behind my wardrobe. I have been trying to keep a diary as the prime minister has instructed but I run out of things to say.

The house is like this (I write this as I walk so you see exactly): you walk inside and this here is the hallway where you hang your coat and then there is a stair and two doors (study to the right, drawing room to left). The drawing room has the biggest mirror above the mantelpiece and it makes everything look 2x. The dining room is here and then there is the kitchen for which you have to go down two stairs. The kitchen is old and has very high ceilings and smells like oil which I do not like but the fireplace is <u>very big</u> and that is where we keep the fire because Uncle Karel says there is only enough wood for one fire but it is not a nice room. I will leave it now. We have had dinner in the dining room every evening. We had potatoes, and cauliflower, and one time meat: a piece of meat each!

The garden goes around in a big circle. Everything snowed in the night. Louis says we will play badminton there in the spring if we are still here in the spring. When will you come? I have heard 5 planes today, and saw 1. Uncle Karel said last night my face was too rough for a little girl and that I should practice in the mirror to make it nicer

*so I won't end up a sour maid. Hendrik cries every night
and keeps us all up. Louis gets very angry with him but I do
not. There's a girl who lives on the farm down the road who
came to the house to ask for food and I said I didn't know
where the food was and she said her father died because he
went into the woods and was shot in the head by a German.
I said, That's terrible! I felt bad for not giving food. Now I
don't think anyone should go into the woods. I have chosen
the best room for you. It is the biggest, and looks out two
snow-covered firs which is your favorite tree which you
have once told me I remember which is why I chose this
room for you.*

    Write soon, come soon!
    Your daughter (Isabel)

Her mother had kept this letter with all the other ones, and
Isabel's halted and confused attempt at a wartime diary, in the
locked drawer of her secretary in her bedroom. Isabel found it a
year after her mother's passing. She was twenty-two, and it was
summer, and she had badly sunburnt her shins that day, having
dozed off on a lounge chair in the garden. She sat by the secretary,
legs chafing on the grain of the carpet, and read each letter she
and her siblings had sent her mother. Hendrik had mostly written
rambling, single-page requests to come and be picked up; Louis
dictated the literal events of the days of the week and fantasized
about joining the army, flying a plane. She read a diary entry of
her own, a Tuesday in October 1945: *counted all the stairs in the
house and there were sixty-four. Hendrik has locked himself up
in the bathroom and won't come out and it's a great bother.*

Isabel, seated on the ground, papers in hand, had locked her
jaw so firmly that the joint of it got stuck in place and she had to
wrench her own mouth open with her fingers.

The war was stored in her memory unclearly, all out of order. In 1939, on a Monday, her father fell down the stairs. On Friday he had a nosebleed in a three-piece suit and was dead before month's end. Nineteen forty-three was the year popular Vera called her shit-breath Isa, and so the rest of the class began to call her shit-breath Isa, too. In 1941 Louis got a little train for his birthday, which had an engine and went around and around and around. Bombs fell on Rotterdam. Trucks rolled over the loose bricks of the Sarphatisstraat, where she and her mother got their pickles. She went to school, she walked home. Bombs fell on Amsterdam.

Their years in the east following the war were louder: chaos at the train stations, hollow-faced people wandering the streets on bare feet. Craters that filled up with rainwater, bunkers shaded green with moss. People showing up at the driveway to their new house to ask for coal, for food. Once, one cold evening when Isabel was thirteen, they were having dinner and there came a loud knock on the door that wouldn't stop. It was 1946 and the war was over but Isabel's mother closed all the windows in a hurry and said *Go upstairs*, and Isabel and her brothers had to go upstairs while the food cooled on their plates. They watched from the bedroom window as outside an upset woman banged on their doors and windows and screamed and screamed. Her shouts were unintelligible, desperate. She had a young woman with her who did nothing, who stood to the side, arms crossed, head down. Isabel had asked Louis in a whisper—*What do they want?* And Louis, staring out the darkened window, had said simply: *Our stuff.* Once, a man went to his knees and began laughing uncontrollably in the middle of a shopping street. The police came to take him away. Isabel was inside a store, watching it happen. She was fifteen when she first heard about the camps. She and some classmates were waiting in a classroom for the teacher to show up, and one of the girls said: *They treat us worse than Jews here*, and one of the other girls said, *God, I wish they'd gas us, at least that'd be a way out.*

They kept Uncle Karel's house after the war and never went back to Amsterdam. It was better for them, Mother insisted: the green, the land. The space. Louis never forgave Mother for that, mourning all the friends he left behind in the city, and Hendrik didn't seem to care much either way. He was an unhappy child, no matter where. Cried often, hid a lot. Isabel didn't mind it, the move to the east. She hadn't any friends in the city, and hadn't any friends in the country, either. It wasn't as bad as everyone made it out to be, all worried about her, fussing over her being alone in her room. But it was fine: she read, she took walks, she and Hendrik made up stories about the people who drove by in cars. And then Louis moved out and life got quieter, and then Hendrik ran away and life got quieter still. Rooms turned cavernous. Mother got sick. Mother passed away. Isabel, freshly in her twenties, directed several maids about the house: the sheets needed changing, the windows needed cleaning. Dinner would need to be served by six.

The day after the funeral was a bleary-bright one: mist over the meadows, weeds looking purple. There was a plate of leftover sandwiches on the table in the dining room, covered by a kitchen towel. Flies hovered over it. The house was empty, except for Isabel. Louis had driven back the previous night and Hendrik would not come into the house, had booked a bed-and-breakfast near town. He had brought a man who lingered outside the cemetery, waiting for Hendrik, umbrella in hand.

Isabel had never known loneliness like that, one that arrived without the promise of leaving. There was no one now, no one to walk through the door unannounced, no one to open and close a drawer in the other room. Outside, meadows. Outside, land and more land. Isabel sat by the window with a cup of tea and was overcome. Terror rose up slow and thunderous: Mother had died so quickly, so easily, and Isabel had had no say in it. Her uncle might die, too, just as suddenly. The deed will go to Louis, and Louis might decide to marry, and Louis might decide he wanted her out—anything could happen at any given moment and she had no say in it, not in any of it. She belonged to the house in the sense that she had nothing else, no other life than the house, but the house, by itself, did not belong to her.

The tea cooled. She had decided, right then, to put the issue forward to Uncle Karel—the issue of what might become of her and the house. The issue of could she perhaps have some hold on the deed, something, a promise, a certainty of being kept in safety. But then Uncle Karel came by for dinner one bleak winter day, and he sat at the big table in his dandruff-speckled jumper, leaned in, and said: "You will understand, Isabel, now that your mother is gone, that you must be your own guardian. You must make your own connections." He wiped at his lips with a napkin. "Don't be a burden to your brothers, they will have their own lives. You can't ask too much. And I won't be here, I'll have my own business, you understand. I'm not saying this to be harsh. I am saying it because it's how these things go, and there is no one else who will tell you." He was nodding so that she might nod along; she did not. She watched him, unmoving. He said, "Yes?"

She stared at him until his nodding stopped.

"Yes," she said, and swallowed, and went to take away the dishes so he wouldn't notice how fast she was breathing, or the trembling of her hands.

And then he left, and again it was only she and the walls. The doors, the windows. She went around the house and closed everything, locked everything, the shutters and the curtains and everything that could be pulled over herself like a cloak. For a moment, for a brief and raging moment, she thought: *Let him. Let him try to drag me out of here.* She saw herself clawing into the walls, taking root.

She was ready for it that first year. Every time Louis met a girl, every time he came by to visit, she waited for it: for him to look around the house and say, *I actually think I might have it now.* But he never did. He never seemed to notice it, even: he sat in rooms as though they might be any space, looked out windows as though they might be any windows. The house, it seemed, was a blur to him—walls in the way any place might have walls, roof like any building might need a roof.

Relief set in by increments. They never spoke of it, of her never leaving, of her living in the old house, but she wondered at times. Wondered whether it was a purposeful silence on his part—that perhaps he wanted her to have it, keep it. A year passed, two. Three. The house was still Isabel's. The house would continue to be Isabel's.

Once a year, on the day of her mother's passing, Isabel would breakfast off one of Mother's plates, a rarity. Two slices of bread with aged cheese. The hares would appear in fragments from under her meal: a tail, a foot, an ear. When she'd finish she'd wash the plate and dry it and put it away where it belonged, in the cabinet, with the doors locked.

3

EVA TOOK UP SPACE WITH A LOUD RESTLESSNESS, A bee stuck in a room with all the windows shut. She touched things, talked about the things she touched, asked questions about them—*Is this painting supposed to be the Veluwe? Was this your mother's vase?*—took to circling the gardens with a cigarette in hand, put her fingers to the petals of shrubs, the trunks of trees. Isabel avoided her. Isabel watched her from an upstairs window. Isabel dug her fingers into her wrists and breathed steadily through her nose.

Neelke, the maid, came by first thing on Monday. Isabel hurried her inside with a list of things that needed to be done. First it was a relief to do so, to have another person in the house, a more familiar one, distraction from the annoyance that was Eva. And then Neelke went to fill a bucket with soap and water and Isabel's relief turned sour. Now there were two people in the house. Now Isabel had to keep her mind on two people in her house, anxious all the more about the potential third—Johan, on his day off, coming up the driveway, hands in his pockets, his slow walk, his dripping way of leaning in and saying, *Missed me?*

Neelke was eighteen. She wore sundresses, had a tight, plump mouth that she often picked at when nervous or in thought. She was the youngest sister of a girl called Silke whom Isabel had gone to school with. Isabel had liked Silke once, because Silke was

35

quieter than the other girls and usually had a book with her—and Isabel could forgive that they were only ever novels, only ever romantic ones. For a little while in year three they biked home together after school, mostly in silence. Silke's high ponytail would whip in the wind, eyes squinting against the gales. One time, Isabel asked her whether she wanted to come over: they could read in her room together. Silke said yes. But Louis had been at home that day, listening to some radio play in the kitchen, and Silke kept making up reasons to linger: could she have a glass of water, and would he be having tea, and could she have some, too, and did Louis always listen to this radio show, and did he know much of radios? He must be *so* smart. Did he know *her* brother? Her brother, too, had graduated last year.

Louis answered the questions without looking at Silke straight on, only from the corner of his eye.

Eventually, up in Isabel's room, all Silke wanted to talk about was Louis. And when Isabel said, *It's really boring to talk about my brother*, Silke then proceeded to talk about every single boy in their class instead: the one with the good hair, the one with the soft eyes, the one who looked like he'd grow to be taller than the rest. She seemed to like them all, even the ones who Isabel had decided with flat certainty were ugly or obtuse. Silke had a nice, sighing thing to say about every single one.

It ended in a fight. Isabel snapped, said, *Are boys really the only thing you can think to talk about*, to which Silke went red and gave a breathless speech of: *Well, at least I talk about anything at all, at least I'm not weird and boring!* And when Silke stormed downstairs, Isabel followed her. And when Silke reached past her to get her coat, Isabel bit her. Her arm was just—right *there*, sleeve pushed up to her elbow. Her skin looked smooth, like the flesh of an almond. No freckles, only the grain of golden hairs. She had been so rude to Isabel. She'd called her *weird*.

She had said Louis's name so many times up in Isabel's room, *so many times*. Silke screamed when Isabel bit her. She screamed even when Isabel let her go, she screamed like she would die. Isabel's mouth left behind a spit mark.

Isabel still had two years left at school after that. They were long and boring. Silke had told *everyone* about what had happened. Some of the boys barked at Isabel during lunch breaks; the girls avoided her with pointed distaste.

When Neelke came by to interview for the job, she wore a knitted cardigan over her dress, held her sleeve ends over her wrists, arms covered. She smiled with her mouth closed. Before she left, she lingered in the doorway, eyes down. She said: *You were in Silke's year, right?* She used the honorific *you*: a deference, a humbling. She looked so much like Silke had back then.

Isabel had confirmed with a single *yes* and had nothing further to say. Isabel gave her the job with a heady satisfaction—like she'd won something. It didn't last long. By the end of Neelke's first week Isabel was checking the windows for missed spots. She rewashed the dishes where she thought a stain had been left, locked her jewelry box, counted her mother's rings.

Eva woke up earlier than usual. It was still very late. Her habits seemed to Isabel a natural extension of her personality: she was loud in the night, talked in her sleep and then slept in, ate in small bites throughout the day, never in one meal, often didn't finish her plate. She left her things carelessly behind and then forgot where she'd put them, would stomp through the house trying to find them. Sometimes she'd disappear for a while. Sometimes she'd be everywhere all at once. Her perfume bullied itself around the house.

Isabel was still finishing her breakfast when Eva came in. She had her hair wrapped in a scarf. Her eyes were puffed with sleep, skin dry around the mouth. She was in her houserobe. She put out a plate for herself, poured some coffee. Isabel said, "You're early," and Eva said, "Hmm?"

Upstairs, Neelke was washing the windows.

"You're early," Isabel repeated. It was a judgment now.

Eva arranged herself a few slices of cheese. Cucumber, tomato. "It got too bright in the room. Someone was—stomping around. I couldn't sleep." Her voice was rough.

"Neelke came to change the sheets today." And then, tapping the crumbs from her fingers, Isabel said: "I suggest now will be a good moment to move your stuff."

Eva looked up at her. "Move my—"

"You won't be staying in Mother's room."

"Your mother's—"

"There's a guest room on the third floor. I've left the windows open so it's aired. Neelke will show you where to—"

"I'm sorry." Eva hitched a breath in the shape of an apology. "Why would I be moving?"

Isabel had decided not to explain herself. "As I've said. You won't be staying in Mother's room."

"It's where Louis said I could stay."

"Well, Louis is not here, and does not live here."

"But it's his house." And then, purposefully kind: "As much as it's yours."

Isabel kept her gaze steady. She arranged her fork on her plate, put her hands neatly in her lap. Eva looked back at her, a questioning smile, eyebrows up. They were a dark brown.

Isabel stood quickly and went to get her jacket from the hook by the back door. "It's not up for discussion. Just do it," she said, and arranged her collar. "I'll be gone today. Don't get in Neelke's way, she'll be busy. But . . ." She hesitated. Eva considered her with a frown. Her night scarf had slipped back and the line of her hair, now visible, came down in a window's peak, brown bleeding into bleach. Isabel cleared her throat, said, "Don't let her roam."

"Roam? Your maid? What, do you think she'll—"

"I don't think anything. I'm just telling you. If—if you see anything, if she, if she takes anything you think isn't hers, just—"

"*Oh!*" Eva said, and then laughed. Put her hands over her mouth like she hadn't meant to.

Isabel looked at her, teeth clenched, and Eva said, "Oh, it's just that Louis had mentioned—" But Isabel didn't want to hear what Louis had told her. She left to the sound of Eva's "Isabel, no I—" and shut the door behind her, marched across the gravel. She took the car to the city. Saw the butcher about tomorrow's order, picked a fabric for the new curtains in the study, then drove to Assen to visit an old friend of her mother's. *Tante* Rian had no children of her own and lived in a big house that was all brown on the inside. She reused coffee grinds instead of making a new pot. Every now and then she would break silences by saying, *Oh, you used to adore me when you were a child, you and your brothers all.*

Today, Isabel sat on the couch and listened to Rian talk about an issue she had with an old neighbor, something about an oven dish that may or may not have been given as a gift before the war. The old neighbor wanted it back, and Rian thought it was so tiring, to still insist fifteen years after the fact. Isabel only half listened. She had left a silk shawl on a hanger in the entryway and she worried about it: she should have folded it into her jewelry box, the one with the lock. In the car, on the way back, the moment Louis said goodbye to Eva it stuck to Isabel's memory, like a feather to a honeyed finger: Eva leaning back against the doorway, and Louis leaning over her, kissing her mouth, a hand on her breast, kneading, murmuring something, kissing her again. Isabel could see the slip of his tongue between their mouths. Eva smiled through it all. Her hands were loose on his side: up and down they went. Up, down.

Isabel had been up on the first landing, crouched, watching them between the slats of the railing. Louis whispered, *Will you be good?* And Eva whispered back, *I'll be incredibly good.*

After he left, Eva stood there for a while, blankly staring at the wall. The smile was gone. Her mouth, kiss-swollen, was slack. She looked vacant. And then, as though with the snap of a rubber band, she was back in her body, and walking, and rounding the bottom of the stairs. She saw Isabel up on the landing and startled. "Oh God," she said, and put a hand over her heart and laughed. "Oh, you scared me."

It was early evening by the time Isabel got home from Rian, arms full of paper-bagged groceries. The shawl was where Isabel had left it, on the peg. Neelke's bike was not outside: she'd gone home.

The house smelled clean. A breeze came through—the windows had been left open. Isabel found Eva in the lounge, on the sofa, paging through a Bijenkorf catalog. The radio was on. She was in high-waisted trousers, hair in two short pigtails. Her legs she had folded under her. The bottoms of her socks were dirt-dark. She looked like a child, like she was making a child of herself. She looked up at Isabel and smiled. She did it slowly.

"Hello," she said, and put the magazine aside. "Do you need any help with those?"

Isabel said "No" and readjusted the groceries. She realized now she had come into the room, and she had come to a standstill and had remained there: unmoving, staring. Eva said, "How was your day?" And Isabel said, "When did Neelke leave?" And Eva leaned forward and said:

"Oh, she's just the sweetest thing, isn't she? So shy, too, I said oh, let me help you when she was peeling the potatoes and she was so worried you'd not—"

"You *helped* her?"

"Well—" Eva leaned back. Her leg slipped out from under her. "Yes, why not? I'm here. I'm not doing much."

On the radio a quick-beat song came on. It wasn't a station Isabel ever listened to. "I'm not paying *you* to peel potatoes, I'm paying *her.*"

"Oh, come on, Isabel." This was said with exasperation, like Isabel was being silly, like this was a recurring theme between the two of them—Isabel being silly, Eva suffering through it.

Isabel left the room quickly. She went to the kitchen to put the groceries away. Eva followed, shuffling steps. She didn't lift her feet properly when she walked. She said, "Do you really not like Neelke?"

Isabel polished each apple with a towel before putting it in the basket. "Of course *you* do."

"What do you mean?" She sounded mild. Isabel didn't answer. She polished an apple, put it in its basket. A heat was coming up the back of her neck. Eva came down the steps into the kitchen proper. She asked it again: "Isabel. What do you mean?"

Isabel could imagine who Eva would have been in school: loud, happy, beloved. Not unkind, necessarily, but the kind who would still giggle with the rest of them for unknown reasons, pointing at someone. The kind who sighed over boys with good hair, over those with bright eyes. She would not have noticed Isabel, not in a good way.

"I watched her, you know," Eva said. "Just like you wanted me to."

Isabel put the soap under the sink. She had to make space for it between bottles and packages. Eva said, "She's just a girl. Harmless."

Isabel put the green beans in the vegetable drawer.

"Oh, what's this?" Eva wandered over to the mantelpiece,

41

reaching for the broken piece of Mother's plate; Isabel had placed it there, at a loss of what else to do with a sliver of a memory. She couldn't throw it away. She couldn't place it in the vitrine with the rest of the set. Eva turned the little thing in her hand, inspected it. "What animal is it supposed to be?" she asked, not looking up. "A rabbit?"

"Don't touch that," Isabel said. "Put it back."

Eva turned to her, amused, it seemed, to have got a reaction from Isabel. To have found something. Isabel marched over, took the piece from her hands, put it back where it belonged. Adjusted it, balanced it against the wall. Eva watched her do it, didn't comment on it. Didn't move away, either. She smelled like she'd been drinking coffee. She smelled like hand soap. Isabel glanced at her quickly and found her closer than expected. She was so short. She had a way of *looking*.

It made Isabel's heart trip into a frightened speed. A moth under a dome of a glass.

Then Eva said, "Louis called earlier."

Isabel moved away, fussed over her skirt, said, "Did he? Well, is he coming to pick you up already?" Work must be covering his phone bill, if he could call from abroad. She put her back to Eva. She hoped her neck wasn't as flushed as it felt.

"No. He was just checking in on me. He asked if you were being nice to me. If you were being decent."

Isabel stilled.

Eva said, "I told him you were lovely."

Isabel didn't know whether this was humor. She looked at her, and then away, and then left—with a breath and a huff. Her skirt was rough over the skin of her legs as she strode through the house, up the stairs, into her room. And changing her mind and leaving her room again, stopping, stranded in the hallway. She held herself by her waist.

A breeze passed through one room and into the other. The door to her mother's room creaked. Fresh sheets, the lace vitrage curtain in the wind, the wide bedframe and the old secretary and Eva's nightgown, silk folded at the foot of the bed. Two of her skirts over the back of the armchair, all of her perfume bottles in a row, makeup bag spilled over the open secretary desk. A leather-bound notebook with a pen keeping place in the pages.

Isabel went to it. It looked used. A diary, perhaps. A log of—

"That's mine," Eva said. She was in the doorway. Isabel had the book in her hands, about to open it. She put it down quickly, said:

"I told you to move your stuff to the guest room."

"I know," Eva answered. "I talked to Louis about it. He said I didn't have to."

"Louis doesn't *live* here."

"Is it so important, Isabel? It's—I know it's your mother's room, and that you cared for her of course, but I mean it's been . . ." She gave an affected gesture: a deep sigh, sympathy. "Gosh. Don't you get lonely, Isa? All alone in this big house?" She was using that voice again: higher than her own, tighter. An actress in a bad play.

Isabel said, "Isabel. Not Isa. You call me Isabel."

Eva's smile was gentle. "Isabel," she said.

"This is not your room."

"Of course it's not."

"Move your things to the guest room."

"I'll sleep here for now, Isabel. It's only for a little while, isn't it? I'm only a guest. I'm not—taking anything from you. You know that, right? I'm just passing." She took a step into the room, another. "Don't you know that?"

Isabel's heart climbed, was tapping fast under her ear. Eva stepped toward her, reached, and Isabel thought she wanted to touch her, do something to her, squeeze her at the waist again. Isabel took a stumbling step back, bumped the chair, but Eva only wanted to reach for her diary. Eva said, "Oh—" as the chair teetered. It didn't fall.

Eva took the book and in a series of quick beats she put the book in the secretary drawer, closed it, turned the lock.

It was the drawer where Mother had once kept her children's letters. Isabel's childhood diary had been kept there, too.

Back in her own room, Isabel slammed her door shut. She looked around, frantic, her shirt too tight, her skirt cinched too close to the skin. Her breath came in rough drags. Her fingers were going numb. She went to her wardrobe and rummaged and grabbed and stuffed the white undershirt in her mouth, as much of it as would fit, and bit down. Clenched. The strain at the hinge of her jaw, the prickling in her eyes. She sat at the foot of the bed and breathed through her nose.

The shirt, when she pulled it from her mouth, was crumpled, spit-wet. Isabel could see herself from the dresser mirror: face red, mouth like a violence. She looked like she'd been crying.

Neelke had left dinner—an oven dish—in the oven. Isabel ate in the study, alone.

That night she couldn't sleep. The house creaked. The house always creaked. In the next room, Eva was having a nightmare of some sorts: huffing, mumbling. It stopped, eventually, and then a silence descended. Footsteps, she thought, but when she went to look the hallway was pitch-black and all the doors were closed. Silence. She went back to bed, dozed in a clammy hold, and startled awake to a sudden knock at the door. She shot upright and wasn't sure: whether it had come from within a dream, whether it had come from outside. Whether it had been loud or quiet.

She kept a torch next to her bed, always, and let it guide her way down the stairs in a bright circle of light. There was no one standing at the front door, no one standing at the back door. The garden stared back at her, blues and grays, asleep. A breeze pulled at the hem of her nightgown. The arms of the lilac shrub swayed. In the kitchen Isabel lit a small fire against the snapping cold of the night and turned on the radio at its quietest. She had a glass of water. She sat by the window and breathed. A single bird warbled at the first note of dawn.

Isabel took the spoons from the drawer and laid them out in the same order as before: biggest to smallest. They lined up so neatly. She counted them: eleven. She counted them again: eleven.

She breathed hotly. Counted them again: *eleven*.

One missing. One spoon missing. She took out the drawer and opened the cabinet and looked in all the spaces where a spoon might have fallen. Eleven.

Eleven.

I watched her, Eva had said. *She's just a girl*, she'd said. *Harmless.*

The next morning, Isabel was waiting for her: laid out a plate for her, a glass, cutlery. When Eva came in, sleep-rubbed, Isabel followed her movements closely—sitting upright in her chair, eyes dry at the edges. When Eva went to the drawer, Isabel said, "No need," and gestured at the table: everything was ready.

Eva looked about, confused a moment. She said, "Oh." And, "Thank you," uncertain. She sat down, taking in the breakfast table. The glass of milk. She said, "Is Neelke coming today?"

"No," Isabel said.

"Right," Eva said.

"It's just us today."

Eva looked up. "No errands today?"

"No. I'll be staying home. All day." She nodded at the food. "Eat," she added, a command. "It's for you."

4

A WEEK HAD PASSED AND ISABEL WAS COUNTING down: three more to go. She sent Louis a quick note tracking the extra costs incurred in the household due to Eva's stay. She called Johan and told him she would be too busy, this week, for a visit, and he said, *Oh, come now, Isabel*, as if she was playing a fun game. She insisted, heart beating fast, that she could not come to him, that she had a guest in the house.

"A guest?" he asked, that same dripping way, words stretched out. "Should I be worried about my Isabel being stolen away from me?"

A roiling, seasick feeling. Nerves, Hendrik said. She hung up and sat at the telephone desk and in a notebook she made an inventory: divided the house into floors, the floors into rooms, and each room had three columns—items, how many, placement. She filled the page and then tore it out, filled the back, too, cramped writing to fit it all. She kept the paper, folded up small, in her pocket. Sometimes she'd reach for it: not to take it out, not to check anything, but just to touch it.

Eva came to find her in the garden and asked whether she could borrow one of the bikes in the shed.

"Why?" Isabel asked. She was on her knees, cutting stems off the rhubarb, placing them in her basket.

"I thought I'd go to town."

"What do you have to do in town?"

"Oh, I don't know. Get an ice cream, send a letter." Eva tipped a finger to a purple rhododendron bulb. "And it'll be nice to go somewhere a moment, really, I don't think I've ever been just in one small place for so long—I mean it's a big house, of course, but what I mean is . . ." She trailed off. "Would you like to come with me?"

A strand of Isabel's hair was stuck to her cheek. She could feel it. It was a warm day and she was sweating. She said, "No." And then, a beat later, "You can take Hendrik's old bike. But it'll be too big for you."

"I don't mind."

"You'll have to roll up your trousers," Isabel said. "The chain will dirty the hem."

Eva looked at her blankly. It lasted a moment too long, too silent, and so Isabel said, "You don't even know the way."

Whatever thought Eva had sunk into now lifted with a snap and she said, "Oh, I'll figure it out. You can tell me. I'll ask someone along the way."

"The bike wheel wobbles."

"I'll be fine," she said, and stood there a beat longer. She didn't fidget. She barely seemed to move at all.

A bead of sweat rolled from Isabel's cheek to her neck. Eva followed its track, eyes slow, and Isabel wiped it away. She cut one more stem of rhubarb, then got up to show Eva to the shed. She kept her arms to her body; she didn't want Eva to see the sweat stains, or where her blouse stuck to her back. Eva wrangled Hendrik's old bike out of the shed. It had gone unused for years, was so rusted that a puff of dust came off it when Eva clapped the saddle. The bike was indeed too tall for her: it took her a few tries to get on, and when she biked, her toes barely reached the pedals. She waved at Isabel, cycling down the gravel path. "I won't be long!" she shouted. She had a small linen bag hanging from her shoulder. Her hair was up in a short pony-tail. She'd painted her lips that same heart-attack red as the first night they'd met.

Isabel watched her disappear around the stand of trees and then rushed inside, upstairs. Eva kept Mother's room in a mess—sheets rumpled, clothes piled. Bottles, tubes, cakes of powder. Once, when Isabel was twelve, her mother found a pile of blood-soiled stockings Isabel had kept under her bed, and for the mess Isabel received two strikes over her wrists. It had been her first period, and she thought she was dying—no one had told her about bleeding. No one had told her what to do with the mess. Mother had no patience for mess.

Isabel went to the secretary, crouched, tried to open it: locked. The drawer too—locked. The key was gone. Isabel up-turned some things to see whether she could find it and came up empty. She did glance over a letter, sent by Louis earlier that year, apparently written soon after they'd first met. He was an awkward writer, tried to expound on Eva's beauty but seemed unable to come up with any word other than *heerlijk* to describe any part of her. *Delightful*. Her delightful face. Her delightful voice. The delightful way her delightful bosom pressed against—

Isabel put the letter down. On the nightstand, stuck into the edge of her mother's picture frame, Eva had wedged a different photograph. It was a woman. Dark hair and a broad smile, look-ing up from a book. She, too, was lounging in a garden. In a chair, in a white dress; one shoe was dangling off her foot, held only by a big toe. The picture was taken hastily—a little blurry, a little out of focus. There was no name, no date. She looked like a harsher version of Eva: eyes more deep-set, cheeks more pro-nounced. Pretty, still. Family.

It seemed obvious, but Isabel hadn't considered it: Eva had

to have come from somewhere. Had once been a child, toothless and wobbling. Isabel plucked the picture from its hold. She fingered the scalloped edge, trying to imagine, and then abruptly stopped. The mud was caked under her nails and her knees were stained from the earth: she had dragged the garden into the house. Isabel tossed the yellowing thing back at the table and left. She tried to find calm in the quiet of the empty house. A bug bumped its body against the glass, once, twice. Three times. She had spent the week since Eva's arrival wanting that emptiness back, longing for it with a hollow belly of desire. She wanted Eva gone, at times so badly she thought she'd just snap, grab Eva by the back of the neck, and drag her out—lock the doors behind her.

But she was restless now. Eva wasn't gone, she'd only just stepped out. She'd be back any moment. Isabel washed her hands and changed her clothes. She unfolded her inventory and walked through it, room to room, and made sure everything was accounted for. A pencil box was missing. Neelke had dusted in the study yesterday. Isabel made note of it. She stood in the dining room, paper flat on the table, and thought. The grandfather clock clicked its tongue at her. On the wall opposite, a painting of a landscape. A purpling dune, a horizon of windblown pines. It was, as Eva had guessed, the Veluwe.

Isabel took the car to the city, parked behind the church. She walked with her chin slightly up toward the Nieuwe Markt, the post office. At home she'd scribbled a quick postcard to a cousin in Brussels. She had meant to send word for weeks.

It was a slow day, the building empty. Quiet conversations echoed under the high ceiling. A man was pushing a cart full of post across the hall. Isabel asked for the right postage, asked the woman in the booth—as an afterthought—whether she'd seen a young woman earlier. Bleached hair, short.

The woman, watery-eyed, thought about this a moment. "Maybe," she said. "Froukje? By the name Froukje?"

"No. Thank you," Isabel said, cleared her throat and left.

Back at the house, Hendrik's old bike was parked out by the gravel, on the edge of the grass bed. Eva was inside: in the kitchen, at the table, writing in her black notebook. Eating a pear. The juice ran down the back of her hand. When she noticed Isabel she turned the notebook over, put it down face-first. She wiped her hand on a kitchen towel. Her lipstick had rubbed off.

"You were gone," she said, and said it in such a way that for a second Isabel thought Eva had seen Isabel in her car, had seen Isabel scurry in and out of the post office. Had stood around a corner, perhaps, smirking to herself, knowing, about to make fun of Isabel for—

Isabel touched the back of a chair, took her hand away again. She said, "Yes."

There was another pear, left in the middle of the table, propped like a statue. Eva said, "I got one for you, too."

Just the one. Not a bag of pears, or several for the fruit basket. Just the two: one for her, one for Isabel. *I don't want it*, Isabel wanted to say. She said, "Thank you." She took the pear. Put it in her pocket.

Eva looked amused. "You won't eat it?"

"Later," Isabel said, and then, with a few aborted movements, fled upstairs. In her bedroom, Isabel—sitting on the edge of her bed—held the pear in the cup of her hands. If she'd eat it now, she'd have to go downstairs to throw away the pits, the core. If she ate it later, Eva might walk by, see her eat it. She did not want Eva to see her eat it. She could throw the whole thing away. She could open the window and throw it away.

It was a water-heavy fruit, full-ripe. The first bite spilled on Isabel's skirt. It wouldn't show: the fabric was brown, checkered.

There was no way of eating it in silence—the sounds it made, the wet. Isabel ate through the whole thing: the flesh and stick and pits and core and all. She made sure nothing was left of it, as though it had never been given in the first place.

Her arms were dripping. Wet all around her mouth. She had to wash her face in the basin afterward.

The spot on her skirt where the fruit had stained remained throughout the day, a cloying brush to the back of her hand.

One silver candle holder went missing. There were two of them, an unappealing set, stumpy and old. Her mother's. Kept in the back of the cupboard, taken out only for occasional polishing. One was gone. It was evening when Isabel found out. She rummaged through the kitchen, dining room, thinking—*This will prove me right, this will—*

She found it under a cabinet: as though it had been placed on the table and had then fallen and rolled out of sight.

Who would do that, Isabel wondered, and felt that she knew already.

Eva was downstairs, writing a letter. Isabel sat at a distance, positioned to watch her. Neelke was upstairs, scrubbing down the bathroom. Every now and then Eva would glance up to see whether Isabel was looking at her, and when she found she was, Eva looked down again quickly, flushing. This went on until Eva stopped midway through a sentence and looked up and said into the space between them:

"You know you don't have to—" And then cut herself off. Isabel waited for her to finish her sentence. She didn't.

"I don't have to what?" Isabel said.

51

"Nothing."

"What don't I have to do, Eva?"

Eva's mouth closed. Her name spoken by Isabel sounded odd to Isabel's ears, badly placed. Eva said, "Never mind, never mind," and folded her letter and went to the garden. Isabel turned in her spot in the armchair: she could still see Eva through the window. Eva looked over her shoulder, marched down the long path. She reached the end, then stopped. Lingered. She stayed there, standing, and Isabel thought, *Something is wrong,* and it took a moment for the thought to catch up with her sight: Eva was shaking. Her shoulders, her arms. Visibly so—terribly so. Then she bent over and held herself, and went down to a crouch, and Isabel got out of her chair, went to the window, and held the curtain further aside and—

She was laughing. Eva was laughing. A hand to the ground to steady herself. It did not stop.

Isabel stepped back. It felt like a déjà vu, like she had seen this before, and had been here before. But she hadn't. There was nothing for Eva to laugh at. Nothing but Isabel, should she want to laugh at Isabel.

She turned away from the window. A moment later, Eva was gone. She stayed gone for hours, hours, and it was nearly evening when she returned—looking sun-pinked and dusty. She entered quietly, uneasily, and as she was taking off her shoes in the hallway Isabel came to her and said: "You can't just leave like that."

Eva did not look up at her. "Oh?"

"What if—" Isabel started, and didn't know how to finish. She recalled, with a sudden stark brightness, how Eva stood at the end of the drive and laughed. Her face had been twisted in a grimace.

She looked normal now. Tired. Her hair had frizzed up in a mess. She appeared to consider Isabel—how Isabel kept her hands fisted at her sides, how she stood so much taller than Eva. Her gaze went down, up.

"Did you worry?"

Isabel did not enjoy being looked at. She made herself stiff, said, "I did not worry. It is—not proper, for a guest, to just—to—"

Eva's smile was the smallest thing, a sad pull of a lip. She said, "I'm going to wash up. When is dinner?"

It took a moment for Isabel to answer. "In an hour."

Eva went upstairs. Neelke had made a mashed potato dish with pork *slavinkjes* and green beans. Isabel occasionally took her dinners with Eva in the dining room. Eva had been excited for her company at first—spent an evening peppering Isabel with questions, a child asking, *What does that mean, what does that mean!* What did Hendrik do for a living, and what did that mean, and what did her father do, and what did *that* mean, and when did they move, and what was Isabel's favorite subject in school, and did she have good friends in the city, and did she have a boyfriend, a *liefje*, would she ever want to—

Isabel either didn't answer, or answered in a way so dull that Eva let go of her line of inquiry. The thought of Eva knowing about Johan turned her stomach over, something unsavory about it, something unwell. That first dinner ended in a long stretch of silence. Eva said once, "Don't you have anything you want to know about me?" To which Isabel said, "No."

After that the dinners turned into sober affairs. Eva, every now and then, either out of habit or out of desperation, would still ring out into the silence with a question. *What year was the house built, do you know?* To which Isabel said: *I haven't a clue.*

Tonight was even quieter. Eva pulled apart her meat, ate half, pushed the rest around her plate.

Isabel watched her at it. "That's disrespectful."

Eva put down her fork. She seemed to be considering a thought. Then said, "Does nothing bring you joy, Isabel?"

"What kind of question is that?"

"A simple one," said Eva. She sounded resigned.

Isabel took a halted breath. An answer was at the back of her throat—she would speak it, she knew. If she did not stop it now she would speak it. She ate her potato and swallowed and still, words came. Unbidden, they still came: "What does it matter, what brings me joy. What a question, what brings me joy. And who are you, to think I have no—To assume I—"

"Oh, then tell me." Eva leaned forward, toward Isabel. Something about her lit up, a moment: like Isabel had given her an inch there, and she wanted more. "If I have it wrong, then tell me, really, tell me what—"

"Nonsense," Isabel said, and took her plate to the kitchen. She stood at the counter, arms locked. There was a track in the ceramic of the sink, fixed last winter, and the filler was a different color: a gray lightning bolt of a shape. She rolled the word *joy* around her head like an insult. She knew no one who spoke of it, of joy, unless in jest. Hendrik saying *what a joy* at an especially long line at the bank; Rian saying *what joy do you bring me today* and herding her into the house, and telling her about a neighbor who'd been rude and a woman at the store who'd been rude, too.

Her mother would sometimes call her a joy. *Geluk*. What a joy you are. When Isabel was a child, at bedtime, her mother would sit at her side and drag a fingertip in a line from the top of her forehead to her chin. She would do this over and over again, whispering *Allez-hop!* every time she passed the slope of Isabel's nose. Pretending it was a playground slide. She did this until Isabel fell asleep.

One day, during their first winter here, Hendrik fell asleep in the cradle of her arms. She'd been reading him a book, on the couch, and he fell asleep. He'd been under the weather, had a slight fever, and his cheeks were puffy, red. Isabel held him and felt his heartbeat through the line of his spine. He was ten. She wanted to seal him in something, wanted to cover him in hard metal, him and her together: hidden and forgotten and underground. Airplanes whistled overhead and nothing was allowed to touch him. She thought that might have been joy, or something like it. Something that feels sad as much as it feels like love. When Isabel was twenty-two, the year after her mother's passing, she got a dog, Haasje. Little hare. The animal wasn't very clever—chased everything into the water, even the things that meant danger. She made Isabel laugh when so few other things ever did. Haasje died, too, barely a few years old. Too young for a dog. There had been a tumor. What was joy, anyway. What was the worth of happiness that left behind a crater thrice the size of its impact. What did people who speak of joy know of what it meant, to sleep and dream only of the whistle of planes and knocks at the door and on windows and to wake with a hand at one's throat—one's own hand, at one's own throat. What did they know of not speaking for days, of not having known the touch of another, never having known, of want and of not having felt the press of skin to one's own, and what did they know of a house that only ever emptied out. Of animals dying and fathers dying and mothers dying and finding bullet holes in the barks of trees right below hearts carved around names of people who weren't there and the bloody lip of a sibling and what did—what did she *know* of—what could she *possibly* know of what it—

A thimble from her sewing kit. Isabel could not find it. It was such a small thing, could've gone anywhere—could've rolled under the bed, could've ended up in a pocket, and then in the drain after a cleaning.

It did not prove anything. It was only a thimble. It did not prove—

Isabel caught her in the office. Eva was taking something from the desk, something shiny. Isabel marched in and the door bounced off the wall, causing a loud bang. A figurine fell over, a vase teetered on the top shelf. They both turned to the noise, eyes up, watching the vase still itself. Then Isabel looked back and glimpsed the tail end of a movement: Eva trying to hide her hand from view, to put it in her pocket. Isabel went to her, grabbed her wrist in a tight grip.

"Isa—" she started, and Isabel held her wrist higher, tried to shake whatever was in it from her grip. "*Ah!*" Eva stumbled—steadied herself, hand back against the desk. Isabel was so much taller. Eva looked up at her, face flushed. The bones of her wrist felt delicate like that, ground together in the circle of Isabel's hand.

They remained for a moment. Eva's stuttering breath close, Isabel's heart a rush of noise in her ears. Their knees knocked together. Eva wouldn't let go of what was in her hand. Isabel took it, then—took her hand, turned it over, wrenched open her fingers. Eva began with an "It's just my—"

An earring. A fake golden earring. Isabel didn't recognize it: it wasn't hers, not her mother's. Neelke, she thought in a frenzy, didn't have her ears pierced. She looked up from Eva's hand and saw—the other earring, hanging from the tender drop of Eva's ear. The late-day sun painted the room in low light, and it caught the peach fuzz on Eva's jaw, the pierced lobe. The flesh of an almond.

"My earring," Eva said, so quietly, breathless. "I dropped it. I was looking for it."

Isabel's eyes went unfocused, focused. Eva's crooked tooth under her full lip. Isabel pulled away, let Eva go. There was a red mark where she'd held her—and she had held her, so very tightly.

Eva breathed quickly. She looked at Isabel and almost spoke, and stuttered first before saying: "What did you think I was doing?" she asked. "Did you think—that I was stealing something?"

Isabel's mouth went dry. She had been so sure. She had thought: *Now I have you.* Eva had been a warm line of heat and Isabel had thought—*Now I have you.* She had imagined the rest in loose flashes: police outside the house, Louis with a shocked expression, Hendrik saying, *Oh, Isa, you were onto her, you really did know that she*—

Eva was putting her earring back into her ear: passed the metal through the flesh, the pierced slit. She clicked the hook into place, eyes on Isabel. On her face—her nose. Her chin. She must have seen something in Isabel's reaction, because she started on a breath, saying: "Oh, you're very protective, aren't you? Of your family, this house. Of Louis. I understand. I also have things I . . . And it suits you, you know. It's very noble, in a way, I think, but Isabel . . ." She was scanning her now, looking for something. "You worry too much. You shouldn't worry so much. What danger am I, hmm? Small as I am?" A soft smile now, and she reached out: in the scuffle a strand of hair had come loose from Isabel's bun—fell over her brow, eye. Eva brushed it aside, tucked it behind Isabel's ear. Her fingers were colder than the room, nails cut short. "Sweet Isabel. What could I do to you?"

Isabel jerked away. The words felt as if they had been shouted across rather than hushed in the small stretch between them. *She knows*, Isabel thought, wildly, and then—*what? Knows what?* She had no answer.

Up in her room Isabel sat at her dresser. There was a cloud of bugs by the open window, catching the setting sun, dancing up, down. In the mirror Isabel tried to see what Eva had seen. She pulled the strand from behind her ear, arranged it over her eye again. Pushed it back, hand slow, smoothing it back. She touched her cheek, the corner of her wide mouth. Her fingers to her lips: she pushed two inside, over her tongue, the ridge of her teeth, and then a door slammed shut downstairs and Isabel got up and dried her fingers off on her skirts and swallowed three times. She could still taste her own skin. She rearranged herself, looked from the window to the wall to the bed.

She knows, Isabel thought, and flushed from the inside out—mortified, a shuddering shame at something she couldn't name. She pushed her head out the window into the chilling evening, hoping the air would take it away from her.

That night, she woke up with the dredges of a dream still hot in her mouth: a pooling heat in her belly, the drag of a hand, the puff of breath on her neck. She thought someone had been in her room, but there was no one. There was only she.

5

AND THEN, OVER THE COURSE OF SEVERAL DAYS: an engraved cake knife, missing. A decorative tile, a letter opener. A napkin ring.

Isabel sat through a long Sunday morning in the church's pews. Around her the congregation mumbled along to a song and Isabel stared ahead, unseeing, at the blurry space between the piano and the pulpit. Before her: a big wooden cross. All around: the inlaid windows. Dust caught in motion. Two more weeks to Louis's return. Yesterday, Isabel, in a fit of worry, had taken out all the good china from the vitrine and laid it out on the table. She filled a bowl with soapy water and took each dish in hand: wiped a wet cloth over the surface, collected the dust. The hares went around and around in a circle and Eva came and stood nearby and watched. She had come to the kitchen for something else, and seemed to have got distracted by Isabel and her cloth. Isabel did not address her. Eva did not seem to mind. After a while, she said, "Ah."

Isabel was wiping gently over the ear of a milk jug.

Eva said, "You do that with such care." It came out quietly.

Isabel held the jug in the dip of her palm. The night had made the space between them odd, hushed. Isabel met Eva's gaze and said, "A house is a precious thing."

Eva didn't answer at first. She was looking at how Isabel was holding the little item—in a cloth, in her hand. There was something hazy about her eyes. Her mouth was slightly open, her tongue pushed behind her teeth. Isabel could see it, did not want to see it.

"Yes," Eva said at length, on an intake of air. "Yes."

The pastor was speaking of St. Augustine and his pears. Something about youth in a pear grove, something about stealing for stealing's sake, something about the seduction of disobedience. The faint taste of pear rose in the back of Isabel's throat. The pastor was quoting, looking down at notes from the pulpit: "*It was foul*, St. Augustine wrote of his childish actions. *It was foul and I loved it. I loved my own undoing.* And so in considering our own—"

A grip caught on Isabel's lungs. She had to shuffle out of her pew, making people stand. *Excuse me*, she said, and thought she would faint. She did not faint. She stood outside, hands pushed to the wall, and tried to slow her breath.

Eva took to spending the afternoons tanning in the garden. She preferred a spot by the hedge, where the firs didn't cast shade, and dragged her chair there: laid out in her two-piece, sunglasses on. She was turning a freckled brown, her hands the darkest. It made the beds of her nails stand out in pink. Isabel noticed it when she reached for something across the table, when she held a pen to write scribbled notes.

Neelke swore she didn't take anything. She gave Isabel a teary speech: *Why would I take anything? Why would I take, we have everything at home?* And Isabel said: *To sell, to pawn off, I don't know why a thief would steal, you tell me.* And Neelke said, *No no no no!* And cried, sobbed, at which point Eva came in smelling of suntan lotion. She looked bewildered by the scene, asked,

"What—" And to Isabel, immediately: "What did you say to her, Isabel?"

"None of your business," Isabel said, and Eva turned to Neelke with a "Sweetheart, what—"

"I have to go," Neelke said, even though she was only halfway through her tasks for the day. Isabel and Eva watched her leave, watched through the window as she ran off with her bike in hand: still teary-eyed, still wiping at her face.

"Be nicer to her," Eva told her, nostrils flared, and Isabel thought, *Why?* And said as much to Hendrik over coffee at a small Utrecht café, their midway point between their two homes—her driving down from the east, him driving up from the west. Hendrik was slow-limbed and happy looking that day— no jittering legs, no murmured conversations with himself. He was having a good week. He hadn't yet mentioned Sebastian's mother, or her health.

"Neelke is not stealing from you," he said. He held his coffee by the rim, a cage of fingers over the mouth of the cup. "And Eva is just some girl Louis picked up somewhere. This is not a mystery."

"But—the spoon. The—"

"Things get misplaced. Things get misplaced all the time when you live with other people. God, what do you think half my arguments with Sebastian are about?" He had to pull in his long legs when someone wanted to pass, then unfolded them again—sprawled into space. "Stop that," he said, and pulled Isabel's pinching fingers from the back of her hand.

"I don't live with other people," she said. The implication was: *unlike you.* Unlike Hendrik and Sebastian. It had been seven years and she avoided saying it out loud as such, admitting it as such— Hendrik and the person he was living with. The person he was—

"I know. But for now you do. For now." He saw her face and

laughed apologetically, said, "Oh, not for long, Isa, she'll be gone before you know it."

Isabel could find no relief in the thought. They took a walk along the city canals. Down by the water a man was hewing a sculpture of a body out of a log of wood. Next to him a willow bent heavy under the curtain of its bloom.

"How's Johan?" Hendrik asked, and Isabel said, "Oh, stop it, stop it," but the question flustered her immediately: Johan had called, just a few days ago, had complained about being abandoned, about never getting to see his girl anymore. He had invited her out for dinner. Just the two of them this time. Not at his mother's, not at hers, but a restaurant in town. It was one that Isabel had never been to, which in itself was an upsetting prospect—a new space, unknown crowds.

Along the streets of Utrecht the sun had spread her arms wide open. Boats bobbed by, an idyll. Isabel was anxious for the day trip to end: she imagined the house with only Eva in it, walking around in it, rooms full of things that weren't hers and her touching them and taking them; putting them in Mother's secretary, locking them away. Doing something with them, Isabel didn't know what, but doing *something*, doing—

"Stop that," Hendrik said again, and took her hand in his.

The first thing she heard when entering the house was Eva's voice in the other room. Isabel was hanging up her hat, her jacket, and inside the house Eva gave a hearty laugh, a giggle; she said, "Stop—stop it! No, I mean it, you can't, I won't allow, you'll just have to wait until you're here and then—"

She was in the drawing room, on the phone. Isabel lingered by the door and listened. There was a pause: on the other end of the call, Louis was talking. Then Eva took a breath, lowered her voice, said:

"Yes." And, "Yes, of course." Another long pause. "Me too.

62

Mm-hmm. Oh, my darling . . ." Eva exhaled the words: *my darling. Mijn lief.* Isabel's mother used to whisper the phrase to Isabel during storms or dark nights or on days when Isabel ached for reasons she couldn't name—when she was young and empty-feeling and wanted to put her fists through things, wanted to bite, wanted to cry. To be held. *My dear. My dear. All is well, shh, my darling.*

Isabel put her forehead to the papered wall, looked in through the gap of the door hinge. Eva sat on the arm of the couch, phone to her ear. She had her hair up. Her dye job had missed the patch at the nape of her neck, and there it was soft brown hair, a few curls. The top knuckle of her spine jutted out above the collar of her blouse. Of her face, Isabel could only see the curve of her cheek, the shape of her smile.

Perhaps Louis was truly in love with her. Perhaps Eva was in love with him. Perhaps it all was real and Hendrik was right. A clamp of a hold tightened on Isabel's lungs. Eva hung up but stayed where she was: hunched, sitting. Her smile shrunk slowly. She touched her cheek, kept her hand there. Took a deep breath.

Isabel, from her hiding place, took it with her.

A yellow egg cup, a paper weight, a children's book.

Isabel went to Uncle Karel for a visit that afternoon. They sat at the garden table for a long time in intermittent silences: he listed all the things that were considerably more expensive now than they were last year this time, then went quiet. Isabel named several things that had needed fixing in the house recently, and then went quiet. It went on. By the time she was back in her car, the earliest of twilight was pulling the sky from a robin's-egg blue to a blush. A wind rose, trees along the path gossiping with shaking leaves. They were so full this late spring. So proud.

Isabel returned home and Eva and Neelke were in the kitchen

sharing a bottle of wine. It was late, Neelke was supposed to have been gone long ago; she was not supposed to be in the house. The radio was on loudly, a popular channel playing songs with skittering beats, guitars. Neelke's skirt was all gathered up around her thighs, one leg bent under her on the chair. Her shoulders were sun-browned. She was sitting close to Eva, hair loose, and Eva bent to push Neelke's hair this way and then that: *You could wear it like this*, she was saying, *or like that. But if you cut it at this length you could—*

The inside of Eva's mouth was stained wine-purple. She was wearing Neelke's cardigan. She said something, and then they both laughed loudly, and Isabel's harsh tumble of a heart shoved her forward: down the two steps into the room. She could feel the angry heat in her face, saying, "What's this? Why is Neelke still here? What are you two—what—"

Neelke jolted, wanted to rise from her chair but was kept in place by Eva's hand—a grip to her arm. Eva turned in her seat to face Isabel, still holding Neelke by her elbow. "Hello, Isabel," she said. "How was your evening?"

"What *is* this?" Even her ears were burning now. She wanted to take the wineglass from the table and throw it against the wall. "What's she doing here?" She nodded at Neelke. Again, Neelke tried to get up but was again kept in place.

"I invited her," Eva said.

"You *invited* her?"

"Why don't you join us, Isabel? Sit down. Join. There's wine, there's—"

"I know there's wine. That's my wine." Her breath was coming fast and uneven through her nose. "This is my kitchen. This is my—"

"House, yes, we know," Eva said. "We know. This is your house." She was defiant—jaw cocked, looking up at Isabel. She'd winged her eyelids today, had painted her lashes. She was still holding on to Neelke.

"Let her go."

"I'll go," Neelke said.

"You stay," Eva said.

"Let her *go*."

"Oh, I think—I think I should—Eva, please, I—"

Eva's attention—steady and hard on Isabel—broke a moment, and then she saw Neelke: unhappy, trying to pull away. Eva murmured, "You shouldn't let her scare you like that," and let go. She took off the cardigan, passed it back to Neelke, who took it with a scramble: collecting her things, her bag. She had taken off her shoes at some point. She was stepping back into them with a frenzy.

"She's not going to fire you," Eva told her.

"I'm not?" Isabel said.

"No." Eva's eyes flared. Her back was a sharp line. "You won't."

The door bounced off its frame: Neelke let it fall shut behind her as she rushed out, not too steady on her feet. Then Eva got out of her chair—a harsh scrape on the floor—and Isabel took a step farther, ready, and both of them spoke at the same time, Isabel with a "—getting *the maid* drunk under *my* roof while—" and Eva with a "—like a tyrant, as if no one is allowed to *breathe* when you're—"

They fell silent.

"I'm losing my *mind*," Eva said. Her tone changed: less angry, more tired. "I'm *locked* in this house, I don't have anything to do and you—you follow me around, you won't leave me alone but you won't even *talk* to me, and the only person who looks at me is an eighteen-year-old!—"

"And whose fault is that? Whose idea was it, to have you come here? To have you *stay*, to—"

"What does it matter!" She laughed this out humorlessly. "Who are you so angry at, Isabel? Is it me? Is it Louis?"

Isabel tightened her arms to her sides. "The maid is not your playmate. Neelke has a *job*, she's here to—"

"Christ, are you even listening to me? You're not. You're not listening."

An indignant sound rose from Isabel. *Not listening*, Eva said, as if Isabel *could*, as if the sound of Eva's voice was a choice for Isabel to make. Every day, she had listen to Eva. Every moment spent in the house and everything about her was too big to avoid: the glare of the sun off her hair, the ring of her laughter, the way her words went high when she put on *that act*, her night terrors—huffing and restless in the dark, so loud that Isabel could hear her through two closed doors. Isabel couldn't *help* but listen, wished she could, wished she—

"This is my *life*," she ground out. "Do you *understand*? This is my—"

"And what a life it is! You *must* be bored. Isabel, I am bored beyond measure and I've only *been* here for a minute. Oh, if you'd just let me—just let me *in*, let's— We could talk, we could take walks, wouldn't that be fun? Wouldn't that be so much better?" The apples of Eva's cheeks looked tight and blotchy. She walked around the table as she spoke, walked toward Isabel. She was in a skirt, a loose shirt with straps. One of them slipped off her shoulder, and there: the pinched elastic of her bra, the way it dug into her flesh. It was pink.

"I can't," Isabel said, "think of anything worse."

Eva came to a standstill. She breathed a few quick times, chest rising. "Why are you so *determined* to dislike me?"

An invisible hand on Isabel's back, pushing her. *Forward*, it said. *Go.* Isabel pushed back against it. She said, "You're wrong. I—"

Eva's expression nearly cleared for a fraction.

"There's no determination there," Isabel said. "I dislike you—quite effortlessly."

Eva's reaction was a punched-out sound. It could have been amusement—it could have been frustration. It rolled through her once, twice. "Right," she said, and then looked up at the ceiling, the empty game rack. She blinked rapidly, throat working. "Right," she said, and walked by Isabel, making to leave. Isabel caught her by her elbow—it happened without her intention.

They both looked down at Isabel's hand, the dig of her fingers. She was holding on tightly.

"Let go," Eva said. Her voice was rough now.

Isabel let go.

The room was overfull, the room was empty. Eva was gone. On the table: a half-drunk bottle of wine. The glasses, a bowl of peanuts, peeled, a bowl of shells. She had used one of Mother's set: the legs of the three hares peeking out along the rim.

The heat of Eva's arm remained cupped in Isabel's hand.

Johan came to pick up Isabel in his car. Isabel dressed neatly, her idea of neatly: an ironed-out dress with mother-of-pearl buttons, a pattern of mustard flowers, her hair pinned down to the back of her head. Her mother had once taught her how to make a proper bun; that's what she called it, *netjes*. Proper. All of Isabel's hair in her mother's hands, gathered and gathered and twisted, twisted, the skin of her scalp pinched. It gave her a severe part down the middle of her head, pulled her features straight out of her face: big bug eyes, pale and gray. Her wide mouth. Her nose, straighter than straight. As a child she'd wanted one that went up at the end, and would try to bend it up in front of the mirror, hoping it would stay like that.

Isabel didn't like to look at herself in the mirror too long. It embarrassed her, her own reflection. She had strong ideas of beauty that she did not find in herself: how tender the face must be, how thick the hair. She had strong thoughts about what it meant, to care too much about beauty. To *want* it, to *search* for it in oneself. In another. They weren't nice thoughts.

Johan, however, was handsome enough. He did his best tonight: a fresh shirt and a good jacket, a pair of trousers she hadn't seen on him before. A pair of shoes she hadn't seen on him before, either. He'd pushed his sandy hair back with product. He did have a nose that went up, that took his top lip with it, showed his big front teeth. His parents knew Uncle Karel, and they lived nearby, and when Mother was still alive and they were all a little young, the family would occasionally come over for dinner. Johan got along with Louis, and didn't get along with Hendrik in a way that felt pointed. Johan hadn't noticed Isabel at all until a year or so ago. What happened was that Isabel was biking to the Van den Berg home and had got rained on, and on arrival had to take down her hair to let it dry. Johan had watched her sit by the fire, combing her fingers through the tangled length. He was smoking out the open doors to the garden. It was still pouring outside. He would not look away from her.

"That's a good look on you," he said when his mother left the room for a moment.

"What?" She said it sharply: he made her nervous. She knew he would say something to her. She expected it to be mocking.

"You look nice," he said. "Drowned little cat."

"Excuse me?" She shivered. She was still cold and her dress clung uneasily. She crossed her arms over her chest. He laughed like she'd made a joke. He showed up often after that when she was around. Sometimes when he visited her at the house he brought by something his mother sent along: a tin of cookies, a pot of preserves, a hat she used to wear, and didn't wear anymore, that she thought Isabel might appreciate.

He never liked to leave. He never seemed to know when she wanted him to leave; he'd stay with one elbow up on the doorframe, asking her inane questions. Did she bake the bread herself? Did she keep the house herself? Isabel would say of course she didn't, what did he take her for, she bought her bread and had a maid, and all the while she spoke Isabel fussed about, not wanting to meet his eye.

And then there were the times he touched her. Once, he kissed her neck, and a shiver like nausea ran through her. She had mentioned it to Hendrik, under the blur of several glasses of wine. Hendrik said: *Oh, that's not bad, that's good!* And Isabel said, *It is?* And Hendrik said: *That's how you know you like someone. When you're shaking and can't think and maybe you're going to throw up if he comes any closer.*

Johan turned the radio to a slow channel. He said, "I love this song."

Isabel did not know the song. She hummed in affirmation as though she did. Eva had been quiet and avoidant since the night in the kitchen. Her face seemed scrubbed of paint—paler now. Once, Isabel walked into a room and Eva picked up her book and walked right out. Once, over a tense dinner, Isabel's foot bumped against Eva's and Eva looked up, away, and all Isabel's mind provided was the echo of—*follow me around, you won't leave me alone but you won't even talk to me, and the only person who looks at me is an eighteen-year-old!*

It was a Friday evening and the restaurant was loud. Isabel was distracted the first few minutes trying to figure out where the kitchen was in relation to the bathroom in relation to the exit. Johan said, "What are you looking around like that for?" like she was entertaining, and she cleared her throat, said:

"Sorry." She touched her hand to her neck to make sure the pins were still in place: they were. "Where is the menu?" she asked, and Johan pulled the folded menu from under where she'd placed her elbow. This, too, amused him. "You're funny," he said. She really wasn't.

He talked a lot. About anything, it seemed to Isabel: himself, yes, his work, a colleague called Willy, Willy's boat called *Marcella*, the reasons why Delft was better than Tilburg. When the food came he talked about the food. He didn't like it: why were they so precious about their potatoes, about their meat? He liked a good honest meal, is what he liked, and Isabel should come by when the *opperdoezer* potatoes were in season because his mother made the *best—*

He ordered wine for the table. He made a point of saying: *Beer is my drink, but for you . . .* She drank. He touched his foot to hers under the table and she thought about Hendrik saying, *That's not bad, that's good.* The restaurant was loud. She drank some more. He went to the bathroom and passed behind her, brushed his fingers to the bare nape of her neck, and her stomach gave a jolt. She moved away from the touch and pretended to press the napkin to her lips instead. She hadn't said much more than a full sentence that night. While he was gone, she considered his empty chair, the smear of gravy on his plate. She imagined looking at his empty chair more often: at her home, or at his. Waiting for him to come back from work and tell her about Willy and his boat. Every day, tell her about Willy and his boat. The wine made her woozy, tired. She rarely drank this much, this fast, only it was so loud, and hot, and the oil left a shiny trail over his fat bottom lip and when he spoke she—

If he tries to kiss me, she thought during the car ride back, *I will let him.*

The windows down helped, but the rocking didn't. He put

the radio on again. Said again, "Oh, I really like that song." And then, putting a hand on her knee, eyes on the dark road ahead: "How lucky am I? Every time I turn on the radio there's a song I like."

She closed her eyes at the cool night air. It smelled like grass, like water. Crickets sang into the air. It was the third week of June. Johan pushed his hand up, pushed up the hem of her dress with it. His big fingers dug into the flesh of her inner thigh. He said, "Are you lucky, Isabel?"

Isabel stopped his hand: her grip over his. She opened her eyes. He glanced at her, licked his lips, and she took his hand from her leg—held it, awkwardly, in hers, fingers laced. He squeezed, smiled. Her stomach turned. Hendrik said it was a good thing.

At the house he got out of the car with her and walked up the path. She veered off unsteadily and he caught her with a hand to the small of her back, kept it there. At the door he said: "You had a good time, didn't you?"

There was one dim light on inside the house. It looked quiet, unmoving; it looked as though the house had gone to sleep, and the light had been left on by accident. Isabel held herself up against the doorway and had forgot what Johan had just asked, and he seemed to recognize, in that moment, how the drink had got to her: laughed quietly, shook his head. Stepped up, closer. He was only just a little taller than Isabel, but he seemed taller now. He ran a knuckle under her eye, her cheek. She smelled the wine on his breath, knew it was on her breath, too. She was shaking all over, couldn't stop it. The doorpost pressed into her back. She could only see the blond sweep of his lashes, the way his nose pulled his Cupid's bow up, kept his mouth open. He breathed into her mouth, and she turned her face from him with a small sound. He kissed her cheek instead. Her jaw, her neck.

She put a hand to his chest—pushed. He pulled away a little, looked at her with cloudy eyes. Pupils blown. He tried to kiss her again. Her hand kept him at bay this time, and she said, "Good night, Johan." She sounded croaky and small. He still could not focus on her face.

"Good night," he said, and tried to kiss her again. She replied with something like a *no*, something like a laugh. She pushed him farther away.

"Isabel," he said.

"Thank you for dinner." She pulled her purse to her. Checked in it, just for something to do. Checked her pins, her hair. Moved a step inside. Johan swayed back, put his hands in his pockets, and then laughed: first a wondering chuckle, and then, as if understanding something, a louder laugh, nodding, saying:

"All right, Isabel. All right."

"Goodbye," she said, and made to close the door.

"Soon? Again?" he called out.

She gave him a vague affirmative, listened to the click of the door. She waited there in the dark, looking through the mottled glass panels in the door: as he walked back to his car, as the headlights swooped over the driveway, as the tires crunched on the gravel, taking Johan away. The house fell still again. The glass was cool against Isabel's forehead. She swallowed several times: her mouth was dry, wine and dust.

She went to the kitchen for a glass of water. Her heels sounded loud against the hardwood floors; a familiar sound, a foreign one. Her mother had heels like these. Isabel took them off as she walked, took off her hat, left her purse in the dining room, and paused on the steps to the kitchen: Eva, at the table, illuminated only by the orange stove light. She was reading the same pulpy paperback she had been reading all these weeks, was still only just a few pages in. Her face was clear and shiny. She hadn't done her hair: it was curly, frizzed, pushed off her face by a ribbon-wrapped band.

Eva looked up—froze. Said, "Forgot I was here?"

"No." Isabel went to the sink. She fumbled with a glass, with the tap.

"Bet you wish you could," Eva said. She left the book on the table, came to linger back against the counter, watching Isabel fill her glass. Drink it. "So. Fun evening?"

"Have you—" Isabel swallowed a breath, a hiccup. "Taken to lurking in corners now?"

Eva shrugged. She was quiet a moment, eyeing Isabel. Then: "He sounded handsome. I could only see his back from the window. What's his name?"

Isabel drank more water. And then, all at once, felt too hot: unbuttoned the top button of her dress, took out a few pins. Eva asked, "So are you two . . . ?"

"I'm not having this conversation with you."

"Oh, come on, Isabel, don't be boring now. Finally something *exciting* happened in this tomb of a house, *surely* you—"

"Hardly exciting," Isabel said. There was a low scratch in her voice. Her neck felt damp when she touched at it. Eva hadn't talked to her in days. She was talking to her now.

"He kissed you," is what Eva said next, said it as if she wasn't sure Isabel herself understood this.

"He didn't." Isabel turned. The rim of the sink dug into her back, a cool discomfort. She said, "He tried." And then, to Eva's silence: "I'm not a schoolgirl."

Eva took a long moment to respond. The length of the pause was filled with the croak of a frog outside. With the electric hum of the stove light.

"Do you . . . not like him?"

"I've known Johan forever. Of course I—Our families are friends."

"No," Eva said. She'd gone softer, a soft that Isabel did not recognize on her: her body turned to Isabel now. Her face, unclear from the corner of Isabel's eye, seemed blurred into sympathy. "No, I mean: do you not *like* him?"

Isabel swallowed once, twice. Her mouth still felt dry. She was not in control, she realized: not of the slump of her body, not of her words. There was something about the way Eva said that word—*like. Like.* Isabel closed her eyes, tried to find steady ground. She said, "Why did you lie to my brother about wanting to come here?"

"I—" An inhale. "Pardon?"

"You told him you wanted to stay with me. Because you liked me. Why did you tell him that?"

"Isabel . . ."

Isabel opened her eyes. Eva had stepped closer to her.

"You think that was a lie?" Her face came into focus now. Her crushed mouth, eyes the color of upturned earth. "I do like you, Isabel. I think you're . . . admirable. It's you who dislikes me." She gave a silent huff, an inch of a smile. "Remember? Quite effortlessly . . ."

"I . . ." Isabel felt distantly dizzy: it wasn't her own head spinning, but somewhere nearby something was spinning, and it was dragging her in. Eva's gaze, heavy in the dark. She had never been called admirable. The kitchen felt so small.

"Is that so strange a thought?" Eva asked. "That you should be liked?"

The heat went, the heat returned. She was unsure of what the conversation was about. Where it had started, and where it was going. She swallowed again, wet her lips: that dryness, that parch.

74

Then Eva said, "Do you not *want* Johan to kiss you?"

Isabel took a breath to answer and then stopped. She said, "You mean to make fun of me."

"No, no I—" She moved. She was near. "I've been kissed by boys I didn't want to kiss, in the past. That's all, that's all I wanted . . ." She trailed off on an inhale.

"How," Isabel started, "how can you know?"

"Know?"

"If you want. Or if you, if you're . . ."

"Well . . . Well, sometimes you just know, of course, and sometimes you have to try, and then you know."

Isabel turned her face away. She was sure it was flaming. Isabel did not know what that meant at all: what it was to know, *of course*.

"You should just let him," Eva said. "Next time he tries. Find out."

Isabel kept her face tilted away. "I meant to. I intended to, tonight. I thought I would. And he—was very close and I . . ." She had said too much: she knew it the moment the words were out. More than she had told anyone, more than she ever imagined telling this girl, this burnt-edged girl, this tight-seamed girl. Eva smelled like she'd eaten a fruit: tart and sweet as she spoke. The night did not seem quite real. She had been so angry with Eva, exactly here, only just a few days ago. She had grabbed Eva's arm, and her skin had been warm, a burn to her palm. It felt far away now, a different story, muffled.

Eva said, "You worry about it too much. It's nothing, really, a kiss. It's such a small thing, you wouldn't believe."

Isabel looked at her now, quick and scathing, meaning to say something about not being stupid, about having kissed before, though she hadn't, but Eva was waiting for her there: a puff of a laugh and then she darted in, pecked Isabel on the lips.

"See! The smallest thing, isn't it? Nothing at all."

Isabel stared. Her mouth felt branded: lemon to a wound, salt. She could not take a full breath. Eva, before her, babbled around words with panicked eyes, saying how she barely remembered her first kiss, and how most boys weren't good kissers at all, and you needed to search for the good ones or train them yourself and that Isabel should be fine, should be fine because she had "good lips, you should be very glad to have good lips, not all girls . . ." She lost her train of thought, unfocused. Her eyes were on Isabel's mouth.

She was so short this close. So warm. She had made Isabel so angry and Isabel's face felt heavy, and a foreign thing pulled at her from behind her navel. Pulled. She turned to Eva—a fraction of a movement. Eva swayed, leaned first away and then, all at once, toward—tiptoes. She kissed her again. It was a press of a mouth this time: Isabel's sharp inhale, Eva's top lip between hers. Heat, the quickest bloom: the pressure of Eva's fingers to her shoulder, her chest to Eva's, her kiss. Their lips clung when Eva pulled back with a raindrop of a sound.

"Oh," Eva said. "You resemble him so much."

Isabel leaned away. Eva's hand fell from her shoulder. Her heartbeat a storm in her chest, her throat. She had never—she hadn't—

She touched her mouth briefly, and then said: "I'm not." Lowered her hand. Said, "I'm nothing like my brother."

"I—" Eva was breathing fast. Her mouth seemed redder, though all they'd done was press close a moment: a cushion of a touch. "I'm—sorry, I—I didn't mean to—"

Isabel was too muddled, all of a sudden too muddled. She turned and held her hands to her face and then righted herself, back straight. She needed to go to bed. She needed to shower, to wash herself. To sleep. To wake up and not remember this with the same clarity. She said, "I'm—" And cleared her throat. "Going to bed."

Behind her, Eva whispered: "Yes."

Isabel left, and Eva followed: a sober procession through the house, up the stairs. Isabel still felt Eva's presence like a bruise. Isabel's hand on the stair rail was clammy. Neither of them turned on the light, and so the hall remained dark, eyes slow to adjust. Up on the landing, Isabel passed a hand along her door, looking for the handle. Behind her Eva wasn't moving, wasn't making a sound. And when she did, it was very quiet, barely a breath: "Isabel."

Isabel found the door handle. She held it in her grip. She felt sick, shaking. *Don't let her come a step closer*, she thought, and Eva took a step closer. "Isabel." A touch, a reaching thing: two fingers to the dip of her spine, barely there.

Don't let—, Isabel thought, and turned, and Eva was there, right there: a hot shape in the dark. Isabel either pulled or was pulled—a rushed and clumsy embrace. The kiss happened without her knowledge, with her understanding the steps it took: how they swayed in the middle of the hallway the one moment and found wall the next; how Isabel came to hold the curve of Eva's jaw, thumb to the bony joint when Eva opened her mouth for her, did so with a stutter of a sound for her; when Eva came to fist a hand under the heat of Isabel's hair, when she came to move against her, puff against her. Isabel pushed in closer. She wanted to push Eva through the wall, wanted to push herself into Eva, too. The slide of Eva's tongue made a pendulum swing low in her belly, made something pitch like a whistle. Eva would not be quiet, would not be still, would grab at her and say, "Mm, *ah—*" Sounds from the back of her throat and restless hands pulling, hot mouth wide, putting her teeth to Isabel's lip. The jolt of the bite made Isabel reach, pinch Eva hard at the waist and Eva *gasped* and—

Isabel stumbled back. She was out of breath. Her mind had gone a white-noise hush. She couldn't see Eva well in the dark: only the glint of her eyes. Eva swallowed and her throat made a click of a sound. Isabel touched her own mouth again: swollen. It felt bruised.

Her heart gave a single terrified thump. She moved away, found her door—opened it, closed it quick behind her. Stood there for a moment, forehead against the wood. The terror was as wide as the want: a boulder moved from the gaping mouth of a cave.

She had left the sash open earlier that evening, before her date with Johan. Before—

A breeze whispered in and cooled the sweat on the back of her neck. She waited. Eventually, she heard Eva's door opening, closing. And then: silence. The creak of bedsprings. Isabel's blood rushing in her ears, her breath against the wood. Isabel licked her lips, and they were sore. She did it again, and again.

Sleep, when it came, offered no relief.

PART II

PART II

6

HENDRIK TOOK PIANO LESSONS AS A CHILD AND IS-abel did not. She had tried several times on her mother's insistence but was not very good at it and so was only angered by it. Music, when she heard it, did not sound to her like the sum of parts—it was a finished whole, a unit of cacophony. At the piano, she would put her fingers to the keys and they each rang out like a start and did not come together at all. She disliked it. Hendrik took to it. Mother would make him play jingles when guests came for dinner, which he did, quietly and with a sulk. Louis would then excuse himself from the table and stomp up the stairs, with his heavy teenage body and his heavy teenage legs.

When they were young the piano teacher would come by once a week and Hendrik practiced downstairs. The teacher was a woman in her seventies, with big dentures and hair dyed a shock of black. She never played the piano herself, only told Hendrik how to do it. She always smelled like she'd been in the sun too long—warm and dry. Then, when Hendrik was in his teens, she retired and Hendrik said he wouldn't play again but then Mother found a tutor in Zwolle who used to teach at the conservatory. The man came by their house one afternoon for tea, for introductions. Isabel didn't think much of him. He was tall in the same way all men were tall, had his floppy hair cut in the same way all men had their hair cut. He spoke with a lot of air in his words, like he was about to run out of breath, crossed and re-crossed his legs often.

Hendrik had sat at the table and hadn't spoken and when the piano tutor asked him to say something about his favorite piece to play, Hendrik had blushed violently and said that he didn't know. That he had never thought of it. Which was a lie, Isabel knew, and could not understand, and disliked the man and the conversation and had left the room to make more tea.

Hendrik would continue his lessons. He was sixteen, Isabel seventeen, and school was just a thing they had to bear for a lit-tle while longer and then they would be done. Louis had moved out the year prior, and Hendrik practiced the piano whenever he could, long, rambling hours on the thing and the music would echo up and through the house—a rushed medley of Beethoven on repeat. He would play it fast and loud, like something was chasing him down the lines of the sheet music. Isabel would do her homework and scrub her knuckles at her ears and eyes and ears again as though that could lessen the volume.

The tutor came by on Thursday afternoons. Hendrik would wait for him, sit at the window, at times a full half hour be-fore he was due. Isabel would say, "Hendrik, come away from the window, please," and Hendrik would only answer by saying things like, "Did you know he's played for the national orches-tra? And he's only twenty-seven. Isn't that young? He's met the Queen once, have you ever met anyone who's met the Queen? He's married but only just last year, and he hasn't mentioned his wife much, I don't think they've known each other very long, don't you think it's strange how sometimes people marry just because they think they—"

Isabel would go upstairs. The tutor would come, and music would be played, and the tutor would go again, and Hendrik would stand outside and wave him goodbye and then stand there after he was gone.

And then, one day, the tutor came, and music was played, and the tutor left, and Hendrik was not outside on the drive and his bike was gone. Mother asked Isabel whether she had seen him, and Isabel said no, and Mother muttered to herself for a while and then said that it was soon to be dinnertime—soon to be evening, and could Isabel go and see if she could find Hendrik and bring him home?

Isabel went on her bike. It was a terrible spring day—the air overfull with pollen, the grasses a screaming green, the swallows dipping up and down and the sheep grazing on the sloping fields. Isabel biked over the dike with a scowl. The wind was strong. She found Hendrik's bike tossed to the side near the sluice bridge. The tutor's bike was there, too, leaned on top of Hendrik's. They weren't anywhere that Isabel could see. Down the one side of the dike there were the high waters; down the other, a grazing hill, a farm, a stand of trees.

The sun was bright and Isabel's heart was racing. She left her bike with the other two and wandered. She thought, *I should call his name*, and couldn't. The sheep scattered away from her. She went to the trees and there she found them: in the shadowed patch, on the ground, entangled. She had not made out much of what was happening, only the panting, the writhing, a quick hand, and Hendrik's quiet *Oh God*. The man a bulk of a back hunched over him.

She turned around and walked and then ran and fell and hurt her knee and then got up again. Her hands were shaking. When she got home, the maid was setting the table for dinner, and Mother asked her, "Where is Hendrik?" And Isabel shook her head and shook her head and took loud and rattling breaths.

Her mother said, "Isabel? What is wrong? Isabel?" and Isabel fled upstairs and locked herself in the bathroom. She cleaned the mud and blood off her knees. She washed her face. Her mother knocked on the door. Isabel called out: "I fell. I fell off the bike. That is all."

They were halfway through dinner by the time Hendrik returned. He was rumpled. Bright-eyed and happy and rumpled, came in with a ramble of "Oh, you started! What are we having, *God* I'm starving, hello, Mother," and kissed her on the cheek. Sat at the table. He had mud on his shoulders. Mother asked, "Where have you been?" and Hendrik said, "Oh, just, out," and Mother said, "I was worried," and Hendrik said, "Why would you be worried? I just went for a bike ride." And then, with half a potato in his mouth: "I biked a bit of the way with Edwin. It was a nice day for it."

Mother watched him. Hendrik didn't notice. His collar was folded inward, and there—a mark. The skin of his neck had been irritated to a mottle. Mother put down her cutlery. Isabel went cold in her seat. She finished her plate, and the food sat big and bulky in her stomach.

There were no more piano lessons after that. Isabel overheard a fight where her mother whispered tightly and Hendrik sobbed at the top of his voice and Isabel closed her bedroom door and pushed her hands to her ears. When that didn't help, she sat on her bed and stuffed the entire corner of the quilt into her mouth and then all she could hear was her own breathing.

She caught Hendrik several days later. It was some unclear hour of night. He was trying to be quiet about it, but Isabel was a light sleeper, listening out for sounds: creaks, knocks. She heard him go down the stairs. She followed in her nightgown, feet quick on the icy floor. He noticed her then, and they fought by the front door in whispers, her saying, "You can't—you *can't!*"

And his saying, "Can't I? Are you going to stop me, Isa?" His breath was heavy with drink and he had a bottle of something in his jacket pocket. He was once a child and she had held him through his night terrors.

She said, "Why are you doing this?" And he just looked at her. Swayed on his feet a little. His eyes were wet. He went into the night, the sound of his bike loud in the garden. Isabel stood outside her mother's door, unsure of what to do. The cold sunk into her legs, her thighs. She went back to bed and didn't sleep at all and listened as the night broke, as a blackbird called out, as the rooster from the farm a kilometer away crowed. A car drove up to the house.

There came a knock on the door. Once, then three times in a loud row, and then a voice like authority calling out, asking whether anyone was awake, whether anyone was home. Isabel heard Mother's door open, heard Mother's shuffling, her bewildered muttering and her hurried movements down the stairs. Muffled voices. Isabel pushed aside the curtain to look outside— a police car. A low mist was clinging to the ground.

Isabel sat at the top of the staircase, held on to a rung. She heard snatches of sentences, some man's low burr of a voice: Hendrik had been shouting and drunk. Hendrik had tried to throw stones at a window. He had cried, he had woken up a suburban street.

The only thing Mother said was: "I see." And, "I see." And, "Thank you." And, "Clear. I see."

Hendrik said nothing, was silent through the whole thing. Tea was offered, declined. The officers left. Isabel pressed her face to the railing and closed her eyes. The house smelled like morning, like the oil used to polish the wood. Mother murmured softly to Hendrik, and Hendrik laughed in response; a mean laugh, a drunken laugh.

Mother's voice rose: "I forbid it, Hendrik. I forbid it."

And Hendrik, his words now clear as a bell: "Forbid *what*? Say it, Mother, please say it, what is it you think you forbid me to do? You can't say it, you can't even think it, of course you can't, how can you even *conceive* of such a thing, what life have you lived and now all alone in this house with your maids and your—curtains that need cleaning and the tea at twelve and *God* the boring fucking—"

The slap rang out crisply. There was nothing else that sound could have been, nothing but the rush of a hand to a cheek. Then Mother's gasp, followed by a single startled cry.

Later, in her room, Isabel went to her knees at his feet. She crouched near and pressed a damp towel to his bleeding lip. Dawn was paling behind the curtains. Mother's ring had caught on his mouth, chipped a tooth, broke skin. Hendrik sat obediently on the edge of the bed and let Isabel clean his face.

"He doesn't love me," he told her. He was crying. "He lied, he doesn't love me."

Isabel wanted to not hear the words in the same way she could sometimes blur her eyes when looking at something—decide not to see it in full focus, decide to disengage. She swallowed and lowered the cloth from his face. All of her recoiled from the word *love*. She couldn't keep the rush of sickness that came over her. She recalled: Hendrik, on the damp mossy ground, Edwin writhing over him.

"It's better like this," she said. "It was wrong. It is better that it's over."

"Wrong?" He asked it quietly. Isabel did not answer. He continued, that same small voice. "Have you ever wanted anyone, Isa? You have never. You can't even—Oh. You're just like her, aren't you?"

Isabel wanted to say, *I'm not*. She wasn't sure this was true, only that Hendrik had meant it as an insult. She said, "Perhaps I

am, if it means I know right from wrong. And I know it is wrong
for a man to force a—"

He knocked her hand away from his lap. "Edwin didn't force
me. I *wanted* him. I—" The rest was choked off with a sound. He
pushed her away and got up.

Isabel said, "Hendrik," and he said, "No," and left.

He slept through the next day, and the day after that. And
then he, too, like Louis before him, was suddenly gone. At first
Isabel thought he'd return: he ran away in the night, left a note
saying he could not bear the house—could not bear the thought
of the countryside any longer, and the people in it. He said, *I am
not made for this place.*

Mother did not discuss the letter with Isabel. She locked it
away in her drawer. And then, a week or two onward, Hendrik
sent a message saying he was out of money and had nowhere to
stay. But he would not come back home, and Mother would not
part with money unless he returned, if only for a while. In the
end, it was Uncle Karel who mediated a solution: found Hendrik
a small apartment in Scheveningen, would check in on him at
intervals and report back to Mother. Isabel never did find out
what Hendrik's life had looked like during those years. He would
go on to finish school, eventually. He would study, eventually.
She missed him with a nauseated fear, a gut-deep thing. He had
been half her life for so long, and then all at once he was gone.
Once he was a child and she would hold him through his night
terrors. Now he had grown and cried over the touch of a man
and let him kiss him under trees, on the ground. And in his eyes
she was her mother's daughter, uncomplicated and stupid in all
matters of the heart and the same at seventeen as she was at
nine years old, at thirteen. Unchanged.

The day Uncle Karel sent news that Hendrik was set up in his
apartment, a good month after the whole affair began, Mother

said. "Well, that's that, then. Just you and me now, Isabel." It was noon. They were having tea. Mother said, "Good. Nice and quiet."

Mother got sick when Isabel was twenty-one. First it went slow, and then it went fast. Isabel called Hendrik and Louis back home. Louis came for a day and then left. Hendrik came with a man, tall and handsome and graying at the temples. It was raining and the droplets rolled off the shoulders of his coat—Hendrik held the umbrella.

Isabel said the man could not stay at the house. Hendrik was wild-eyed and pale and he took Isabel aside and barely breathed as he said, "Isabel. Please, Isabel," and Isabel said, "She is *sick*. Are you here to make it worse, or are you here to help?" They were whispering in the study. The man still stood outside, under the front-door awning. Hendrik turned from her to wipe at his face and then went and had a murmured conversation with his friend, whom he then took back to the station.

Hendrik would not speak with Isabel that week. He sat at Mother's side and held her hand and ignored Isabel. Once, the first year when Hendrik did not show for Christmas, Mother had said: "I suppose we all have our priorities." Isabel had held him as a child. He now loved others more than he loved her. His mother was on her deathbed and he cried over a man. Such were things, and Isabel lifted her chin at it, ground her teeth at it, made herself bigger.

Mother passed on a Friday evening. She had done suddenly better the previous day, had sat up in bed and for a second had recognized Hendrik but not Isabel. And so the next morning Hendrik said he would go to Scheveningen for the day. He didn't say why or for whom, but Isabel could guess. He gave her a phone number to call in case Mother worsened, and Isabel said she would, but she did not. She was holding her mother's hand, she could not leave, she could not go to the phone.

It happened like this: Mother was a shriveled heap in bed. Her hands were soft fists like babies have soft fists. She took a quiet breath, and then not the next. Hendrik came home that evening and she told him. He wanted to go up to see Mother and his knees gave out halfway up the stairs. There he was stuck, could not move for a while. His crying sounded more like long inhales. Isabel did not go with him into Mother's room.

Later, in the kitchen, he said, "Why. Why didn't you call." His voice was rough, eyes tired.

Isabel did not answer. She had poured herself a glass of jenever. She drank it and thought, *You were where you wanted to be. I was where I needed to be.*

She thought, *And now you will leave again.*

And he did. She would barely hear from him in the year that followed. Then came a summer, and Isabel found old letters they'd written to Mother as children and sent Hendrik one of his, and he wrote back immediately, thanking her. She wrote back with an update on the house and the estate in general. He wrote back describing his new apartment, saying she should come by, perhaps. She said he was welcome to visit her, too: the roses had come up nicely this year.

They sat in the garden, on the bench under the firs. Hendrik looked well. He was kind to her, and listened in a soft way, and often looked out to the sky and took a deep breath, as though that, too, was joy. Into a lull in the conversation he said: "I've met someone."

Hendrik, sixteen and waiting at the window. Hendrik on the mossy ground, writhing. Hendrik on her bed's edge with his bleeding lip and—

"We live together now," he said. "An apartment, it's not much, but—he is very good. I would like for you to meet him, Isabel."

Isabel did not want to meet anyone. She just wanted this: the two of them, summer. Mother's bench. He read her silence for what it was and then turned to her and took her hand in his and said: "You don't have to be *her*, Isabel." He meant their mother. She knew he meant their mother. He said, "You can be whoever you want to be now. Do you know that? You have all the freedom. She's gone. You're not taking care of her, you're not bound to this house. Go where you want to go. Meet whoever. Love."

Bound to this house, he said. As if it was a tether and not a shelter. And not her own love, too.

She did meet Sebastian, however. Hendrik came one afternoon and stayed for dinner. When Sebastian got out of the car Isabel held her breath. He was short and striking and dark like some of the farm boys were dark—like the men who came from the south and worked in the greenhouses. But he was not a farmer, or a greenhouse worker. He wore an expensive-looking suit. He sounded French but looked different in a way she didn't think was French, in a way she had only ever seen in the big cities. Her first thought was, *foreign*. Her second thought was a jumble of words, things she'd heard said in connection to the word *foreign*—never good things, never safe things—and a nervous coil tightened within her. Hendrik's hand was on Sebastian's elbow, guiding him toward her. Hendrik could barely look away from him. This stranger would come into her house and she had the urge to rush back in and cover everything, hide it all from him: the things, the walls, the paintings. The pictures.

Hendrik didn't kiss her hello. Once he'd been a child and she had held him through his night terrors. She thought, *I am the only one who remembers that.* She thought—*He has forgotten and there's no one left who remembers that.*

Sebastian was quiet in the kitchen. Hendrik encouraged him to ask Isabel specific questions: "*Oh*, ask her this!" Which he then did, verbatim, which Isabel then answered shortly and didn't ask him anything in return. Hendrik allowed this for several minutes before he had enough and said, "Oh, what a boring conversation this is, come see the house!" And then pulled Sebastian from his seat and herded him into rooms. Isabel stayed behind and listened to them walk through the house, Hendrik saying: "So here's where I banged my forehead against the mantelpiece, which is how I got this scar." And, "This is great-aunt Cora in her headdress, a real heartbreaker." And, "This is the rug, it is simply a rug, and this is a vase of flowers Isabel cut from the garden, are you enjoying this tour very much? You should, I'm doing an excellent job."

There had been a moment, after dinner that day, a short and uneasy moment, when Hendrik had left the room for a while and it was just the two of them, Isabel and Sebastian. She remained seated. He walked slowly about the room, a hand in his pocket. The back of his head was neatly shaven. He had a mole right above his lip. He had dressed up to come see her. Isabel knew that Hendrik must have told him all about her: that she was lonely and bitter and took after her mother too much.

That's how this man would think about her, too, now.

He paused by a framed picture left on the side table. He picked it up. Isabel tensed. She knew which one it was: Haasje, the dog. Black-and-white. It had been taken in the garden, the young pup lounging under one of the firs, in the shade.

"There was a dog?" he asked. He was trying hard to work away the French inflection to his Dutch.

"Yes," Isabel said. "Was."

"I had a dog." He put the picture back. "Well, my cousin did. But the dog liked me best. Mother and I moved in with my aunt the same week they got the dog. My cousin wanted to call the dog Sebastian. Some sort of joke, I think. Mother forbade it."

"What did he—call it, then?"

"Lucky," he said, the English word.

It made her blush. She didn't know why. Sebastian turned to her and asked, "What was your dog's name?" in reply to which she stood from her seat and wiped her hands on her skirt and said, "I'll go get Hendrik. You two should get going before it's fully dark."

It *was* getting dark. And they did leave soon. Isabel watched the car drive away with a leaden weight in her chest. She had never shown the house to new eyes: she hadn't made new friends, or invited anyone over. The only strangers who had come over were the maids, who would always settle in like an unease—a grain of sand under the eyelid. It had been Hendrik's pleasure now—to get to show the house to someone beloved. To have a newfound person see him through the spaces where he'd once lived, slept. The walls he'd touched, the house whose shape lived within him, even though he'd left long ago. Even though he didn't even live there at all.

7

ISABEL WASN'T FULLY AWAKE WHEN THE HAPPY
honk of Hendrik's car sounded from outside. She was dressed,
she was downstairs, but she was not awake—stood at the table,
hand over her belly, staring. She had been listening for sounds
from upstairs, the creak of a floorboard, the rush of the shower.
Nothing yet. Eva was still asleep.

It was a bright day, a birdsong day. Insects hissed at the doorway. Isabel put a netted cover over the bowl of fruit. Hendrik
and Sebastian came up to the house with a bustle, bags in hand,
sunglasses on. They were coming to visit for the weekend. Hendrik had told her they would, and she had forgot. Hendrik was
before her and Sebastian close behind him and somewhere upstairs, Eva.

Hendrik said immediately, "Oh, did you forget we were coming?" kissing her cheeks, laughing about this. She said, "No, I—"
and her voice came out rough, scratchy.

"God, it's a gorgeous day!" Hendrik exclaimed, looking out
the window. He took up space quickly, cheerfully. Sebastian arranged their luggage out of the way and greeted Isabel with a
more gentle hand, that look of his: like he had opinions about
her, indecipherable. Everything was happening too fast, everyone was moving too fast: Hendrik called for coffee, and so coffee
must be made, and what was it they wanted to do this weekend?

A plan, he wanted a plan, a drive to the city, a big dinner, a swim out by the lakes, and—

"Oh, where's our special guest? Isn't she here somewhere?" Hendrik pretended to look in a cabinet for her, behind a curtain.

Isabel was light-headed. She had a sudden strong urge to keep Eva away from the two men: not out of embarrassment this time. Out of something else. Out of something dark, and coiling, and—

"She's . . ." Isabel started, "asleep, I think."

"What, still?"

Isabel didn't answer. A weekend, they had come to stay. A full weekend. She itched at the thought, confused, wanted to bundle them out the door again, wanted the moment back—the stillness of the morning.

Eva entered the room. Barefoot, trousers, shirt tucked in. She'd combed her hair back into a puffy ponytail. Red around the eyes. She had a dent to her bottom lip, Isabel noticed—hadn't noticed before. A dent like someone had pressed a thumb to her there when she was still taking shape, and the lip forever kept the pressure of that touch. Isabel wondered, briefly and horribly, what Louis had done to earn his first kiss from Eva. How he had touched her, and whether she'd let him, as she'd let Isabel. Whether she'd touched him in return, whether she'd taken him to her room, whether they'd not waited at all before they—

Eva looked at Isabel. There was the length of the room between them. The space felt obvious, so very obvious, but then Hendrik danced back in from the kitchen, coffee in hand, midway into a conversation that sounded like "—too far, maybe we can try Agnieten, it's a lovely—Oh, hello! Eva, hello!"

He went to her, kissed her cheeks. She allowed this, dazed. Said, "Hello?" And then, weakly: "This is a surprise."

"Is it? Isabel didn't tell you we were coming?"

"No," Eva said. Then, "We?" and Hendrik called for Sebastian, who came in and was introduced by Hendrik with a "This is Sebastian, my good friend. Bas, this is Eva, Louis's . . ." He trailed off.

A beat of silence that hung too long.

"Girlfriend," Eva finished then. A glance, quick as anything. Isabel looked away from it. She felt sick. Shame rose up like tar—slow, thick. *Louis's girlfriend.*

"Lovely," said Sebastian. "Is Louis here, too?"

"Louis is away for work. A conference," Eva said. She passed a hand over her hair, to smooth it. No use: the frizz escaped, stood out in a halo. Her surety of the last weeks was gone, leeched—she stood there, not knowing what to do with her arms.

"How nice you're staying here, then." Sebastian nodded at her. "You and Isabel must be great friends."

Hendrik hid amusement behind pulled-in lips. He acted as if he was inspecting something out the window. He must have told Sebastian about Eva, the same as he must have told him about Isabel. Eva blushed, gave a shaky smile that shrunk quickly. "Yes," she said.

Isabel excused herself to the bathroom. She sat there, in the dark, digging into the flesh of her arm. The light came in from under the door, a sliver of a line. When she exited she almost stumbled into Eva, who did not expect to see her—who stepped back wildly, who held her breath. The hallway was narrow. She held herself as if she was frightened: of Isabel, of what Isabel might do. As if it had been Isabel who had preyed on her, who had stolen a kiss, who had taken her in her arms.

Isabel's shame turned itself over into something more familiar: anger took its worn seat. "I am not," she started, a tight hiss, "the sort of person who—"

"Oh, not now," Eva cut her off, and glanced over her shoulder to see whether any of it had been overheard. She whispered: "Not now, Isabel, please."

"I—" Isabel halted. She was tired. She had not slept. She tried to summon the haziness that possessed her last night: the heat in her belly, how badly she had wanted, for a moment. She couldn't. Eva was someone else now: distracted from her, not caring for her. Looking away from her, worried about other people.

She didn't have anything else to say. She bustled by Eva, held her breath as their arms brushed, and when Hendrik asked the room at large if anyone wanted some "nice things" from the baker's, she said: "I'll come with you," and marched herself out the door.

Hendrik drove them to the city. At the baker's, awaiting their turn, Hendrik said: "This should be a fun weekend, hmm."

Isabel was inspecting the display. The sweet things were nauseating to look at: shiny, gelatinous. A fly had got behind the glass. "How do you mean," she asked, though she knew what he meant, whom he meant.

"Just that she's so silly, isn't she?" Hendrik's turn was next, and he rattled off their order.

Isabel said, "She isn't silly." She said it too seriously, too quietly, and Hendrik didn't hear her and he said, "Hm, what?" and so Isabel had to repeat herself, louder:

"She isn't silly." Isabel was blushing. She meant to say: *She is horrid.* She meant to say, *I think she's stealing from me,* and then thought of the kiss and blushed more angrily. Hendrik accepted their bagged order from over the counter.

"She isn't?" he said. He wasn't looking at her but he put on a tone: light, as if she could be tricked into thinking he wasn't paying attention.

"Never mind," she said, and went to take the bags from him.

She insisted on carrying them to the car. Hendrik only held a single baguette aloft.

On the drive back he said, out of nowhere: "So we've decided on Paris. I wanted to let you know. We've decided—" He stopped himself. It really was a beautiful day, the sun beating off the road in a blur. "His mother is . . . well, you know how it is. You remember. So we're going, soon. Before summer's end. I don't know for how long, of course, but Isabel, listen, I want—I want you to know that you can come visit. I want you to know that Paris isn't—"

"No," she said. "I can't just leave. I can't just do whatever I want, I can't—" And immediately a flash of last night came to her: her mouth slippery on Eva's, her hand on Eva's thigh.

Hendrik lifted a hesitant hand to her shoulder. "Hey," he said.

"I'm fine." She reemerged. She felt bare suddenly. Too obvious.

Hendrik took his hand away. "It won't be indefinitely. It's not permanent."

"I know. Let's talk about something else."

He thought about this for a while. Then, "Oh, hello, how did your big night with Johan go!"

The crops in the field to their right stood young and knee-high. The horizon beyond, uninterrupted and endless. "Fine," Isabel said.

"Well? Must I save the date? A summer wedding, an autumn wedding?"

"Stop," she said, and he turned to her in humor, ready to poke more—and noticed she was serious. He retreated, and they drove on in silence for a while.

"He *is* nice to you," Hendrik said eventually. "Isn't he? Because if he's not, then—"

"He's fine," Isabel said. "Johan is . . . fine."

Two swallows, twirling up against the bright sky. Hendrik said, "Will you ever tell me anything, Isabel?"

She looked at him, quick. Her heart beat fast. She wondered, frantically, what it *would* be like to tell him. Hendrik's eyes were on the road. He sighed, said, "Very well, then."

Behind the house, on the lawn, Eva and Sebastian were playing badminton. They'd unearthed the net somewhere, found two rusty bats.

"What in God's name," Hendrik said. He and Isabel crowded close at the kitchen window to watch them. The game was being played badly and in some kind of hysterics on Eva's part. She missed a hit and lay herself down in the grass in reply while Sebastian bowed to accept his victory. He was smoking a cigarette out the corner of his mouth.

Hendrik shouted out the door, "I leave you alone for one second!"

Sebastian waved, said they were out of ways to entertain themselves. Eva got up. She tried to wipe a grass stain from her knee, pouting at it. Hendrik gave Isabel a look that somehow communicated the word *silly*, and Isabel—Isabel turned away. And then, all too quickly, it was all of them inside, preparing for lunch, dancing around each other: putting plates on the table, then cutlery. Eva was keeping a distance in a way that no one else would notice, and Isabel, spiteful, did the same. Hendrik said, "Where did the small bread knife go?" And the question echoed in Isabel from a muffled distance: where did any of the things in the house go when they disappeared? She thought, *I will tell him about the list*, and could feel none of the indignant anger from before: only the same muddled sense of loss, as if she herself had been taken and placed where she did not belong. She was woozy with the thought a moment, and then Sebastian put a hand to her arm and asked her to get the glasses that he couldn't reach, so she did. Eva, at the round table, was peeling an apple. She cut it into four parts. She placed a part on each of their plates.

"Oh, aren't you sweet," Hendrik said, and ate his slice in one big bite. And then, with his mouth still full: "Where *did* you learn to play badminton so well? Or are you an autodidact? Either way a natural."

He was making fun of her. He was making fun of her the way he had that night at the restaurant. Isabel thought it had gone over her head then. She had been wrong. Eva knew what he was doing and was caught off guard by it; tried to smile still, and couldn't.

Isabel said his name. Once, and in warning: "Hendrik."

He didn't expect it—gave Isabel a confused look. Sebastian spoke up with a quick "Hendrik only teases because he's the worst player of us all." He leaned back and was amused, and said in his low voice: "You know we'd summer with a family in Geneva and one of my cousins, a menace, insisted we play and then would toss the shuttle as far off as he could. So most of the afternoons were spent not so much playing but with me looking for the damn thing. The son of the hotel owner took pity on me, gave me private lessons. So he wouldn't have to scavenge the garden for shuttles, mostly." He said, "Now I am proficient."

Eva smiled at him, closed-mouthed.

The table went quiet.

Isabel picked up her slice of the apple. Again she felt exposed: her harsh reply to Hendrik, his confusion. Isabel brought the apple to her lips. The fruit was tart and sour. Eva, Isabel imagined, must have gone to sleep last and woken up this morning with only a vague recollection of what happened in the night, in the short space between the two doors, and thought to herself: *How very embarrassing. Why did I do that? So embarrassing.*

The day barreled on, stops and starts. Fast the one moment, slow the next. Hendrik in his childhood room, on his bed, saying, "Hello, bed." Sebastian shaking out the sheets, a billow of dust. Footsteps up and down the stairs, a house full of snatched conversation: Sebastian and Hendrik, humming voices in the library; the rush of someone turning on the tap upstairs; Eva and Hendrik smoking out in the garden, talking slow and serious. He was overtly nicer to her now, and she allowed it.

The four of them went for a walk through the fields. Hendrik wanted to wade into the high corn, Sebastian told him not to because snakes might live between the stalks. Eva said, "Snakes, what nonsense!" and then disappeared between the green, yellow head bobbing above. Isabel said, "No, don't—" which no one heard, because then Eva gave a shout and ran right back out, swatting all around her, saying, "Something—oh, something brushed my—" Which had Hendrik in tears.

Isabel stared at the back of Eva's head on the walk home. When she turned to say something, her profile was smiling, cheeks tight. She had gone bright in the hours since Hendrik and Sebastian's arrival: a bird puffing, preening. She was making herself funny, interesting. Clumsy.

Embarrassing, Isabel thought, and as though on cue Eva cast a quick glance back at her. Isabel held it a moment. Hendrik asked Eva a question, and Eva blinked, said, "Hmm, what?" Hendrik had to ask his question a second time.

Isabel fell back. Sebastian came to walk beside her, hands clasped behind his back. The silence was companionable, at first. Then Sebastian said, "You've heard about my mother."

It wasn't a question. Isabel took a moment to say, "Yes." And, "I was sorry to hear."

He, too, turned his reply over in his mind for a while. "You were there, when your mother . . . when she fell ill, no?"

100

Isabel nodded once. He said, "I think about her all the time. It's odd, I would go days without thinking about her before. Now I worry. It's as if I'm there already, in mind. But I'm not. I'm . . ." He paused. Isabel wanted him to not say anything anymore, wanted him to join the others. He didn't. He said, "She's still lucid. She might get better yet."

Ahead, Eva took Hendrik's arm and briefly leaned into him.

"You're leaving soon," Isabel said. "Hendrik said before summer's end."

He wiped the back of his hand over his forehead. It was a hot evening. "Unless she improves, yes. Isabel." He said her name as if imploring. "Did you find—When did you find that you—" He was halting. He had never spoken to her like this, uncertainly, seeking. "When did you decide that there was no—that it was hopeless, that you knew she would—"

"I don't—" She closed her mouth. Tried again, voice lower. "You should speak to Hendrik about these things."

Another beat of silence. Sebastian recovered his stoic self. All calm, he said, "In fact, Hendrik said to ask you. That you would . . . He wasn't there, at the end, was he?" Sebastian looked at her. "You were."

Isabel did not answer. *We are not the same,* she thought. *We are nothing alike,* she thought. He had Hendrik, and Hendrik was coming with him. She had been alone. The room where her mother died had stood empty for years. Eva slept there now. A picture of her own mother on the nightstand.

Isabel said, "Excuse me," and doubled her speed, overtook the murmuring Hendrik and Eva and walked ahead of everyone: a fast-paced step toward home.

Wine was poured before dinner. Wine was poured during dinner. All of them clustered at one end of the long table, conversation moving quickly and loudly from *Could you pass the—* to *So you said you grew up in—* to *Where's the big spoon, I could've sworn it was—*

A slow headache was pulsing at the back of Isabel's head, getting worse. She ate little of the food. They all had left her alone after they'd returned. Sebastian hadn't tried to continue the conversation and now he and Eva were discussing the merit of good eyes, good brows. Hendrik lounged in his chair, smoking with an expansive sprawl, watching the two indulgently.

Sebastian said of his eyebrows, all seriousness, "I think I'd like mine thinner," and Eva said, "No, but you have a good shape, do you know what it's like to pluck an eyebrow that has no shape? No, don't touch them, they're perfect."

"Ah," Hendrik said, leaning into Isabel's space, whispering: "A compliment. Now she'll have him forever."

Isabel wanted to answer, but Hendrik then opened the conversation to the group: "What about *my* eyebrows? What about Isabel's, how do ours hold up, what have we been saddled with?"

Eva considered him—hmm'd at this. She turned her attention to Isabel. Isabel tilted her face away, not wanting to join in on the game. This made Eva laugh, a sound between kind and mean. It was the drinking, Isabel thought, that made her like this. That made all of them like this. Eva leaned forward and said, "Isabel, look at me a moment. Let me see."

Isabel passed the back of her hand over her brow, hiding it. "No, it's silly," she said, and Hendrik, next to her, tugged her hand away and said, "Oh, just let her!" and Isabel pulled away from him, annoyed, but now Eva hitched up in her seat and reached across the table. Her hand was a heat, hovering near Isabel's face. The pad of her thumb passed over Isabel's brow.

102

Fingers curled in, knuckles to Isabel's cheek. She did it again, smoothing the grain of hair.

Isabel moved with the touch a fraction. Eva pulled away.

Dinner came to an unclear close and Hendrik heralded them all into the sitting room to put on a record, to dance. The heat of the day lingered: rolled-up sleeves, shiny foreheads. A few flies were stuck inside, bounced from window to ceiling to wall. Isabel meant to clear the dishes instead and was told she was not allowed: *Come dance!* Hendrik insisted. *Come on, come on, we'll wash up later, come dance!*

Isabel would not dance. She sat in the armchair and watched the others sway, uncoordinated and drunk, all about the space. They pushed the coffee table aside, made a dance floor. The records were old, ones that Isabel's brothers bought as teens and left behind when they moved away; Isabel did not buy music. She didn't know how. Hendrik chose an American singer for the party, something poppy and familiar. They danced and smoked and shimmied on socks, and then a fast song turned slow, and Hendrik took Sebastian's hand—in good humor, at first. Then serious, then with purpose. Sebastian went with a small smile: settling against him, face turned, cheek to Hendrik's shoulder.

Eva seemed lost a moment. Out of breath on the edge of the carpet. She noticed, and then *noticed*. She sat down, eyes on the two men. Her hair had come loose and was sticking to her face, the sheen of sweat. She was blushing fiercely. Not just from the exercise, Isabel thought. Not just from that.

Hendrik held Sebastian close. Sebastian hummed a small word, hand to the small of Hendrik's back. There was no mistaking, none. It was obvious what they were now. Who they were. Isabel held her hands tight in her lap. Her heart hammered, something to do with fear.

103

Eva stared at the dancing couple. *Say something*, Isabel thought, a flare of daring. Eva's mouth was parted, puffed breaths.

She looked at Isabel as if in answer. The dip of her lip, the glint of her crooked tooth. The night blurred. Had Eva gone dancing with Louis often? The one song ended, the next began. Isabel drank in silence and the dancing continued. At some point Sebastian got tired and sat down with a happy murmur, a "Go on, go on, I'll just rest for a moment." It wasn't a moment: soon he was dozing against the armrest. Hendrik danced with Eva by holding her hand at a length and letting her pass under it, a twirl. When he announced his retirement, Eva said, "Noooo!" Said, "No, don't leave me, one more. Come, one more."

Hendrik, with two damp spots under his arms, turned to Isabel: "You take her from me. I can't," he said. "I can't. I'm old, I can't."

Isabel did not take this seriously. She was still in the same chair, still sitting primly. Again, she had drunk too much. She hadn't danced a single song and felt as though she had—overheated and short of breath. Hendrik sat down next to dozing Sebastian, gave a quick kiss to the side of his head.

Eva stood before her, holding out two hands: "Dance with me," she said.

Isabel looked at her. The offer, the upturned palms. Eva's trousers were cinched too tightly at the waist, button pulling. They would leave a mark, surely—folds of fabric pressed against her skin. They would be felt long after undressing: a relief, then an ache.

Isabel rose without accepting the hands held out. Eva watched her stand at her full height, eyes going up, up. It was a bop of a song, a lyric that went, *I'd bounce to you, I'd bounce bounce bounce!*

"Dance," Eva told her. She began shimmying. Her shoulders

moved, her hips. Isabel didn't know how to do that, only knew to stare. Eva laughed nervously, shook Isabel's arm playfully: "Go on! Move a little."

Isabel didn't. She wasn't sure what sort of game this was: to be pushed away, to be pulled again while others watched. Was Eva pretending, was she drunk, was she—

The needle hissed into the next song. Slower, much slower. Eva paused, said, "Ah." She stood before Isabel. Hesitated, looked lost, then decided—on a joke, or a play—and reached for Isabel, clocked her reaction. Told her, "Come. It's just a dance."

She took Isabel's hands now, put them at her waist. Warm, skin under cloth. Isabel looked to Hendrik, a panic, and Hendrik was slumped into Sebastian—head turned away from them, murmuring. Not paying attention. Isabel tried to pull away, but Eva's hands held her fast by her wrists. She was making sure Isabel wasn't letting go. Then—she touched Isabel. Up, up her arms, to her shoulders. A hold, a dance. She was moving the two of them in a swaying slur. They went in a circle. Eva had to arch her back a little, to keep her arms around Isabel—pressed her chest close, a heartbeat, the soft give of her breasts. Her breath was a cool puff to Isabel's throat.

Isabel pulled her in. She didn't mean to. She was a belly full of wine, was two hands holding the good dip of a waist. She was a touch, trailing up—up Eva's spine to the back of her neck. Goose bumps, damp skin, whorl of hair. She breathed her in. She fisted her fingers in—grabbed.

Eva's reaction was whispered to the shell of her ear: "*Isa.*"

Isabel's arms were full and then they were empty. She jolted away and escaped quickly, went to the dining room. She began to clear the dishes and didn't see what she took. In the sitting room the song played on. She made it to the kitchen somehow, no memory of her feet carrying her. And then Eva was there with her, taking the dishes from her hands and pulling her along, saying, "Come—just—"

Feet tangling, arms. Around the corner, hidden from the doorway. Eva's mouth was close, messy against Isabel's cheek. She was putting Isabel's hands where they'd last been: at her back, her neck. "Like this," she breathed. "Like you did, like—"

Isabel did it again: fingers into the heat of Eva's hair, pulling. Eva shuddered against her, and all Isabel saw of her was a spill of dark lashes, an open mouth, and then nothing—the red dark of closed eyes. Eva tasted of the wine, of the mint candy she had rolled around her mouth while dancing. She was hot, so hot through her clothes—fingers tight on Isabel's shoulders, pulling her down, pushing herself up. Her head went back easily under Isabel's tug. The kiss happened fast and then held—held. Slowed, by increments—built itself back up. The dry chalk of the wall behind Eva's head, Isabel's hand caging her in. The hidden pocket behind Eva's ear, thin skin; the slide of her tongue, the pulse at her throat, heavy under the press of Isabel's thumb. In the distance, the record ended, needle hissing and then skipping, lifting. Quiet in the house. In the kitchen only the rustle of clothes, the sound of movement, the slick of their kiss. Eva's quiet *Ah!*—the hot puff of it.

The world pooled between Isabel's legs. She stepped away and put a hand to her own face—her cheek. "I have a fever," she said, and was sure she did. "God, I think I've run a fever."

Eva followed her, took her hand away, said: "Let me feel, let me—" She cradled Isabel's face, back of her fingers to her forehead, her temple. "You're fine," she said. "It's not a fever. Darling, my darling. Oh—"

Isabel swayed back into her. In the crook of Eva's neck, she found a heartbeat to put her lips to.

8

THE NEXT MORNING HENDRIK DECIDED THEY would go swimming. He packed everything into the car while the early sun climbed bright behind the firs. The garden smelled like evergreens, and Hendrik wasn't wearing his sunglasses, so he kept his eyes squinted in the light—occasionally blocking it with a hand.

Isabel watched him as she leaned back against the car door, arms crossed. She said, quietly—only for the two of them, "You were careless last night."

He wasn't paying attention. "Hm?" was his answer, tightening the towel over the picnic basket. And then her words reached him, delayed, and he said, "You mean in front of Eva? Isabel, come now."

"Don't tell me come now. You're too easy with these things. You're too—"

"Darling, she knew, she knew, what's this?" He closed the trunk. "Where is this coming from?"

"Knew?" Isabel repeated. The dress she had chosen to wear was already proving too hot for the day. She had been distracted in dressing herself. She had spent the morning searching for marks in the mirror, marks on her face. Anything to indicate what she and Eva had done. She had found none. "What do you mean, she *knew*?"

"I don't know, she just knew! She asked me something about Sebastian earlier and—oh, I can't recall, she just understood, we didn't speak it out loud. It's not so outrageous, Isabel. She's a modern girl and there are other people like us in the world and perhaps we're not the first ones Eva's met or—"

"I *know* there's—" She stopped herself, lowered her voice. Eva and Sebastian were inside, clearing up breakfast. The window was open, and sound carried easily here. She said, "Never mind."

Hendrik came to stand next to her. He lit a cigarette, said, "You're letting her sleep in Mother's room, though."

"I'm not *letting* her anything." She said it and felt the words churn on themselves. A lie, of course. She *let* Eva. She had *let* her a lot. She added, quickly, "Louis told her she could stay there."

"Hm."

"What, *hm*?"

He shrugged. There was a discoloration forming on his middle finger, right where he always held the cigarette. He said, "It's just that I've never known you to allow anything you didn't want in the first place." He added, "She's good for you, I think."

"*Good?*" A heavy thud in her chest as she said this. Images from last night, quick and terrible and overlit. "What do you mean, *good*?"

Hendrik was amused by her anger, said, "She's loosened you. It's nice."

Isabel could only look at him. Could only widen her eyes, a baffled breath, and Hendrik continued, "You danced last night, now you're coming for a swim. Who would've thought!"

"*Loosening.* As if I'm—a bolt, a rusted—" Her voice did something odd. She calmed, said, "I thought you didn't like her. That you thought her silly." She recalled the way Hendrik kept on saying the word *gauze* on their walk back from Louis's place. She recalled it very clearly, how he only wanted to be mean about it.

"No," he said now, gesturing at her with his cigarette. "You didn't like her. I played along for fun."

She opened her mouth to disagree, and just then Sebastian and Eva walked out toward them—hands up as well, shielding from the sun. "Are we ready?" Sebastian said, and Eva said, "The weather's so nice!" And took Sebastian's arm as they walked on. She wore the same trousers as yesterday. Last night, in the dark of the kitchen, Isabel had her hands over the band of that waist—had dug her fingers in, had felt at the tight seams.

Her heart had raced then. Her heart raced now still.

It's not a fever, Eva had whispered, mouth close, but Isabel had continued to shiver. Eva touched her, hushed her, and then Sebastian had stumbled into the room—half-asleep, there for a glass of water. They'd jumped apart. Isabel went and stood facing the wall, a hand over her mouth. Eva went the other direction and began a quick and cheery chatter. There was a tremble in her voice. Sebastian was too slow to keep up. After a few moments he said, "Are you all right?"

"We're clearing the dishes," Eva said.

"In the dark?" Sebastian asked.

"Oh!" Eva laughed, and Isabel turned enough to see her consider the room. "I hadn't noticed. Silly, silly."

Over breakfast Eva avoided looking at her straight on. Now, in the back of the car, they were back to this: sitting widely apart. Eva hooked her arm out of the window, face into the wind, eyes closed. The reeds stood tall at the foot of the dike, puffy tails swaying. Sheep in the field, bits of their wool clung to the fence's wires. Isabel placed one hand in the empty space on the seat next to her. Farther, farther. Left it outstretched.

"You know, Eva," Hendrik said, turning enough to direct his words to the back of the car. "Louis has done well, for once. Where *did* he find you?"

Eva laughed loudly, a clattering sound. "Find me!" she said. "Am I a lost glove?"

Isabel put her hand back in her lap. *Fool*, she thought at herself, and closed her eyes tightly. She swallowed against the sudden rise of sour.

They hadn't decided on a lake. Hendrik said they'd just drive up toward the Black-Water rivers and see what they ran into—somewhere quiet, somewhere fun. The rivers in this region reached into the land like fingers, slowed into narrow streams or rushed into man-made lakes.

They drove by a big, broken-down shed that had not been rebuilt since the war. A series of bunkers, all in a row, up the high shoulder of a dike. The concrete had turned green in the years since their last use. The metal stuck out like rungs. Kids in swimwear climbed up on them, made it to the slanted roof, would catch the sun up there.

Sebastian said, "How about there? That looks nice. Young people." And then, to Isabel, "Is it to your liking, Isabel?"

He was trying to be nice to her and still it felt like a jab at her expense. She said, "Here is fine," and didn't look at anyone in the car.

The lake was new, a slow end of the river that had been widened by a bomb: a crater that filled up, connected itself with the river overtime. Along the grassy shores: young people. Girls walking along the water's edge in two-pieces, boys jumping in from a makeshift plank; someone had made a campfire for roasting; someone had brought a radio and turned it on loud.

Isabel had her bathing suit under her clothes but she did not take off her dress. She sat on the blanket, on the makeshift shore, and watched the others strip, still chatting, perfectly at ease. Legs and arms and a strip of belly. A playful breeze chased down

the dike; Sebastian used the picnic basket to hold down the edge
of the blanket. Hendrik lit another cigarette.

Only once the others were gone did she unzip herself, peel
away her dress. She was never this bare at the mercy of others.
She kept her gaze away from everyone, read a book while the
rest ran in and out of the water. They came back for a drink, for
a piece of fruit, bread, stood and dripped for a moment—"How's
the book, Isabel?"—and then ran right back.

Isabel stared at the same page for over an hour and did not
recall a single word. *Like this*, Eva said last night. She had felt
restless in Isabel's arms, like she couldn't wait, like she needed
something—something, panted short and quick into Isabel's
mouth, had pushed her body as close as she could get. Isabel
pinched the rough skin over her knee until the memory lessened. She kept her thighs tightly pressed. Out on the lake, Eva
ran along the shallow end while Sebastian followed leisurely,
smoking.

Hendrik came to join Isabel, collapsed on the towel. His skin
brought with it the chill of the water, carried on the air. He fumbled with his discarded trousers, looked for his cigarettes, found
them. They sat together for a while, watching Eva and Sebastian's play as it unfolded: Sebastian suddenly running, catching
up to Eva, Eva shrieking, delighted, a tug-of- war, Eva allowing
herself to be caught. Held, laughing, laughing.

"Aren't they a sight together?" Hendrik said. He was leaning
on one elbow. His hair was wet, water running down his neck,
and his smile was an odd one; sad, or happy, or tired. But he
was right: they did make for a sight, something from a movie
scene—Sebastian's broad back, the sun's glint in his dark curls,
his forearms darker where he'd rolled up his sleeves in spring.
He'd wrapped his arms around Eva, her back to his chest, and
she held him by his wrists. The line of her thighs, the stretch of

skin over ribs, the bump of her soft belly under her swim shorts. They both stood out in the lake's crowd—darker-skinned, more defined. Sharp. Nose, chin. Italian youths, perhaps, if one were not to look too closely. From this distance the off-yellow of Eva's hair didn't seem so bad. The frizz of it pressed into Sebastian's cheek when she turned her head to say something. He smiled, a show of dimples.

They looked like a couple on a honeymoon.

"Ah," Hendrik said. "A pretty deception."

Isabel did not touch herself.

Arousal, when it came, was an inconvenience—a wrench in the routine and a distraction. It was a heavy blanket weighing her down in the night, it was the drag of honey into lungs. It was never bound to anyone. Not a face, not a body, not the promise of a touch—never the promise of a touch. It rose and fell with the same unpredictability of a fever caught outside the house, the same disembodied mystery—who had it been? Who was it that coughed, passed this on?

And much like with a fever, she would sweat the worst of it into the sheets. It was rare that she gave into it. She hated the headiness, the wet, the excess of the experience. But then, on some summer nights—on some winter nights—when the house hummed with its own emptiness, cavernous rooms upon rooms upon rooms—she would dip into herself. She would make sure she was still there; a body, a heartbeat, a toppling hunger between two legs.

She would be quick about it, impatient for the thing to break, for the illness to crest. She would stuff the hem of a sheet into her mouth, find the folded seam of her underwear, bunch it up, pull, *rub*. She would think of nothing, would keep her mind wide and empty. Only sometimes, on the edge of the peak, a thought would come to her—not an image, but a voice. *Please*, it said. Just that, nothing else. A breath, a release. *Please!*

Isabel dove into the water—a shock of cold sucking her in. She stayed under, swam until the air ached in her chest. When she resurfaced, the day had shifted around her: the breeze blew with more purpose. An angry waving of gray up the horizon. Above, the afternoon sun still beat down heavy and full-bodied, but a chill crept in on the breath of the wind.

She swam more and watched the bad weather inch near. Treetops were swaying.

The others were up on the embankment, sharing food—bread and cheese and grapes. A rumble in the distance, and the whole lake turned its face in unison. Swallows, dots of black against the summer storm, swooped and climbed and swooped.

Isabel hurried back up the incline, dripping and shivering, arms tight around her chest. The first fat drops began to fall. Hendrik was tossing everything back in the basket, and Sebastian handed Isabel a towel and said, "Quickly, quickly."

They ran back to the car, half in clothes, half out. They were all inside already except for Eva, who was wriggling into her trousers, laughing incredulously at how quickly the weather had turned. "God, that came out of nowhere! Out of nowhere!" Her shirt clung to the wet top of her bikini—two wet marks.

Her arm brushed Isabel's when she got inside: cold, a damp touch. She closed the car door behind her. The windows fogged up immediately. Hendrik wiped the windshield with his arm. The rain drummed on the car roof. Other parked cars took to the narrow road; poor bikers pushed through the rain, some still in swimwear. Sebastian wondered whether they should head back home and Hendrik said, "Why should we go back! Why should we let the Dutch summer chase us away!"

They would look for an inn, a café, somewhere to sit out the rain; they'd dry and they'd warm and they'd drink something. They drove slowly, pointing at buildings in the distance—a roof spotted over the peak of a dike, a windmill that might be a brewery. They found an establishment at the end of a small two-street village: an impressive old country house, repurposed as some sort of hotel, some sort of tavern. Several couples were running toward the entrance with newspapers over their heads. They were decked out in tennis clothes. The lawn was well-kept, bright green.

"This looks nice," Hendrik said, and the rest were quiet for a moment.

"Very nice," Sebastian said. It was either wry or genuine; it was hard to tell. "You should probably put your trousers back on."

"Ah," Hendrik said, looking down at his bare legs. He was handed back his trousers. It was a clumsy show, wedged behind the wheel. They all ran from the car at once. It was raining even harder now. Eva cried out some exclamation, her face wet.

There was a bar at the back of the establishment and they were not the only wet guests to have sought refuge. Something like humor hung about the place—a commiseration over a sunny day lost, an amusement over shared misery. There was a tall fireplace against the wall, and someone was lighting a fire. People cheered when the flame caught. A few kids went to stand by it, hands outstretched, and the room grew damp and humid.

The four of them settled into a booth. Sebastian went to order their drinks and came back pulled tighter than when he'd left—tense, jaw clenched. He remained standing and Hendrik said, "What? What happened?" and Sebastian said, "Nothing, could you pass me my wallet?"

Hendrik reached for him. Sebastian moved away from it, irritated, said, "No. Just—give me the damned wallet, please, if you want your drink."

Hendrik gave him his wallet, then stood—made to walk with him to the bar. Sebastian said, "No, sit down," and Hendrik said, "I can't come with you? Is that not allowed?" to which Sebastian said, "No scene." It was a command. Hendrik, when he replied, replied to something else altogether: "Look, you can't carry everything back by yourself."

Sebastian relented silently. Isabel kept her eyes on the table. High dark varnish, chipped in places. Under the varnish the glimpse of wood was lighter, much lighter. It was only she and Eva at the table now. Eva was still breathing like she was recovering from the run.

"They wouldn't serve him," Eva said, out of nowhere and into nothing: generally and vaguely at the space between them. She said, "They wouldn't serve him unless he paid beforehand."

Like she was telling Isabel. Like she was making sure Isabel knew, understood what happened. It wasn't the first thing she had said to her since the night before, but it felt like it.

"I know," Isabel said. It came out harsher than she meant it. She swallowed, and then on that wave of emotion: "I'm not as clueless as you think."

The back of the room was an open conservatory. The rain blurred the view, and the outside was just a shapeless green, the splatter of water on ground. The ceilings were high, the echo bad. Eva put her elbows on the table. Her hair was still dark with the wet, her eyes stern. She said, "All right. So what is it that you are?"

Isabel was reminded—a bathroom of a restaurant, something from another life. Isabel had told her Louis would tire of her. Eva had answered, in that same tone as now: *Hm. We'll see.*

"I—" Isabel started, and was cut off: Sebastian and Hendrik's return, hands full of drinks. Eva turned to them, smiling, expression cleared, not a trace of what had just passed. She tried to ask Sebastian something quietly, and he only said, "Let's just drink our drinks, please, thank you."

Eva was pushed further into the booth, and now they were seated in twos: Hendrik and Sebastian a pair, Eva and Isabel—a pair. Isabel shifted, kept her distance. Her mouth was dry, and she drank too quickly, felt it rise fast. She was tired from a day in the sun, from the water, from a sleepless night preceded by a sleepless night preceded by Eva's presence in the hall across—constant and pressing on her brain like a thumb. Pressing, pressing.

A conversation was taking place. Eva had asked Sebastian about his childhood, and Sebastian answered with compact phrases at first, short bites of information. He was still locked up in discomfort, still ill at ease, and answered Eva's questions as such: he was born in Algiers. No, he remembered none of it. No, he was four when they moved to Paris.

Eva hummed and didn't push. Isabel had heard parts of the story before, flashes of it, and knew that Sebastian never spoke of any of it: not of the move or what had been left behind or of the news that occasionally lifted out of the radio and into living rooms, disembodied and distant: civil war, independence. None of that. He only ever mentioned his mother, not his father. Daughter of a French politician, a family of very important people. She had not been allowed to marry whom she wanted to marry. She raised him alone. They lived with her sister's family. *C'est comme ça,* is what he'd say of it when he tired of questions. *It is what it is.*

He didn't say that now. He loosened unexpectedly. The drink,

116

the melancholy heat. The slow way Eva eased the conversation out of him. He spoke of his mother: how beautiful she had been in her youth, movie-star beauty. How she had been too young to have him when she had him, and heartsick, still, and how she tried her best. To raise him, to have the family accept him, the brown child they desperately tried to pass off as white. He said again, "*Bon*, she tried her best."

To this, Hendrik added a quiet "Her best wasn't damn near enough."

Sebastian said, "It doesn't matter now."

Isabel knew what she'd thought when she first met Sebastian. *Foreign* had been the word. She hadn't wanted him in her house. She hadn't wanted him touching her things. She knew, too, what she thought of Eva when she first saw her.

She knew what that made her, what kind of person that meant she was. She ran hot with it now, indignant and embarrassed all at once, and then Eva said, "Hmm. I had an aunt in Algiers."

Sebastian went quiet. He said, "Had?"

Eva nodded and drank to the bottom of her beer.

Hendrik asked, "Where's your family nowadays, Eva?"

"Oh," she said. "Nowhere." And then looked around as if waiting impatiently for the next round of drinks. "Or some of them are somewhere, who knows. Ah! More drinks?"

"All of them?" Isabel asked. "All of them gone?"

Eva's attention snapped back to her. She was half turned in her seat and now faced Isabel. "Yes," she said. "All of them."

Isabel had not meant it flippantly. She'd not meant to insult. She wanted to say as much, but Eva took a breath. Eased, continued: "We were just the three of us, me and my parents, so it's . . . not a lot to begin with. And they both, well, you know. Yours are gone, too, so, you know what . . ." She took a shuddering breath, kept it in. Pressed her lips closed.

117

The table went quiet. Eventually Eva said, "Oh, let's not talk about death! It's sad and boring. Let's have more drinks, shall I get more drinks? Shall I—"

More drinks were had. Food was ordered, food arrived. Sausages, fries. Evening closed in slowly: the rain unrelenting, the bar crowding up. Isabel's swimsuit was still wet under her dress. Her thighs rubbed together sticky, tacky. Eva's forearm was a line of heat, a hand's width away from hers, leaned on the tabletop. The conversation took another nostalgic turn, despite Eva's request not to talk of it: Hendrik was now telling a story of *their* mother. About the time Hendrik fell into the canal, and their mother, refusing to wait for help, went into the water herself, in skirts and everything. She fished him out, and the two had to walk back home drenched to the bone. She was a tall woman, elbows and knees like sharp corners, and her clothes clung to her like a dog whose true size is revealed from below the pomp of its coat: all skin and bones. She walked Hendrik back home, and he shook, cold and miserable, and Mother kept her hand on his shoulder the whole time. When people looked at them, two drowned miseries, Mother would shake Hendrik and say, *Nose ahead*. She meant: Don't mind others. Only look ahead.

Eva was listening with a soft look. On the table, her hand was tight around her glass. "An impressive lady," she said.

"Oh, yes."

Eva let go of the glass. Placed her hand flat on the table. "She loved rabbits? I noticed, around the house, all the—"

"Hares," Hendrik corrected.

"Hares," Eva agreed.

A moment for everyone to sip their drink. The bar was playing some local radio, sad music, the kind that rose and whined. Eva said, "My cousin got a hare once. A terrible idea, of course, to keep a hare inside a house. She wanted one so badly, and

118

then on her birthday my uncle just . . . showed up with one of those, those reed cages and—a hare. A living hare. Everyone was screaming, the children loved it. The poor hare—we chased it around. It jumped around from room to room, into the garden, scared for its life. Gosh. Got up on the table somehow. Smashed a few plates. Our best china. We thought it was hilariously funny at the time, but . . . Poor thing."

"What," Isabel asked. "What happened to it?"

Eva gave her a sidelong look. "They released it," she said. "After a few days. They couldn't keep it." She put a nail to the groove of the wood—a chip in the varnish—poked at it. "It's not a thing to keep."

The room heated up. The fire, the people. Hendrik lolled sleepily against the backrest. Sebastian yawned. Isabel said, "We should head back."

"Oh, I can't," Hendrik said, dramatic, head loose on his neck. "I'm too tired. Too full."

"I can drive," Isabel said, but wasn't sure she could: she was muddled and heavy-eyed, unwell in her own body. The rain was coming down still, and the day was turning dark, and she wasn't sure of the way home.

"Let's stay here. Let's stay here, they have rooms, don't they? It'll be a vacation. What do you think? Come on, let's do it. Let's ask, who knows, they might have rooms, let's—"

"Oh," Eva said, "I'm not sure that's a—"

"I'll just ask, what's wrong with asking? I'll ask, I'll ask," Hendrik said, and no longer seemed tired: pushed Sebastian out the booth ahead of him, left to ask someone about rooms.

"We don't have anything with us," Eva said, quiet. She seemed uncomfortable. "Clothes or . . ." She looked out the conservatory into the gardens, the downpour, the frown of the stormy evening making it look later in the night than it was.

There were rooms available. Hendrik booked them in without asking first, carried the news back to the table with triumph. Two sets of keys on leather rings.

"Two rooms?" Isabel asked, a little thinly, and Hendrik babbled in reply: "Hmm, yes, they said both have a shower, God, I could kill for a shower right now, I feel like I've been sitting in a shallow pool all evening, and it's—"

The rooms were identical: heavily carpeted, two beds pushed widely apart, green sheets, a wardrobe, a bathroom. Good nights were lost in a hubbub of tired excitement, and then the doors were closed. They were alone. The overhead lights were off; only the bedside lamps were on, a green-glass glow to an already green room.

It'd been two days since her dinner with Johan. Two days since Eva first took her mouth in a kiss. Two days and they've been running in short sprints at each other, starting, stopping, toward and away. Catching slatted-fenced glimpses of each other.

The room had the effect of a glass bauble—quiet, voices coming through the walls muffled and indecipherable. Eva stood with her back to her, hands at her waist, head down. She'd put her hair up once it had dried, and it bared the stretch of her neck.

Isabel sat down heavily on the edge of one of the beds. She waited.

"It's," Eva started. She wiped her hands along her ribs. It was a nervous gesture, and Isabel had seen it on her before. "It's been an odd few days."

"Odd," Isabel repeated, flat.

"We've just been—" She turned to face Isabel, and she was all nerves now, eyes restless and a trembling smile. "Oh, we've been a bit stupid, haven't we? Just—so silly, with—But it's, it's just, we shouldn't think about it too much, right, Isabel? It happens, kisses are just—things, and they happen, and . . . Perhaps best if

120

we—just. How about we don't speak of it at all? Wouldn't that be best? And Louis will be back within a week or so, of course, and we'll—we'll be like sisters, and . . . So it's best if we . . ."

"It was a game to you," Isabel concluded for her. "You meant to make—fun of me."

"No! No. Not a—" She put two hands over her face, over her eyes, made a sound of despair. She said, "I don't know, Isabel! I don't know any better than you."

"You don't know what it—" Isabel's voice had warped itself. She had to stop, swallow, say: "I've never . . . You don't know what it, what it meant to me, to . . ."

"What are you doing?" Eva looked at Isabel's hands—where she dug her nails into skin, was pinching it raw. She stepped to her, said, "Stop it," took her by the wrist. Isabel let her. Looked up at her, slow. She was close. She smelled of wet cloth. She was heat, too. Her belly, so near, the rapid rise and fall of it.

Isabel tugged at the hold Eva had on her, did so gently. *Closer*, it said. She opened her legs. Eva held, a levered counterweight— then yielded. She stepped into the bracket of Isabel's knees, a hiccupped sound, and Isabel swayed, put her face to Eva—her soft stomach. It gave so gently, skin so warm through fabric. She remained there a moment. Moved, the smallest gesture: nosing in, opening her mouth. Eva's muscles jumped, and a hand went into Isabel's hair, and they both shared a breath—a sound, a soft breath in unison—and then Eva was gone: stepping away with a hiss. She walked to the bathroom, closed the door behind.

At first—nothing. Silence like the stretched skin of a drum. Isabel sat in it, a sob stuck in her throat.

Then the rush of water, the shower turned on. It went on for a long time. Isabel did not move from her spot. When the shower ended, and Eva came out in a tightly cinched robe, Isabel did not meet her eye. She got up and rushed by—not a spared look, not

121

a word—and locked herself in the bathroom in return. The heat was locked, the steam made it hard to see.

She undressed herself, peeling. She took down her hair. It had grown too long over the summer, now reached halfway down her back, sticking to her skin. She shook under the shower, shook under the heat of the water. She reached down and held herself between her legs.

9

A SOUND WOKE HER UP IN THE MIDDLE OF THE
night. The storm had calmed, the room had settled, all quiet shadows and the blank faces of closed doors. Shallow sleep, strangers'
footsteps in the halls. And then that noise: a choked gag, a gasp.
Isabel was upright in bed, heart racing, catching up with herself,
with the dark and her body and where she was, who she was.

And whom she was with: Eva, tangled in the bed across the
room. She sounded like she was suffocating. There was a fraction where Isabel stared wide-eyed into the room, looking for a
cause—a huddled figure in a corner, outstretched hands, a men-
acing. But there was nothing, nothing but Eva, jerking under the
sheets. Isabel couldn't see her face, couldn't make out the rest
of her.

She went. Her feet were unsteady. She sought Eva out with
flat palms, sought out her shoulders, her neck, looking for
something—a necklace, a ribbon, something that was doing this
to her. There wasn't anything. A nightmare, then, and Isabel
shook her, said, "Eva. *Eva.*"

Eva woke up and grabbed Isabel by the throat.

It was a good grip. Isabel struggled against it, and Eva tightened her hand, eyes wild and unseeing in the dark. Isabel scrab-
bled at Eva's fingers, strangled out an "Eva—" And Eva's wrist was
warm. She was panting. Isabel choked out, "It's me, it's Isabel."

Eva's touch slackened. Slackened, then loosened altogether. She said, "Isabel?" It sounded small. Isabel said, "Yes, it's me, it's—" and got into the bed. Eva's hand was still on her throat, now just a curling of fingers. Eva began to breathe loudly and Isabel held her. The robe had come slightly undone in the night, and now slipped under Isabel's grip. She pulled Eva in. She said "Shh" when Eva sobbed, she said: "It's me, it's me." And Eva said, "Isabel. Isabel," and said her name like that: a statement, a reminder.

"Come here," Isabel said, tried to tilt Eva's face up. "Eva. Show me your face." And when Eva wouldn't, she held her closer. She said, "Look at me."

A faint light through the window: perhaps an emergency lamp at the back of the building, a car with the taillights left on. Eva raised her face. Isabel wiped at Eva's cheeks.

Isabel had never known an embrace like this. Had never been so close in the night. She put her forehead to Eva's—damp sweat, hot skin. Their noses brushed. Her hand was on the sash of Eva's robe, tightening. It wasn't a kiss, it was only a nearness. Isabel could feel the heat of her lips. It wasn't a kiss.

Eva whispered, "You should go back to your bed."

The words brushed Isabel's skin. She answered: "No."

Eva made a sound, a whine. "It's no good," she said, and fisted at the collar of Isabel's robe. "It's bad, Isa."

Isabel wasn't sure what she meant: the two them, or the night, or Louis, or everything. Eva fell asleep like that—in Isabel's arms, her face to Isabel's throat. The twist of a hand she'd put to Isabel's robe loosened in her sleep—but still held.

Isabel stayed awake. Every now and then a shudder began, and she would not let it rise. She remained unmoving, not wanting to stir Eva from her sleep again. She seemed so small, and real in a way she wasn't always. Her skin was soft and warm, her heartbeat close below. She was rounded at her hip, had the soft give of fat over her ribs. Isabel wanted to dig her fingers into her. Eva shuddered in her slumber, goose bumps rising. Isabel stroked a thumb down the side of her neck. Isabel's heart went wide, went tight. Went wide and tight again. The morning came with palest of skies. The shadows lifted as though they'd only been glimpsed under the hem of a skirt—the lift on an arm, secrets of the body that only unfolded for the night.

The bed, when Isabel woke, was empty. It still held Eva's warmth. She did not know the time. The day was too loud: the sun too loud, the birds too loud, the people outside the hotel and in the hallways and in the far distance—too loud.

The room was hot. Isabel could not get her hair in order. She stood before the bathroom mirror and tried to comb it through with wet fingers and could not get it in order. The skin around her mouth was irritated. She looked as though she'd woken from a sickness.

She found the others at the restaurant, in the same seats as the previous evening—Sebastian leaning back, Hendrik telling some grand story that included gestures and reenactments. Approaching, all Isabel could see of Eva was her back: the slight slouch of her, the press of her spine against the white of her shirt—each bump, all the way up.

Hendrik greeted Isabel with a big *hey-ho!* He clasped her shoulder, pulled her into the group. Eva was in profile, eyes down, unreadable. Breakfast was brief and Isabel took it at a different table. Hendrik laughed at this, said, *Oh, it's like that!* and Isabel could not respond. She held a cup of coffee like a buoy, nose to the rim. Yesterday's dress was creased, still held some damp.

On the way out Eva walked ahead as if in a greater hurry than they were. She held the picnic basket at her side, short legs going fast. At the car, she waited for Hendrik to unlock the doors, and when he did she claimed the passenger seat quickly, which made Hendrik laugh, and made Sebastian pause and look and say, "All yours, then."

Isabel closed her eyes in the back seat and did not open them until they were already driving. All the windows were down. The wind pushed through, a hot breath, a bright warm palm of sky to her face. Sebastian quietly asked her, once, "Are you all right?" And Isabel said, "Of course," sternly. The storm had left its marks on the landscape: trees felled, branches tumbled down dikes. In reply, nature screeched into the day: insects rubbing noise out of wings, blackbirds running and cawing, flying and cawing.

The journey back was quiet, a tense and reserved mood settling between them. Sebastian and Hendrik had half-spoken conversations about picking up their stuff at the house and immediately continuing on to Den Haag. *Do we have time to stay for tea? We don't have time to stay for tea.* Isabel realized she'd put a hand to her throat and was holding herself like that. She put her hand back in her lap with a jerk.

At the house there was a car parked up the long driveway. Isabel recognized it quickly. She knew, in that moment, whom they'd find waiting for them, and she was right: Johan, over by the hedge, smoking a cigarette and looking like he was kicking the root of the plant—shoving his foot into it. He looked like he'd been there for a while.

Hendrik slowed to a stop, a good distance away. Everyone in the car was silent a moment, and then Hendrik said, "*Oh*, Isabel. What have you *done* to him?"

"I," Isabel began, and then stopped. A blush rose quick and true, a bodily thing, hot up into her face. Johan noticed them.

Isabel said, "Hendrik. Hendrik, go to him. I can't—I don't want to—"

"Go to him? And say what! He's here for you, obviously, what do you want me to—"

"I don't care! Go, *please*, he's almost here, please just—"

Hendrik went—with an incredulous huff, a laugh. A quiet *I guess I must!* and he got out of the car. He stopped Johan up the path by blocking his way, saying, "Neighbor Johan!"

Isabel couldn't hear the rest of the conversation from the car, only the cadence of talk—of voice, of bass. Isabel put two hands on her knees and waited for it to be over. She glanced up once, caught Eva's eye in the rearview mirror, realized the gaze had been on her for a while—and looked away.

Ahead, Johan nodded and nodded at something Hendrik said. Then he smiled and shook Hendrik's hand, and then waved at her—at the three of them. No one waved back. He left, went back to his own car. Drove by them slowly, window down to say: "See you then!"

Hendrik wandered back at a leisurely pace. He began to unload their luggage from the trunk. He'd lit himself a cigarette. They all got out of the car and Isabel said, "What did you say, what happened?" And Hendrik said, "Oh, he was adamant, he was *adamant*."

"Adamant about *what*?"

"You'd promised him another date." Hendrik had his bag over his shoulder, the beach blankets over an arm. "Apparently."

"I didn't—" But something of the like had been said, Johan asking, *Soon?* and Isabel only humming, a vague yes. The smell of wine on his breath, his hand too close to her breast. "I meant *eventually*. Not—not within days!"

Hendrik shrugged. "Well," he said. "He's coming for dinner tonight, so that's that."

"*Dinner.*"

"You didn't give me instructions, Isabel. You just sent me at him." He walked toward the house. Isabel went after, half a step behind, angry and saying he had no right to invite anyone on her behalf, and that she could not cook, that Neelke was gone for the day and that she had no means to make dinner, and that she—

"Go do groceries, Isabel. Figure it out." He opened the door awkwardly: smoke between his lips, arms occupied, only one hand to shimmy at the key. "Besides," he said. "He'll expect you to cook for him sooner or later, anyway."

Sebastian was following behind them, slow. Eva did not. She remained behind, picnic basket at her feet. She looked like a chastened child.

Isabel said, "What do you *mean*, sooner or later?"

"What do you think," Hendrik said, and went inside. Isabel stood, frozen in the entryway. Sebastian, when he reached her, said, "It'll be all right, Isabel." He touched her arm—a squeeze, a comfort. Isabel looked at it. Looked at him. He let her go. He cleared his throat and went after Hendrik.

Across the path, Eva remained, eyes down. Isabel waited. Mouth dry, throat dry. Eventually, Eva picked up the basket, made her way over, too. She took her time, rearranged the weight, from this arm to that arm, back and forth. At the door, several steps away, she stopped. Said, "I can help you cook, you know."

Eva's night of bad sleep showed on her face, too. Her hair was a yellow dusting catching the noon light.

"No," Isabel said.

"I can."

"Why would you?" She meant the question seriously. She wanted to hear the answer.

Eva said, "Perhaps . . ." She hesitated. "Perhaps it will be a good thing. Better than— Oh, it'll be good for you to have the company of . . . You'll enjoy it, it'll be fun, you'll see. You'll have fun, and you'll see that—you'll see, you'll see that . . ."

Eva could not finish her thought. She wanted Isabel to understand something that Isabel did not understand.

"I'll see what?"

"Isabel." A quick glance at the door—back. "Isabel. He *likes* you."

It was the way Eva said it: big-eyed, pleading almost. She wanted Isabel to move in a direction—away. She said, "You want to be rid of me."

Eva didn't reply. She made a sound, a cut-off sound, and Isabel did not wait for the rest: "Understood," she said, and walked away—down the path, down the road. Beyond the house: into the farmland, two cows on a field. The horizon, cut only by a stand of trees. She looked behind her once and saw Eva, a distant dot, unmoving, still framed by the darkened doorway.

Isabel walked for an hour. Her dress dried on her skin. She tried to call some cows over to pet, and only one came, and left soon when she understood Isabel had no food to offer.

Hunger pushed her homeward. She came in through the kitchen. Eva was there, an apron over a clean dress. She was cooking. A pot on the fire, the door open to let the steam run out. Isabel's heart gave one heavy, sad thump.

Eva turned to Isabel quickly, wiped her hands on a towel, took a step like she wanted to say something—fall into an explanation, a conversation. Isabel did not allow as much, did not want to hear it and have to face what was happening: the ruse of the dinner, the way it seemed to be designed to push Isabel away. Hand her off to someone else. She went to the pantry, said behind the door's protection: "Hendrik and Sebastian left?"

"Yes," Eva said. A high-chested breath. "They said to say good-bye. They said . . ."

Isabel held on to the door handle. She felt the sun's mark on the back of her head. "They said?"

"Ah. Hendrik hoped that you could . . ."

Isabel took a half loaf to the table. She did not sit down, buttered a slice standing up. She pushed her hair back one-handed, sweat on her forehead. She ate too fast. An embarrassed heat crawled up her cheeks as Eva watched her. She said: "Hendrik hoped you would come to thank him later."

Thank him. Humiliation wrapped itself tight around her throat. Isabel held the last piece of bread in her hand. "How kind."

"Isabel. I do . . . I do care for you, you know. It's not that I—"

"Don't make a mess of the kitchen. Clean up after you're done." Isabel put down the last bite, wiped the crumbs from her fingers. Her voice was hard and steady, just as she wanted it. "Don't touch the china in the cabinet."

Upstairs, in the bathroom, she wiped at her face with a rough towel, ran a bath, and lowered herself in. There was a bruise on her thigh she could not place. Sunlight came in through the crocheted curtain, patterns on the water, on the floor. Steam rose. The ventilation connected with the house below, and over the quiet lap of bathwater Isabel could hear the clattering of pans, of pots. Of spoon to the rim of a bowl. Of the gas being turned up high, the rush and then catch of fire.

She was not wanted. That was the long and the short of it: she had learned want, briefly and hungrily. A span of a day, two days. She had learned the shape of it, the quick taste of it. She had reached out, foolishly, and she was not wanted in return. She was not Louis. She was not Hendrik.

And in a house not too far from here, in a room with a window

130

overlooking a rose garden, Johan was thinking of her. Getting ready to come to her.

She stood before her closet in her underclothes. She remembered Johan's hand on her leg, on her bare skin. She chose her one pair of trousers, the one she wore most often for gardening. It was high at the waist, loose at the knees. An old blouse that had been washed a dull gray over the years, and was missing a button at the collar. She plaited her hair quickly, purposefully messy. Plaits did not suit her, looked starkly childish against her severe features.

The house smelled like food. Isabel's stomach turned over on itself. The tail of her wet braid stained the back of her shirt. Isabel had half-formed plans to send Eva away, to do so cruelly—demand she eat her own dinner in her room. That she not come down for the rest of the evening. The idea alone was miserable. Triumphant and miserable.

But Eva had already set the table herself—outside, in the garden, under the shade of the parasol. She'd set out two plates of her own accord, not three. She was arranging the glasses, and then saw Isabel had come out of the kitchen, and then froze. Confused a moment—eyes quick. Her gaze lingered somewhere at the height of Isabel's waist. The button of her trousers.

Evening was settling in slow. The air smelled like the warm bark of pine. Isabel said, "Are you done?"

Eva nodded. She took a moment to say, "You should—tell him you cooked. He'll like that."

"What will you do?" Isabel asked. She had intended to command, and instead it was only a question. "When he arrives?"

"Oh, I'll—Don't worry about me."

"I don't," Isabel said.

Eva smiled at that, unhappy. She had done a lovely job of the garden table: a cloth, two candles. A bowl over a plate. The good glasses, the etched crystal. She had not yet changed out yesterday's clothes. It could not have been comfortable. Isabel weathered the sudden and rattling rush that demanded she go to Eva, that she put her hands on her—and Isabel remained where she was, a tree upright in a storm.

It was Eva who came to her. Starting and then stopping—a quick step, a pause. There was an arm's length between them. There was a blush mottling Eva's jaw. "Your plait is crooked," she said, and it sounded uncertain: as if she herself did not know why she said it.

Isabel looked at her.

"God," Eva said, a sob. And then, all in a blurry rush: "I don't, I don't want to be rid of you, but what can we do, Isabel? What can we have? Louis is—The house—Isabel, can't you see? In the end there will be nothing. Can't you see how it'll be just—"

"I can't," Isabel said. "I can't see. There must—"

A car approached. Eva swallowed a word, an exclamation, turned away, went to arrange her face with her back turned to Isabel. Isabel took a step, took her elbow, said, "Don't leave us. Eat with us, please, don't leave me with him, stay, you must stay."

"I can't," Eva said.

"You can," Isabel said. "You can. You will."

The look Eva gave her was wide and dark. Her mouth set as though in anger. It wasn't anger. Isabel recognized it this time. Found it echoed in herself, a shiver. It wasn't anger at all.

She went inside and fumbled with a plate, a bowl, a third seat at the table.

Johan shut the car door in the distance and came toward them. His hair was combed back with water, oil. He carried with him an overwhelming cloud of cologne. He raised his hand in hello before he said hello. He noticed Eva quickly, seemed curious about it, vaguely annoyed about it. He greeted Isabel first: leaned in close, kissed her cheeks three times. He did it slowly. He put a hand to her waist. "I waited for you," he said, low, in her ear. There was still a shiver in her, which he mistook for thrill, and grinned at her.

To Eva he gave a hand. "Hello," he said. "A friend? On your way out?"

"Eva is staying," Isabel said before Eva could answer. "She's—staying. With me, at the house." A shiver, too, to her words. She could not get them under control, could not get them to lie flat. "She'll be staying for dinner."

"Oh." Johan saw the table: three spots, one haphazardly laid. "I thought, Isabel, that we would get the chance to . . ."

"I could—" Eva started, and Isabel cut in with:

"Eva is a guest. She'll be eating with us."

"Ah," Johan said, and rocked back on his heels, put on some nonchalance and said: "The more the merrier, I suppose. And a chance to meet Isabel's friends, of course, a privilege. I'm sure you two have been cooking away all day, working hard, no? A treat for me. Aren't I lucky?"

He went into the kitchen, rubbing his hands together, saying how good it smelled. Saying how he was hungry already, how he couldn't wait. Eva closed her eyes the moment he was out of sight. Isabel touched her hand on passing: her smallest finger to Eva's smallest finger. A touch, a hook, and gone.

How quickly did the belly of despair turn itself over into hope, the give of the skin of overripe fruit.

The heat drew into the evening. Frogs from the low canals tottered onto land, onto the estate. The dinner scratched by in increments, each of them painful, each of them slow. And though the air was light and the candles burned lovely, Isabel sat, locked in her body, waiting for it to end. Johan did not seem to notice.

He sat close to Isabel, legs wide in his chair, and talked. The same stories as the other night: his mother, his colleague Willy, the boat. About the food he said again and again, "I'm picky, you know. I'm very picky. But this is almost good, I'll give you that. Very well done, very well done."

Eva had made some sort of sweet loaf in the oven. Had made some sort of potato dish, fried and shredded. Had glazed carrots with honey. It was good, it was very good. Isabel tasted little of it. On the other side of the table, Eva spoke up only to say: "Isabel is a very talented cook, it's true." And Johan said, "Is she?" And Eva said, "The best I know, really."

She kept saying things like that, breathless and in between sips of wine. "Doesn't Isabel look lovely tonight?" To which Johan said, "Very," with a low-eyed glance at Isabel. Eva said, "Haven't you always admired how well she keeps the garden?" And Johan said, "Now that you mention it . . ." Eva said, "You know what I've always admired about Isabel?" And Johan said, "I'm sure you'll tell me," and Eva said: "Her honesty."

Isabel ran hot. She went inside to refill the carafe of water. Out of view, she wet her hand under the tap, held it to her cheek—her other cheek. *Let it be over*, she thought. *Let it be over. Let it be over. Let it be—*

She returned and Johan rose from his seat. He was arranging his jacket over his arm, then said, "Shall we go for a walk, Isabel?"

Eva was still in her seat, collecting the plates, stacking them. She didn't look up at her, kept her face tilted away.

Isabel said, "I—I should. Help clear the table."

"Eva said she didn't mind." Johan held out his elbow for Isabel to take. "Didn't you, Eva?"

"Don't mind at all," Eva said on a fluttery sound, an imitation of a laugh. She still wasn't looking up. "Go, go, you two! Go, have fun."

"Eva," Isabel said.

Eva slowed in her cleaning. A trembling misery. A certainty, too. She said, "*Go.*"

The night had got away from Isabel. Her mouth opened on a silent word, closed. She was tired. She took Johan's arm. He made a pleased sound, gestured to say: let's. He guided them down the path. The muscle of his arm pushed against the seam of his shirt: chosen a size too small. His cologne, this close, was so strong she thought she could taste it.

He picked a path by a reed-flanked canal. The stalks were yellow and high, and swayed slowly against the blazing sunset. Johan said, "Your friend adores you."

Isabel could not answer. She could only hum, a broken little "Hm."

They walked on. Then he said, "You look lovely tonight. Your hair like this." He reached across her to push her plait back over her shoulder. To push a strand behind her ear. She moved her face away from the touch. He took it as shyness and tutted, indulgent. "Though I do prefer you in a dress," he said, and put his hand over hers where she held him—his arm. The press of his hand was heavy.

"Let's go back," she said.

"In a little while," he said, and guided her all around the pasture, trapped at his side.

By the time they got back to the house the night had settled darker than before. The garden table had been cleared. Eva wasn't there. Isabel made to pull her hand from him, to say her good night, but he wouldn't let her go. She said, "Johan," and he said, "*Isabel*," like it was a game. He walked her backward a few steps. Her back against one of the trees. He pressed his body close, purposefully. She could feel him through his trousers— the shape of him, raised and excited. She gasped, and again he

misunderstood, leaned his face to hers, said, "I like you, Isabel."
He huffed, something like a laugh. "You play these games . . ."

"Johan," she said once more, and knew how it sounded:
breathless, pleading. She had been on edge all night. She had
sat with her heart beating fast, had flushed, had gone wet and
wanting at someone else's nearness—the memory of Eva's hands
in her hair, how she had pulled. The pooling shadow of a look
when Isabel had said, *You can. You will.*

Her desire got tangled and Johan's hand on her ribs made her
arch, crossed wires, and then he kissed her. She let it happen a
moment, and then turned away from it. His tongue had been
heavy in her mouth. He kissed her jaw, her neck. She panted
under him. One light upstairs was on, and when Isabel looked
up, the curtains drew close—quick as anything.

She pushed him off. "I have—" She pushed him again. "I have
a guest, Johan."

He slumped away, slumped next to her—shoulder against the
tree trunk. "What," he said, looked at her with a smile. "She can't
see anyway. She won't mind."

Isabel smoothed down her shirt. She wanted to wash out her
mouth. She wanted to be back in the house. "Good night," she
said.

Johan groaned. "Isabel!" he said. He had two hands in his
pockets, the fabric tight over his crotch. She walked away, dizzy.
He said it again: "Isabel!" and laughed. "Are you walking away!
Really!"

"Good night," she said, and didn't look back.

"Good night," he answered, incredulous.

She locked the kitchen door behind her. She was trembling.
Felt oddly vulnerable with her hair down, in her trousers. Somewhere in the house—Eva. Somewhere in the house, alone. The
doors were locked. The lights were out.

Isabel waited in the kitchen until Johan drove away. She counted nine whole minutes on the clock. He honked as he left, and the sound juddered through her.

Her lips had gone dry. She took out her plait—nervous hands, itching, wanting to shed something. She went upstairs. There, at the end of the hall, the door to her mother's old room was left ajar, ever so slightly. A soft beam of light. Eva was sitting on the edge of the bed, in her sleeping clothes—powder-pink silk. It caught the orange of the bedside lamp like a high sun over sea.

Eva's hands were on her knees, an unnatural position. She had been waiting for Isabel. She knew Isabel would come for her.

Eva looked up. Isabel stepped inside. The door closed behind her.

10

FOR A BEAT, THE DISTANCE TO THE BED STRETCHED like an open field, a thin horizon; she looked at it and did not know how long it would take to cross it. She looked at it and thought, *This will go on forever.*

Then Eva said, "You let him kiss you."

The doorjamb dug into Isabel's back. She leaned away from it. She said, "You let him take me away."

A flicker of an emotion. Eva tightened her jaw, said, "Did you—" She was still sitting primly. "Did you enjoy it?" She said it and then turned her face away. She meant the kiss. She meant Johan's kiss. She looked like she didn't want to hear the answer at all.

How do you know, Isabel had asked her, mere days ago—had asked her a little drunkenly, a little out of her mind. And Eva had said, *You should just let him. Find out.*

And then she had kissed Isabel herself. And kissed her, and kissed her, and kissed her.

"No," Isabel said now, an emphatic rush of sound.

"You blushed very prettily for him tonight. Could barely speak a word around him."

The three steps from the door to the bed snapped into nothingness. She went, she fell to her knees, she said, "That wasn't for him." Between Eva's legs, grabbing her knees, sliding up her touch—under the fall of the hem of Eva's shorts. Isabel's hands had gone cold in the evening and Eva's skin was a heat, was a rasp against the grain of hair. A punch of air from Eva's lungs, she opened her legs to Isabel and Isabel told her: "You know that. You know it wasn't for him."

They were at eye level like this: Isabel kneeling, Eva perched on the bed's edge. They were close, and Eva had two hard hands in the flesh of Isabel's shoulders. Their noses brushed, cheeks pressed, and Eva turned her face away. Turned it back. Isabel made a sound, tightened her grip on Eva's thighs, and Eva panted—a hot thing on Isabel's lips.

The carpet itched under her knees. Through fabric, through trousers. Sweat at the line of her spine. All she could see of Eva was the downcast of her eyes, the fan of her lashes. She was looking at Isabel's mouth. She was digging her fingers into the back of her neck.

"Tell me no." Isabel's voice rumbled between them. "Eva. Tell me yes or no."

"I can't," Eva said, and opened her mouth over Isabel's. A rolling movement of the body, the press of her breasts to Isabel's. There was something maddening to her kiss, wide-open the one moment, and then hesitant the next, pulling back. It made Isabel want to barrel in, want to break the hinges, push the door from its bolts; she nipped her lip, she sucked her in, she pushed her hands up Eva's bare thighs and pulled. The movement skid Eva to the very edge of the bed, it opened her legs wider, it pressed her heat to Isabel's stomach—Eva's crotch, the hard bone of her mound.

Eva's mouth slipped off hers with a breath. Isabel chased it, and the next kiss was faster, frantic. Isabel had a fanned hold at the fold of Eva's leg, the join of her pelvis. Her thumb touching the elastic of her underwear. The thin skin had gone damp there. Isabel kissed her harder. She tugged on the elastic. She didn't know what she wanted; she knew what she wanted. She didn't know and knew at once, a blurry shape turning sometimes sharp, a loud Klaxon of *yes*; and answering the question *Where?* with: *Anywhere. Anywhere.*

Eva couldn't close her mouth anymore, couldn't coordinate the kiss; jaw cocked open, rolling her hips, pressing into the soft hill below Isabel's navel. A wetness had seeped through. Isabel let her, let her grind, guided the movements with her hands. The world had gone a high-pitched silent; only Eva's shuddering, choked-off moans. Isabel kissed her neck, her throat. Her thumb was trapped between them. She wanted to push it in. She wanted to move. She wanted—

"Touch me," Eva said, slipped into a messy half-kiss, clutched at her and ground against her and said: "God, just, *please*, can you—"

"Tell me." Isabel hid behind her ear. She made up for her embarrassment with a bite to Eva's earlobe. "What to—"

It happened quick, the one moment inseparable from the next. Eva took Isabel's hand and sucked two fingers into her mouth, wet them, pushed the hand down the front of her shorts—the bare space she allowed between them, pressing small kisses to Isabel's bottom lip. "Like this," she said. "Like this." She was hot there. Soaking against the cotton panel of her underwear. She curved Isabel's two fingers into herself, silent, as though a syllable was caught in her throat. Isabel moaned in her stead. The sound of her fingers inside Eva—the wet ticking of it, like the rolling of a hard candy in a mouth. Eva showed her where to press her thumb. Isabel did as bid. Eva tightened around her, pushed against her—arms around Isabel's shoulders, mouth slack to the line of her hair.

"Yes?" Isabel asked, and Eva nodded, managed a weak "Yes,

yeah, ah—"; clutched at Isabel's hair, pulled herself closer, pulled Isabel into her. Isabel held her by the flesh of her ass, the back-and-forth, and they swayed, and they moved, and they fell back into the bed. Isabel's fingers slipped from her and Eva said, "Ah, come—come here, fuck, come here—"

Isabel's limbs didn't move like they were supposed to, everything slow and syrupy. Eva under her, the sleeping shorts pushed down and then caught around one ankle. Isabel was back inside her. Faster now. Her hair was a curtain around them, strands stuck to her face, the sweat. Eva pushed it away, held her face like that. Isabel had once walked in on Louis fucking a girl in his bedroom. Isabel was fourteen at the time, and had never imagined any human movement to go with the word *fucking*—hadn't imagined it much at all, other than the sickening flush at the idea, at the thought. And then she had a flash, just a flash—some girl's thigh from under her dress, her hands dug into the short crop of Louis's hair, the rolling of her hips and his bare backside.

It had only been a second, and then she had fled. Spent the rest of the afternoon digging a hole in the garden with a stick. The image had stayed with her for years. Whenever anyone said the word *fuck*, that's what she saw: earth overturned. She had hated the word. She had hated how it made her feel like looking away.

She didn't look away now, Eva's knee up, her foot pressed under the clothed underside of Isabel's buttock. She allowed herself to think it: *fucking her*. Her fingers deep, buried. *I'm fucking her.* She was pushed up on one elbow, looking down at Eva; the high blotch on her neck, her chest, the shape of her breasts under the shiny cloth—full, spilled to the side. The dark, shadowy space where they were joined, where Isabel pressed in and in and in. Eva's mouth was swollen. There was another reddening mark at the base of her throat. Eva opened her eyes, found she was being

141

watched, tried to turn from it—then turned back to it, unfocused, hazy-eyed. She let go of Isabel's hair, found the waist of Isabel's trousers and pulled at her, the hem of her blouse from where it was tucked, pulled at her waist some more. She wedged a leg between Isabel's legs, pushed it up. And then they were moving. And then they were a twisted shape, both of them, Isabel riding her thigh, fucking her, a frazzled rhythm, and Eva began to talk. Said *yes*, and *ah*, and *that's good that's so good that's—*

Her fingers were twisted in the belt loops of Isabel's trousers, leverage, and that's how she came. An arching, a sob, a gushing around Isabel's fingers. Isabel did not want it to stop. She did not let up, circled and circled her thumb, until Eva had to push her away—had to take her by the wrist and say, "Ah—shh, no, ah—"

Isabel acquiesced. Her arm trembled where she kept herself up. Eva's thigh was still between her legs, where she was heaviest; where she was swollen and soaked and would die if Eva touched her there. She was sure she would die if Eva touched her there.

She did not die. Eva got her to lie down, got her to open her trousers with shaky hands, fingers clumsy on the zip. She lay next to Isabel, on her side, propped on an elbow. She stroked Isabel's stomach, only her stomach, a sugared slowness to her now that she had come. Isabel could barely stand it, could barely stand the ease. The inching hand. Eva spoke to her in small words, sweet things. "You looked so lovely tonight," she said. "God, you don't—know how—" She pushed aside the fly of the trousers, slipped her hand in, over Isabel's underwear. The fabric slipped, drenched. Isabel shuddered, full-bodied, a nervous gasp. She clutched at the sheets for something to hold. Eva said, "Fuck." Said, "No one's touched you like this before? Look at me. Look at me, sweetheart. Let me see your face, I want—to see when you like it, I want to see—"

The discovery was that Isabel could not keep quiet. She had done as much for all her life, in her bedroom, underwear bunched, corner of a pillow stuffed into her mouth. Not a peep from her, perfunctory and quick. She did not manage as much now. She could not keep quiet. She could not. The sounds pulled from her, loud under the room's slanted ceiling; loud in the night, loud in how empty the house was. Eva's fingers were slow on her, sliding round where she wanted them—around, *around*, never quite *there*. She kissed Isabel, trying to quiet her. She said, "Shh, let me, shh," and then never picked up speed, never pressed, never pushed. Isabel pulled at cloth and it ripped. Eva laughed, softly, against her mouth.

Isabel groaned—grabbed Eva's hand, pushed it where she wanted it. She rose up into Eva, kissed her hard, pulled her close. Bit: her neck, her chest. Eva said, "Oh, I—" and tilted to it, arched to it. Isabel fit her mouth around a breast, over fabric, sucked at it. She clutched at Eva, the give of fat over bones, over hips. She wanted to hold all of her at once and couldn't. Wanted to have bigger hands, wanted to envelop, wanted to cover her, contain her—scooping water out of a sinking boat.

She flipped them over. She got on top. She asked with a small touch to the hem of Eva's top—and Eva said "Yes yes yes—" and Eva took it off. She was naked now. Naked under Isabel. Sand-rolled skin, a freckled stretch that was the darkest at her shoulders. At the dip of her sternum, the farthest the sun could reach. The scar, up her side, a pale-taut line; an old thing, a healed thing. Isabel traced it with a thumb. Eva's stomach quivered. Her eyes were closed. The skin of the breast that Isabel had taken into her mouth was reddish now. A light brown nipple. A light brown areola. Two freckles there, too. Isabel's chest went tight at the sight of it: those two freckles, dotting the hidden bow of a breast. So small they were. So unnoticed. She kissed them, and kissed them, and pressed her face into as much skin as she could find. Papery and soft and weathered in places—elbows and knuckles. Skin. All of her skin.

Isabel woke up and it was dark. The window on the wrong side of the room, the space all odd, the sheets too rough on her skin and the shifting heat of a body nearby. Eva was twisting next to her. She was dreaming badly, breath stuck in her throat—choking.

Isabel reached for her. They were both naked, and the knowledge of it pushed through her with a fright—and then was gone. Eva jerked, clutched Isabel's arms, then softened. Exhaled. Did not quite wake up. Isabel was not quite awake herself. She cupped Eva's face and drew a line with her thumb: from the top of Eva's forehead down over the rise of her nose. Over the bridge of it, over her lips, all the way to her chin. She did it again, and then again.

"What are you doing?" Eva whispered. Her eyes were still closed. And then, "No, don't stop, keep doing that." She smelled like deep sleep, like trapped heat.

Isabel said, "My mother used to do this. When I was young, when I had nightmares." The top of Eva's forehead, the line of her nose. Her mouth, the dip below.

"What did you have nightmares about?"

"Airplanes. Bombs." She paused, finger pad to Eva's bottom lip. "Girls at school. People knocking at the door. Wanting to get in."

Eva opened her eyes. It was too dark to see properly, but there was the glint of her eyes moving, the droplet sound of her mouth opening under Isabel's touch. She put the edge of her teeth to Isabel's thumb, did so softly, and then closed around it. Sucked it in.

Isabel inhaled. Held it, held it. Released, pressed her thumb to the wet flat of Eva's tongue. She had never touched another person in want. She had now. She had gulped at the cup of it. Her hands were no longer the same; her belly, her cunt. At Eva's mercy, trapped behind the cage of her teeth, she had grown a new shape.

Sunrise came with the early hand of summer; loud, birds and birds. Eva slept on Isabel's chest. Her back was a good width, a broad width. Isabel ran a touch from the one end to the other end, shoulder, spine, shoulder. Each stroke a dry rustle of a sound. They breathed.

Neelke came at seven. From upstairs, Isabel heard her bike over the gravel, and the opening of the door, and the gentle clattering in the kitchen. She lifted Eva off her as quietly as she could; Eva slept on. Isabel got dressed: trousers, blouse over bare breasts, and that is how she went downstairs to greet Neelke. Her mind was humming, a full emptiness, her body sore and present. She could feel embarrassment just beyond her, out of reach.

Neelke took her in with a brief confusion, eyes sliding over and off her; gaze to the floor as Isabel spoke. Isabel wasn't sure what she looked like: her hair, her face. She could not care much. They sat down and went through the list of what needed doing for the week: the windows, the laundry, the grouting. She said, "I will be taking my breakfast upstairs."

Neelke nodded, eyes down. Isabel said, "Do not go into Eva's room. She's resting."

Neelke said, "Eva's room," as though she was unsure which one that was. She couldn't have been, and yet Isabel told her: "My mother's." She said it sharply, then swallowed, a round egg at the base of her throat. *My mother's.*

Neelke looked at her now. Her eyes were so big. There was a tightness at her mouth, a stillness to the way she held herself. She had noticed something on Isabel's neck.

Isabel covered the soreness with a hand and said nothing of it. She took breakfast upstairs. The carrying tray she had bought when Mother's illness bound her to the bed. She had often made this trip during that final year—balancing a supper, a clattering of plates, glasses, through the drawing room, up the stairs. *Mother's room.*

Eva was still asleep. The day was bright behind the curtains. The room smelled like bodies, like—like how they had smelled, pressed close together. Rubbing, rubbing. Isabel had pulled Eva into her lap at some point in the night. Had sat back against the headboard and kept Eva in her lap, straddled, and touched her like she was trying to figure her out: the slick of her and the depth of her and all that made her go *ah*. Wet had pearled in her thatch of curls. She had kept her mouth slack to Isabel's ear and said, *How do I feel?* and Isabel had answered: *Good. You feel good.*

Afterward, Eva had not looked at her when she'd said: "Louis will come back soon." She was still shivering, still coming down. She had put her face to Isabel's neck. And Isabel had said, "I know," and it had come out roughly, and Eva had said very quickly: "Oh let's not think about it let's have this just for now we will only live now and what comes will come and we won't think about it and—"

Isabel had kissed her. She did not know what else to do. At first she thought Eva had been crying into the kiss, but no: she was laughing. Uncontrollable and terrible. "Shh," Isabel had said. "Shh now."

She put the breakfast down on the bedside table. She opened a window. A ray of light cut across the bed, across Eva's arm;

across her bare breast and a map of marks, red and smarting. She wondered whether Louis had ever done as much, given her as much. Saw her and was undone by her as much. Isabel's stomach churned, a sharp tug, and she turned away from the image and shut her eyes to it.

For a moment she was lost. She walked around the room, she wiped her damp hands on her blouse. She touched things: the edge of the wardrobe, the edge of the secretary. As a child Isabel would crawl under the secretary while her mother was writing letters. She would put her hand to the underside of the wood to feel the scritch-scratch of the pen. There were initials carved into the bottom of the drawer: *EDH*. Her mother's name was Elisabeth, and her mother had probably once been a child hiding under the table, too. Isabel didn't know what the *D* or the *H* stood for, and had never asked.

Downstairs, Neelke was doing the dishes. On the desk, Eva's leather-bound notebook. Isabel put a hand over it, as she would over a Bible. The leather was warmed. Perhaps by the room, perhaps by the sun.

"Don't," Eva said.

Isabel turned. Eva was sitting up, holding the sheets up to her chest, covering. Her hair was matted. She looked fully awake now. "It's private," she said. She meant the book. Isabel had forgot about the book instantly, and now glanced at it. Eva said: "My diary. It's . . ."

Isabel came to sit at her side. Eva shuffled. She was watching Isabel like she was trying to calculate her next move. Isabel said, "I brought you breakfast," and Eva saw the food and said, "Oh, ah . . ." And Isabel said, "Eat something."

Eva ate two grapes. Isabel watched her chew, watched her swallow. Eva said, "Don't just watch me," and took a handful of grapes from the stem and gave them to Isabel. She still clutched

147

the sheet to her throat. Isabel couldn't look away from it: the fast pulse right below the thin skin.

Isabel ate the grapes. She poured Eva water, poured herself water. Bread, butter, cheese. Then she took everything and put it aside, and put a knee on the bed, and came in close. Eva's breath went short and stuttering. Isabel pulled the sheet from her hold. Eva whispered a curse, whispered it again at Isabel's cold hands on her waist. A sound from downstairs. Eva jerked, said, "What's—" And Isabel said, "Neelke."

"Isabel," Eva said into a kiss. "She's—right there, we shouldn't—"

"I told her not to come here. She knows."

"Isabel," Eva said again, bending under the kiss. Shifting back, back—onto the pillows. "It's—ah, it's, I don't—"

"We'll be quiet," Isabel whispered, settling between Eva's legs, rolling in. "We'll be quiet," she promised again. On the bedside table, the glasses rattled; the plates clicked together.

"God," Eva said, nails to Isabel's back, under the fall of her blouse. "*God.*"

Eva watched her garden. High noon was approaching and Isabel was on her knees, her string hat on, gloves. What survived of the gourds needed to be harvested. The tomatoes were swelling. Isabel's shirt clung to her back, sweat under her arms. Eva lay on a towel in the grass, watching her through the mirror-black of her sunglasses.

Isabel sat back on her knees. "What?"

"What," Eva said. And then, "You care for the garden. It's nice to see."

Isabel pushed away her hair with the back of a hand. A strand of it was caught at the corner of her mouth. Mud, sand, somehow the grain of it against her teeth. Eva, on her towel, did not move. Isabel took off her gloves. Took off her hat. Went to her.

That's how the days had passed. Eva had cooked for her last night, moving through the kitchen with a calm, towel over her shoulder and swaying—a step to the hob, a step to the counter. Isabel remained close, asked small-worded questions just to get Eva to say something, to get her to say the next word: *Who taught you to cook?* And, *Did you cook at home?* And, *Do you enjoy it?* And, *What's that?* And, *How do you do that?*

Eva was amused by it all, a half smile tilted to Isabel, and answered as though it was all said in jest: *Who do you think? Where else? Does it look like I enjoy it? This is a spatula, sweetheart. I do it like this. And then like this. And then—*

Isabel, too full to be teased, came to stand behind her. Wrapped her arms around her, pressed her face to Eva's neck and stayed there. Eva's laughter went quiet. She let herself be held a moment. She stroked Isabel's arms. She said, quiet, "Who are you?" She said, "Have you always been like this? Have you just been waiting to happen?"

A small hour was lost in the kitchen. They turned hobs off, left the precut onions sweating on a plate. Eva held on to the counter's edge, panting with Isabel's hand moving fast under the skirts of her dress, working her. Isabel's fingers were still pruned by the time dinner was done. When they went to bed that night, Eva had cleaned up the room. The desk was tidied. The notebook was gone. The drawer locked.

Right before she fell asleep, Isabel spared an edge of a thought to her forgotten inventory: that tightly folded piece of paper left in the pocket of her skirt. An edge of a thought to the things on that list, to the precious things and the places they belonged— and then she was gone. Fell, all at once, into slumber.

Now, in the garden, falling between the lazy bend of Eva's knees, Isabel repeated: "Nice to see." She palmed Eva's thighs. She arranged them as she wanted them: open, around her hips. Hoisted her closer.

"Ah," Eva said, her expression still a blank glint of sunglasses. "Too far, you're—" and pulled Isabel in by the damp collar of her shirt.

After, Isabel said, a statement: "You've done this before." They lay side by side. The towel had bunched under them at some point, had been cast aside. Isabel had a wide-fingered hold on Eva's leg, high up her leg. Eva said, "Hmm," a general sound, an I-don't-know-what-you-mean sound. A tired sound.

"With women," Isabel said. "Other women."

Eva stilled. Then sighed, a tight sound. She was silent for a while. A blackbird rushed across the grass, stopped, raised its tail—called out. Called out. Isabel squeezed her hand at Eva's thigh.

"There was," she started. Finished it with a "Once," which wasn't much at all.

"Who?"

"What, you expect you know her?" Eva gave her a look. Her sunglasses had come off. More freckles with every sunny day—a wild smattering under her eye. "Just a girl. We were . . . young." She was thoughtful about it.

Isabel's hold went soft. She imagined: if she and Eva had met when they were younger. Her heart kicked, hard and hungry.

Eva said, "I met her at a boardinghouse. I was looking for a place to stay, somewhere else, and she had . . . relatives, and said I could stay with them. With her." It was as vague as any story could get. Isabel let her talk. She sounded—far. "Her aunt and uncle. They had an attic room for us. One bed. It was a cold winter. So . . ."

"So?"

"So. So it was a cold winter."

It was hard to remember the chill of winter in the heat. It was hard to shift away from the clamping hand at the throat at the notion: someone else's hand on Eva. Someone else's mouth. It wasn't this girl Isabel was imagining—was jealous of. Louis was due in a few days—they weren't sure how many. He was meant to send word, and no word had come as of yet. When the phone rang, on the occasion that it rang, Eva would go stiff and Isabel would rush to it with a lump in her throat. It hadn't been Louis, so far. Once, Uncle Karel. Once, a wrong number. Isabel did not know what would happen on the day it *would* be Louis— Eva would not speak of it, would only say, *Let's not think about it!* and Isabel swung daily between hope and terror, though she hardly knew what hope would look like; what the worst of terror would look like, either. Hendrik and Sebastian lived in the city, in an apartment. Isabel would not leave the house, would never leave the house. But Eva seemed to like it here. Eva cared for the way the light filled the rooms, cared for the neat order of the kitchen, had watched Isabel work the garden and called it *nice to see*, she could—she might—

Isabel asked, "What was she like?"

"Funny," Eva said. "A habitual liar." Eva smiled. "Lied about everything, even when she didn't have to. Ha."

Isabel went quiet. Went still enough that Eva's attention was called back to her, that Eva turned to her, searched for something between the one eye and the other. "Do you miss her?"

Eva cupped Isabel's face. She said, "Sometimes. Yes." Then, "Sweetheart. Oh—" She kissed her. The sweat was salty between them. Isabel took her inside the house, took her by the hand, wet a cloth under the tap and cooled Eva's hot face with it. The bridge of her nose had been pinched red by the sun.

"That's nice." Eva swayed into her. Isabel turned her face this way, that. Eva let her. Isabel kept her with a hand to the small of her back. She put the wet towel to Eva's throat.

"Yeah," Eva sighed, and shivered. Isabel held her there. A hand over cloth over throat—held her there like that. Held her by her throat.

That night Eva didn't want to sleep in her own bed, wanted them both to sleep in Isabel's. "It's cooler in your room," was her explanation, pulling on Isabel's arm, back-walking them the other direction. "Come on," she said. "Come on, a change of scenery. Come on."

Isabel's room *was* cooler. The sheets crisper, tightly made. The bed a narrow one, not made for two people. Eva would have her night terrors, and Isabel would have to keep her from hurting herself—from hurting Isabel: constrain her arms, hush, tell her, *It's a dream you're okay it's a dream shhh it's a—*

But first, Eva walked around the bed and touched things. The mirror's frame, the picture on the vanity, the bristles of Isabel's hairbrush. On the shelf: fingers along the spines of the books.

She asked, "Has this always been your room?"

"Yes."

"Have you always kept it so neat?"

"Yes," Isabel said. She was watching her intently. Eva took the old tattered stuffed animal of a hare from its perch and inspected it, its worn fur, the spot where its nose had worn down to fibers.

"Sweet," she said. "Yours?"

"Yes." Explained, unnecessarily: "I was a child."

Eva smiled at the hare. Pet it between the eyes. "You must have loved it. To have kept it."

Isabel didn't answer. It wasn't a question, wasn't much else but a statement. She did not want to say *yes*, did not want to agree to something so indulgent. She wanted Eva to put the doll back. She wanted Eva to come to bed. She did not want to talk about her mother.

"What's her name?"

"Whose?"

Eva gave her a look. "The animal's."

"Haas," Isabel said: *hare*. Eva's petting hand stilled. She was looking at Isabel, a steady look, a blank one.

"It's what it is," Isabel continued. She thought perhaps she had said something wrong, and could not think what. "Isn't it? A hare."

Eva put the doll back on the shelf. She was breathing lighter now. "Call it what it is. Ha," she said, a little laugh.

"I'm not," Isabel said, stopped. "I did not have the imagination, as a child, to . . ."

Eva had come close as Isabel spoke, had come close quickly, was moving all fast and blearily and put her hands to Isabel's and her face to her face and said, "Let's not talk let's not talk," and pushed into Isabel. Let Isabel push back into her.

"Harder," she said later. In bed, on her front, hips tilted up. Isabel was behind her, over her, straddling the back of her thigh. They were rocking slow. Eva said, *"More."* Isabel said, "What?" blurry with heat, with skin, and Eva repeated it again and again, *more more more*, until Isabel held her down. Until Isabel put her teeth to the back of her neck.

Again, terrors woke Eva up in the night. She choked into the pillow and Isabel had to shake her awake, then hold her and Eva sobbed into her, into the flat bone between her breasts. "What," she asked. "What are these dreams, what is it, what is it?"

Eva didn't answer. She tired herself out, she fell asleep. Isabel kissed the line of her hair, kissed her closed eyes. Isabel tried to breathe through the misery of holding someone else's hurt within oneself and stayed awake like a guard dog—like there was something to keep out. Like there was someone trying to get in.

Then, on the first of July, a letter from Louis, sent with high urgency:

> *Unexpected delays will send note within a week.*
> *Apologies hope you'll make it without me for just a little*
> *while longer will let you know as soon as I arrive much love*
> *Louis*

Isabel read it first, heart pounding. Eva was upstairs. Isabel waited for her to come down, an impatient and unmoving rod at the dining table. And when Eva did come down, calling hello before entering, Isabel took the letter and held it out to her, gaze down. Eva, too, read it with something akin to terror.

"All right," she said.

"Eva," Isabel said. "We—"

"All right," Eva said again. Her shoulders were straight, her face shuttered. "A few more days. Okay. A few more days."

Isabel looked at her. Eva handed the letter back. "Let's not talk about it. He'll come when he'll come. I'm—I'm going to the city, I want—We don't have leeks, I thought to make something with leeks, have you seen the linen bag, I swear I left it in the kitchen last—"

Isabel folded the letter five times until it was only a very small square. She put it in the paper drawer, a stack of letters from Rian and some administration. Neelke wanted to make dinner but said she couldn't find the small blue oven dish. Isabel thought, *Small blue oven dish*—as if scanning a list, searching—and then shook it off. Shook it off and told Neelke she didn't have to make dinner. Eva had gone into the city for groceries—she didn't have to make dinner. Neelke nodded and didn't know where to go next, walked from one end of the room to the other, unsure.

"The curtains need dusting," Isabel told her, and stepped aside to let Neelke pass.

Eva came back later than she said she would. She had several leeks sticking out of her linen bag, biking up the gravel path. Isabel was outside, waiting for her. Itchy and feeling silly for it. Eva had only been gone an hour. Isabel had spent a lifetime alone. She had spent a whole life without this woman, without her in this house, and now an hour. And now her heart raced at the sound of tires on gravel, the sight of her: first a dot, then a person, then a known shape, coming closer.

She walked back into the house before Eva would notice her waiting. Isabel saw herself for a brief second from the outside in: restless and demanding, and somehow—*needy*. A word she had never ascribed to herself, she had never *needed* anything that could not be easily given. The thought embarrassed her, the glimpse of herself in the mirror embarrassed her, and so she turned away from it all with a firm twist.

Eva cooked: soups and sauces, and she put lentils in the rice, fried the onions to a crisp. She made bread, bread that rose and baked with a smell that pushed through the wall, hot yeast, soft dough. She made enough to last them for two days, all the way through sundown Saturday. Sunday came and Louis had not yet called and Isabel did not go to church. Sunday came and instead Isabel spent the morning convincing herself she didn't want to kiss Eva, then doing little else but kissing Eva into the shadowed wall in the hallway. She put her hand over Eva's breast, a hot flush of shock at her own daring, and Eva pushed into her hand, made a long noise into her mouth. It was like they were hiding here, out of sight of the sun-drenched remainder of the house. It was like they were sneaking around, only it was Sunday, and the house was empty. Isabel said, "Eva," and, "*Eva.*" And Eva said, "What?" She put her hand over Isabel's, squeezed harder, said: "What, darling? Go on. Go on."

Then Johan called the house on the phone and Isabel thought it would be Louis, and it wasn't, and she was so giddy with relief she laughed and happily told Johan he better not come by, that she would be gone to visit family for a while. Eva watched her do it, lingering in the study doorway.

"Will you not let him know?" she asked when Isabel hung up.

Isabel looked at her, caught in a movement. Her heart picked up fast. "Let him know?" She said it like a question, like: finish this sentence for her.

"That you're not interested," Eva said. She leaned back against the wood. She had a tilt to her jaw as if she was expecting Isabel to say, *Who's to say I'm not interested?* which made Isabel's stomach twist fast.

"I've not," she started, stopped. Eased her hands down the side of her skirt. "I don't know how."

"Don't you?" Eva asked.

Isabel looked at her. She took a step, hesitated. Said, "Would you like me to?"

She knew what she wanted to hear, hated how obvious it was: wanting to be told she was wanted. Eva inhaled. Isabel, flustered and unable to keep herself from moving, went to her. Always toward her. Her hands shook on Eva's hips, and Eva looked up at her. She said, "Isn't it about what you want?" Eva arched her back into the hold, easy. "Isn't it about what you don't want?"

"What I want," Isabel said, hovering, lips close. Isabel had never wanted before. And now any day Louis could knock on the door and then what Isabel wanted would no longer matter.

156

Neelke was in the dining room, two doors away, and in a pocket in a skirt in a wardrobe: a list, forgotten. Eva had a small silk scarf tied at her neck. *Neelke will wonder*, she'd said that morning, adjusting the fabric over the markings. She'd been looking at Isabel through the mirror. *Don't look at me like that. She'll wonder, she's smarter than you think.*

"What you want," Eva said now, hands over Isabel's wrists, moving: up her arms, her elbows. Up. There was muscle there. Knees in the earth, back bent over soil: digging work.

They were running out of time. There still were places Isabel wanted to show Eva. That's how she told her this: *I want to show you places*, which made Eva laugh, made her grab Isabel by the shoulder, made her say, *You sound like the bad guy in the movie.* And Isabel had only been to the movie theater twice in her life, and found it all very loud, and all the people had sat too close. She pulled away a resentful inch and said, smarting, *I meant it seriously*, and Eva pushed in that same inch and grabbed her and said, smiling wide: *I know I know I know I know.*

They went biking to the places Isabel wanted to show her. Picture-book places: fields, sheep, cottonwood trees puffing into the air. The whole time Isabel glanced at her from the corner of her eye, sure that Eva disliked the whole idea; disliked the land, the nature, the saccharine summer of it all. They stopped at a teahouse. Eva ordered ice cream, which came in a big glass bowl. She said, "I can't finish it." She held her spoon aloft, beaten. The ice cream dripped down her wrist. And Isabel, possessed by something rough and unfamiliar, briskly took her wrist and licked it off her skin. Eva pushed her away, quick, looking around.

Eva spoke, all amusement gone, eyes turned away: "She can see outside."

Isabel retreated immediately. She rolled the sugar around her mouth, swallowed it away, said, "Who?"

"The owner," she said. There had been an owner. She had told them they could sit outside; she had come to take their order. Isabel had forgot about her, couldn't even recall her face—only something of a voice remained. Accented, the eastern blur, swallowed syllables.

They continued on their trip. Eva in a rumbling silence, a set to her shoulder, and Isabel with a hiss of humiliation, of annoyance. She kept thinking of the sudden jerk of Eva pushing her away, and how her body shocked with it. They arrived: a shallow lake where Isabel would ice-skate in the winters. She thought to bring Eva here for a reason that felt important and was now vague—there was nothing much to see. They left their bikes by the slope of the road. Eva said, "I'm going in," and stood and took off her dress. Nothing could be seen from the road, and here there was only the two of them; only the bubbling of water on reeds.

Eva went into the water in her underwear. A surprised "Oh, it's not that cold!" and then she dove in. Isabel watched her, frowned at her, leaned back on her elbows. She pulled out tufts of grass and watched her some more.

Eva floated on her back. Eva disappeared below the surface, a blur of pink from under the green. She came back out, dripping, shivering. She brought with her the chill of water, standing by Isabel's legs. The fabric of her underwear was translucent, clinging.

Isabel said, "You're done swimming?"

Eva wrung out her short hair, dark and wet. She was panting. She nodded. "Yeah. Yeah, I'm done."

She lay back down. Her skin was all up in goose bumps. She noted Isabel looking at her and closed her eyes to it all the same, turned her face to the sun. "Remember," she said after a while. "Remember when you hated me? Remember when you looked at me like you just wanted me to *die*?"

They were talking around Louis's name. They'd been talking around him all along—touching around the invisible shape of him, across the length of a table, the width of a bed, the length of a bare leg.

Isabel's world narrowed down to a small patch of skin on Eva's shoulder. She didn't look at anything else, didn't lift her eyes. She didn't want to have this conversation. Eva did. Eva said, "You don't remember? It was really only yesterday. Really you don't know me at all." She was talking with a loud kind of voice, like she was telling herself as well as Isabel.

A shiver ran through Eva. Then movement, all at once: she rolled over onto Isabel, kissed her hard and fast and her jaw and her neck, shaky hands everywhere. Eva was still wet from the lake, pushed the water through Isabel's dress, and Isabel could only catch up: could only try to hold her in return, try to gentle the embrace, and if not gentle then match it somehow—match the dig of her fingers, the rhythm in how she moved. Isabel said, "Eva." She said, "Eva," and wanted to say: *I never, I only, I only wanted, I'm*—

There was no one around. It was fast and furtive. Eva kissed sloppily, mouth slipping off Isabel's and coming back again. The press of her fingers was purposeful under Isabel's dress, the damp crotch of her underwear pushed aside. It was quick; she knew Isabel's body by now, knew how to pull her to a frenzied peak. "Is that good?" she asked, Isabel bleary and hot beneath her. "Like that? That's good?"

Isabel came, overwhelmed and surprised by it, clutching at Eva's shoulders. The whole thing had not lasted more than a few minutes. They were both breathing hard, and Eva's face—so close—crumpled a moment. Just a moment and then Eva was gone, pulling away, wiping her hand on her own skin, looking about herself: lost, like she forgot where she had put her things.

Isabel pulled her back in. Eva tried to push her off, and Isabel would not let her, collected her, her elbows, her waist, her face. She cupped her close and said, "You must know. You must know how much I—" Swallowed, said: "Don't resent me."

Eva let herself be held, but did so carefully—a promise of pulling away still. She said, "Resent you for what?"

"That I didn't understand before."

"Understand—"

"What to do with you. What to do with you, Eva."

Eva moved in an odd shudder, as if someone had pushed her from behind, inside. A sound, a laugh or a sob. "And now? What will you do with me now?"

Isabel's answer came from a hidden place, and the words had folded and folded in on themselves over the course of days and so now they came out warped and rough, barely legible: "What will you let me?"

She leaned against Isabel's mouth. She did not say.

11

IT WAS FRIDAY EVENING AND THE RESTAURANT WAS loud. It had been a week since Louis's letter and the days were too short and they were holding on too tightly. Eva had dressed up: a skirt that had a shine in the candlelight, one that Isabel had not seen on her before; something old but well-made. She had curled her hair so it sat at the line of her jaw; she had put on lipstick, but it had smeared. A drag of paint under her bottom lip.

Isabel had kissed her in the car, right before they left. Her mouth, her neck. Eva had put a hand to Isabel's shoulder and said, *Isa, we need to go*, and Isabel had buried her face to the skin behind Eva's ear, breathed her in. Squeezed her thigh, under the skirt, the fold of her leg.

Eva had rolled into it, held Isabel by the back of her head, and still said: *Isabel. Reservations.* And for a moment Isabel didn't know what the word meant—reservations about what? And then the fog of the press of Eva's body lifted a little, and she repeated to herself: *Reservations.* At the restaurant.

Eva had not liked the idea much. *It will be weird*, she'd said earlier in the week, and Isabel had said, *Weird how?* and Eva said, *Two women? Alone? At dinner?* and Isabel said: *Have you never had a dinner with a friend who is a woman?* And Eva said: *Oh, you know what I mean.*

Eva said this often: *You know what I mean*, and Isabel mostly never knew what she meant, not exactly. Only that Eva was frightened, and that she saw people as danger. Isabel understood fear. Isabel rarely considered other people at all. But a dinner could be innocent enough, could be quiet and reserved and polite enough, and Eva had only half agreed when Isabel called ahead and then announced: reservations had been made. Eva got flustered at this, upset in her prickly way, had said, *I didn't even say yes yet, you—you just—you decide these things and then I have no choice to just—*

To which Isabel came close. Came closer still. Loomed with all of her height. Eva had trailed off; had gone quiet, had lifted her face. A distracted film over her eyes. Isabel's hand was on Eva's hip. She asked, *Do you not want to go?*

Eva took a long time to answer. *I didn't say that*, she said, and the words were whispered into the first beat of an open-mouth kiss.

And now their drinks were served, and their food was ordered, and Eva kept looking around like a noise was startling her—like she was looking for a way out.

"What's the matter?" Isabel asked, and Eva looked at her wide-eyed, caught. She said, "The matter?" and Isabel said, "You're skittish." She added: "You're acting as if we're criminals on the run."

Eva gave a strangled laugh at that. She covered it up with a hand to her mouth. She took her napkin and held it to her bare collar; it was a hot night, and the place was busy.

The food arrived. Eva had ordered fish. She ate in a way Isabel had not seen her eat before: overly careful, elbows pulled in, each bone picked up between knife and fork and daintily left on the plate's edge. She ate the fish one flake at a time. Her lipstick left an oily stain on the fork.

"Is it good?" Isabel asked, and Eva nodded and said, "Mm-hmm," and Isabel stared at her own plate for a few seconds and let the feeling build, then said: "You would've enjoyed this better if I'd been—some man, wouldn't you. If I'd been a man and taken you here. You would've had a good time, then."

"Isabel." Eva said it like a hiss, or a command: *Quiet down.* "Please. Don't—"

"I will do as I please," Isabel cut her off, a sharp tone, and then continued to do nothing of what she pleased: throat too tight to swallow, guilt-rotten heat in her belly, down her spine. She did not look at Eva, she did not say anything else. She went to the bathroom with a curt *Excuse me*. With a quick movement: put the napkin on the table, pushed the chair back.

The bathroom was a single stall and the lights were too bright. In the mirror Isabel saw herself: a sheen of sweat, bags under her eyes. She had not been sleeping much lately. And when she did sleep, curled tight around Eva, Eva would wake up often, gasp, kick; night terrors.

There came a knock at the door. Isabel ran the tap as if she was washing her hands, and then closed it. Again, a knock, and then Eva saying her name quietly—through the wood: "*Isabel.*"

Isabel threw away the paper towel. She opened the door, hesitant, a small crack, and Eva said, "Oh, just—" And pushed her way in, locked the door behind her; she was red-faced and angry-looking and still reaching for Isabel: reaching for Isabel's arms, her neck, pulling her in. Isabel pulled away and began to form a question and Eva just shook her head and said, "Shh, don't talk," and "Come here come here," and handled Isabel—her hands, her arms, pulling them around her, all the way around her. "Hold me," she said. "Just hold me."

Isabel did. Isabel folded into her—the both of them clunking messily against the door, Eva's back to the wood, Isabel collecting her: scooping her in, up, mouth to the sweat on Eva's skin. Beyond the bathroom, the kitchen staff shouted at one another; the restaurant continued on in a babble.

"I'm still here," Eva said. "I'm still here." She kissed the shell of Isabel's ear, and then again, and then again.

Back at the table, Isabel asked: "How is the wine?" Her voice was scraped thin.

Eva put down her glass. There, too: the mark of her lipstick to the rim. "The wine is good," Eva said. She continued eating her fish, flake for flake. After a while she paused, said, "What are you staring at me for?"

"You should eat," Isabel said. The words came out muddily, she had to clear her throat.

"What do you mean, *should*? I'm eating." She gestured with her fork. "I'm eating."

"I know," Isabel said, and could not explain herself further.

Crickets accompanied them on the ride home. Isabel turned on the radio and immediately turned it back off again. She parked in front of the house, and Eva reached for Isabel in the moment Isabel went to open the car door and she said: "Can we stay here for a while?"

Isabel settled back. Eva still held on to her arm.

"Here?" Isabel asked. "In the car?"

Eva said, "Yes. I don't—I don't want go in yet. Can we just . . ."

The house was a dark shape against the sky. Two proud firs. A single star came out under the waning moon; a beauty mark dotted under a coy eye. The hot season's night rustled in the way that winter's never did: bugs dry in the brush, things that had business in the dark.

Isabel now felt it, too: the looming. The doors, the windows, and what lay behind them. She could not put a word to the fear, only that it was Eva's, and now it was hers, too.

164

She looked to Eva. Her curls had given up in the humidity, had drooped and then puffed up. Her lipstick had smudged further. In the dark, in the dim light of the night, Isabel could see the line of her profile in contrast: her parted lips, her cheek, her jaw. Peach fuzz and bone.

Isabel took Eva's hand and kissed it. Held it close to her face, her mouth, kissed it: Eva's knuckles and the papery skin on the back of her hand and the webbing between her fingers. Eva made a sound. Isabel closed her eyes and repeated Eva's name into the heart of Eva's palm, the very middle of it.

"I only upset you," she said. "I only want to be close to you and all I do is upset you. Eva. Eva."

Eva cupped Isabel's cheek. Isabel hid that hold, and Eva said, "This is all there is, Isabel. This is all we have. We should make peace with that, yes? Yes, Isabel?" She was quiet about it. "It is what it is," she said. "I will have to go with Louis. You understand that, don't you, Isabel?"

"No," said Isabel.

"Darling," Eva said.

"You can't."

"Isn't it better than nothing?" Eva said. "Isn't it enough?"

Isabel took a breath to answer and found that she had no answer to give. Found that she did not know the precise meaning of the word *enough*, the way Eva used it—not what it meant in relation to another, in relation to *her*. She had held a pear in her hand and she had eaten it skin and all. She had eaten the stem and she had eaten its seeds and she had eaten its core, and the hunger still sat in her like an open maw. She thought: *I can hold you and find that I still miss your body.* She thought: *I can listen to you speak and still miss the sound of your voice.*

Isabel opened her mouth to Eva's skin and then bit the heel of Eva's hand—hard. Eva jumped, hissed, didn't pull away—swayed closer. This, too, Isabel knew about her now: what she liked. How she liked it. Isabel soothed the bite. Eva touched Isabel's face, her mouth. Her teeth, the shape of them under Isabel's lips. The night was foggy and distant.

"Let's go," Eva said.

"Inside?" Isabel asked, and Eva took a while to answer: a hesitation. "Sure," she said then. "Inside. Sure."

The house was a held breath. The windows blank eyes, watching them enter. The furniture was asleep, the fruit in the bowl on the table—asleep. Eva's hand was loose in hers. They parted between the kitchen and the dining room: Eva wanted a glass of water, and the phone rang in the other room, and so Isabel went to pick it up.

She said, "Isabel speaking." She was distracted, her mind in the kitchen still—two steps behind, held away from her. She had an eye on the doorway.

"Isa," said Louis. "Isa, it's me, Louis, how are you? Listen, Isa, listen, I've got a question, I've got something to ask of you, Isa I need to—"

She knew at the sound of his voice. Just that first syllable, and she knew—knew from the inside out. Not exactly *what*, only that it was coming, fast, and that it was going to settle over the night like a freeze.

"What—" She cradled the phone closer to her ear, hid it. Her heart turned over on itself, fast. "What do you want? Are you back? Have you come back?"

"Listen," he said. He sounded harried. He sounded like he was using some kind of public phone. He, too, was cradling the phone near—a rustle, a mouth-sound. "Listen, Isabel, is ah. Is Eva still there with you?"

"Is she— What do you mean? Where else would she be? You—you *left* her here, if—"

"God, I don't have time for this," he said, not to Isabel, seemingly to himself, or someone near—someone invisible. "Hey, listen, Isa, Isa, are you listening?"

"Don't talk to me like that."

"I need you to—listen. Can you, ah." He cleared his throat, shuffled again. "Can you get her out of there? Like, tell her I'm, I don't know, I've . . . drowned in the channel, I'm not coming home, I'm . . . ha . . ." He wanted to be making fun of himself. He was doing it wrong—he was too serious for jokes.

A moment passed. Isabel listened to him breathe, and there—there it was. She knew now. She understood. They'd been here before. "Louis," she said. It was an accusation—it was a threat, too.

"I'm sorry," he said. "I know, okay? I know, I'm sorry, I know, I can't help it, she—We met at the—I was staying with this family, and—it happened quickly. Mary came back with me. Isabel, I swear, I swear I've never felt this way. You have to believe me, Isabel. Do you believe me? I know I've—I know I'm asking a lot, but God, if you could feel what I feel. If you could *see* her. If you knew what—If you'd ever felt this way, God, Isabel, I promise you, I promise you, you wouldn't judge me so much, you wouldn't—"

"Do *not*—" Isabel started, and didn't get to finish because Eva walked into the room with her glass of water and she saw it: something about Isabel's stance, something about her tone of voice. How she was holding the phone.

She said, "Who is it?"

On the phone, Louis said, "Is that her?"

"No one," Isabel said, and Louis told her, "Don't tell her, Isabel, don't—" and Isabel told him, "Shut up," and Eva put down the glass and stepped forward and said:

"Is that Louis? Is that him?"

Isabel put her hand over the receiver, her heart a drummed alarm in her throat. She said, "Eva. Please."

"Give me the phone," Eva said.

Isabel heard Louis say, "Don't—don't put her on the—" and there was a tussle: Eva trying to get the phone from Isabel's grip and Isabel not trying hard enough, arms soft and elbows giving and then Eva pushed her aside—not roughly. Just a push. Isabel went, a single stumble of a step.

Eva said into the phone, "Hello, my darling." Her voice was pitched. It was terrible—wrong and honeyed. She hadn't talked like that in so long. She held the phone the same way Isabel had, cradled and hidden. Isabel couldn't make out Louis's words, only the timbre. It was mostly Eva who was talking, saying, "When are . . . Mm-hmm . . . So when . . . Yes, I . . . Me too, darling, yes, so much, when—hm. Okay. No—sooner. Sooner. Okay. What?"

She was quiet for a while. Louis was talking. Eva was nodding. She had a hand over her chest, over her heart.

Isabel swallowed around a bulb of nausea. She found herself angry, and that the emotion took the shape of an old familiar one: how she had spent the early days and early nights sitting in Eva's shadow; annoyed with her, obsessed with her, unable to look away from her. She'd thought it was hate. She knew better, now. Louis's words skipped and skipped in her mind. *I swear*, he said, *I swear I've never felt this way, I swear I've—*

Eva said, "Okay." She said, "Me too, darling." She said, "I'll see you then."

She hung up. Her head dropped. She put her hands over her face and breathed several times—loud, as if she was about to cry. But she didn't cry. She inhaled, she pushed her hair from her face. She turned to face Eva. "He's back," she said. "He's coming tomorrow. To get me."

Isabel pressed her teeth together. She needed to swallow before answering: "On your request."

"On my request," Eva echoed. She looked pallid now. Her pretty skirt, her faded lipstick.

The whole thing crowded on itself. Eva stood there, a pretense of pride, chin lifted, like she was about to take on Isabel, and Isabel thought: *Who are you?* They were kissing in the car. They held each other. She said: "So he didn't tell you."

"Tell me?"

"Right," Isabel said.

"Tell me what?"

"You want to leave me," Isabel said. "You can't wait to get away from me."

"Isabel," Eva said, an exhausted word.

"You think you love him?"

"Good God." Eva turned—padded the collar of her blouse to her face, her sweat. She said, "What kind of question is that."

"A simple one."

Eva flashed her a look: dangerous. She held her ground for a moment. Held Isabel's eye, nostrils flared, and then she was gone—walking in a non-direction, taking a step and stopping, taking another and stopping. "I need—" she said. "I need to pack. I need—"

"He doesn't care about you," Isabel told her.

"Oh, what do you know, Isabel."

Eva wasn't looking at her. Isabel told her, "He met someone else. That's why he called me. He met someone else. He wants you gone."

"I'm sure he did," Eva said. "I'm sure he does." She didn't seem surprised by it, or offended. She looked distracted, saying quickly, "And Louis will meet another girl after that, and another after that, oh, what does it matter? They will come and they will go and isn't it—And I will be there, I'll be true now, he'll see, I'll stay, I won't—I can't—"

"You think you're the first girl he's brought home?" Isabel said. "You think you're the first girl he's promised to marry?"

"So *what!*" Eva laughed, a thin and sad laugh. "So he doesn't love me! Who cares about that? Who *cares* about—"

"I care," Isabel said. Her voice broke on the syllable.

Eva's face was a grimace around a smile. Her chin was dimpled, trembling. "What use," she said, "is that to me? So you care. I have *nothing*, Isabel. I have not a *thing* in this life. Do you *understand* what that means, to someone like me, to get to—to have the promise of a—"

"So it was about money," Isabel cut in. "You wanted his money."

Eva stopped short. A flicker—something, as if Isabel had snapped her fingers between her eyes, brought her back. She laughed again, that same hollow sound. "Sure," she said, and nodded. "Yeah, it's about money, why not."

"I have money," Isabel said. "I could—You could, you could stay, we could—"

"We could *what*? God, Isabel. You have an *allowance*. What do you think, that you'd keep me? Keep me here? How? As *what*? Your maid? Your—" She swallowed, twice in a row, and Isabel tried to reply with quick-heated words and Eva cut her off with a louder "And then in a week, month, year, when you're bored and done with me—then what? What am I to do then? You'll kick me out? You'll leave me to—"

"I won't. I won't be done with you."

"Oh, you won't? How nice." Eva was sharp now, sharp and fast: "Are you listening? I'm telling you: your word is nothing, it's—it's—air. What certainty in life do *you* have? What certainty can you give me? What *home*?"

"This home," she said. "My home."

Eva shook her head. "No, you can't," she said. "It's not yours to give."

Isabel opened her mouth, closed it. The argument ran around her in circles, and she wasn't sure where it had started, and where it had ended; what she said or hadn't said or might still say. All she wanted was to make a sound—just a sound, a miserable groan—and have it arrive at Eva's feet as an explanation, fully formed and coherent: *Don't go. Stay.*

"God," Eva said, and wiped her eyes on her sleeves. She had painted her lashes: the fabric came away stained. She said it twice more, "God, oh God," and then marched out of the room. Isabel made to follow immediately, and Eva stopped her with a quick hand into the wide distance between them:

"No," she said. "Leave me be."

Isabel stopped. The ground held her: two hands risen up from the floorboards, a grip on her ankles. She couldn't move if she wanted to.

Eva's footsteps were quick clacks across the dining room, across the kitchen floor. A door that opened, a door that closed.

And Isabel, stranded in the empty space between a couch and a wall. A home that wasn't hers to give.

It was a dark dipping moment of night when Eva returned. Isabel was up in her room, listening: the rummaging, the slow steps up the stairs. She could not imagine where Eva had been and could imagine all too well where Eva had been: the neighbors, the town, a bar, someone's car, someone's bed. Louis, perhaps— somehow she could've found Louis, and she had cried in his arms and he could've decided he loved her again, more than this other girl, and he could've taken her home or to a hotel and she could've said, *Oh, I've missed you!* and he could buy her things like clothes and shoes and pretty rings to put in her ears and a roof should he want to and—

Isabel lay in bed in her clothes over the sheets and let herself believe this was true, that Eva had done all of it, had done the worst of it in the span of a few hours. The picture of Eva's mother was still in Eva's room. Eva would not leave without it, she thought. She would come back for that picture, if nothing else.

I have not a thing in this life, she'd said. She had said it before. Isabel had thought she meant—that she had meant family. That she had meant loved ones. Isabel had thought she was saying: I am like you.

She had meant: money. Now she could hear from Eva's tread in the hallway that she was trying to be quiet, trying not to creak the floorboard. Eva was moving like a whisper in the other room. The drag of a quiet something on the floor, the scrape of a chair, the whining hinges of the wardrobe doors. The light in her room was on and it filtered into the hallway like a crack, cast the faintest orange into Isabel's room.

Isabel got out of bed, went to Eva's room. Not Eva's room— Mother's. Eva was on her knees on the ground, packing her suitcase. She was doing a bad job of it. She was making the motions of folding without actually folding, and then throwing in the clothes in heaps. Everything that was on the table was now on the floor: her perfume bottles, her powders, her mother's picture, her diary.

She looked up and her face was—blotchy, rubbed at, puffed. Isabel remembered the voice she'd used with Louis on the phone, high-pitched and syrupy. She remembered noting the bulging seam of Eva's skirt that first night, at the restaurant; remembered the repulsion, the shrill annoyance, the humidity in the bathroom.

Eva continued packing and Isabel said, "Eva." Eva did not reply, did not look at her anymore, and so Isabel went to her knees by her side and tried to still her hands—grabbed at her arms, which would not stay still, pulling away. "Eva," she said again, and, "Please, please, don't—"

Eva pushed her away with a sobbing breath and Isabel took her by the shoulders and turned her, made Eva face her, and Eva slumped. She wept for a few moments, forehead to Isabel's chest; then she came up and said, "We've been so stupid," and Isabel held her close and Eva continued: "We should have never, *I* should have never, what a catastrophe, what a—"

"No," Isabel said. Eva had stopped weeping. She let Isabel bear her full weight, on her knees on the hard floor. Isabel told her: "There isn't a version of me that could've looked away from you."

Eva calmed down at that. "Don't say that." She spoke into the collar of Isabel's dress: "Please stop saying things like that."

They took to bed. It was confused and closed-eyed. Eva said, "Turn off the light, turn it off," and Isabel, half out of her dress already, had to go turn off the light; bumped into things on the floor, kicked something, the clatter of a bottle. Eva's hands shook the whole time. Isabel buried herself between Eva's legs, held her by her heavy thighs, her ass. She was swollen, breathless. Isabel ate her, the loud suck of a full-ripe fruit; she ate the flesh and the seeds and the core and all.

Afterward, Eva fell asleep with an away slant, the line of her spine turned to Isabel. Their feet were still tangled. Isabel swallowed the taste of Eva; swallowed again, and again. Her throat felt dry. She stumbled on her way to the bathroom. She drank with her mouth under the tap; her face was a shark shadow in the mirror, puffy-mouthed and wide-eyed in the dark. The water dripped down her throat. She looked a nightmare.

They slept almost together, a finger's width of space between them. Isabel floated on near dreams, never really resting in full. She gave up with the early dawn, that midsummer's peak, and sat up against the pillows and waited. The day would come and Eva would leave. The day would come and the suitcase would close, and would be taken down, and then the house would be empty.

She put her feet to the ground and found an odd surface, and bent down to see: the diary. It peeked out from under the bed. She had kicked it last night. She bent down for it. The cover was soft, leather, a well-made thing. The first light of morning cast the shadows of the tall firs against the curtains, drooping shapes, heavy branches. Eva breathed a deep sleeping sigh.

Isabel turned the book over in her hands. She opened on the first page, just to see—see the penmanship, see what words Eva wrote in what way, see if it was Louis's name in a rounded swirl of *O* and *U*. The word *apple* with a childlike, open-bottomed *P*.

It wasn't a diary entry on that first page. It was a list. A good handful of items had been crossed off. At the top: *teaspoons*. Eva had written the number between brackets: twelve. The next item crossed off: *bread knife (wood handle)*. Then: *tiles (decorative, hares)*. The letter opener, napkin rings, the engraved cake knife. And on and on the list went, two columns on one page, and into the next—an inventory of a house.

Isabel stared at the list. She held the little book so long and so tightly that her thumb left a print on the page: damp, sticky. The shadows shifted against the curtains. A bird flew off a branch.

Isabel rummaged in the wardrobe, put on her robe, and went downstairs. She made coffee. She counted the spoons: five. There were five left. She hadn't been counting recently, and now there were five left. Isabel reached for a cup for her coffee and accidentally dropped it and it bounced around on the kitchen floor; the ear broke off, a chip off its lip. Isabel threw it in the bin and got herself a new cup.

174

It didn't take long for Eva to come down, haphazardly dressed, sleep crusted at the corners of her eyes. She called for Isabel before she found her: "Isabel?" into the living room, and, "Isabel? Have you seen—" into the dining room, and then at the top stair to the kitchen: came to a halt.

"Good morning," Isabel said. She was sitting at the table, hands folded in her lap. The coffee was steaming on the table. Eva's diary was open, and next to it Isabel's own pages of inventory, the ones she had made in a fit of worry, a fit of paranoia, all those weeks ago.

It was a blindingly bright day. The sun streamed in like a fairy tale. Outside the window bugs stayed low to the ground, wings caught in gold.

Eva said, "Isabel. *Isabel.* It's—I promise, I—"

"You wanted to get to know me. That's what you told him. You just liked me so much, after that dinner. Could barely stop talking about me, he said. I made an impression, he said. In fact, you were the one who *suggested* you stay here while he was gone, weren't you?"

Eva stared at her. Mouth a little open, sleep ruffled. She looked to the diary, to Isabel, to the diary again. She said, "You didn't . . ." She said, "You haven't—"

"You're a thief. You came here to steal from me." Isabel sounded calm. She sounded like she had woken up and realized, and had slowly and evenly made her peace with it. It was what she wanted to sound like.

"No," Eva said, like she was disagreeing with an argument, an argument she was only slowly waking up to. "No," she said again, firmly.

"No? You're not?" Isabel put a hand on the open page. "Then where is my property?"

Eva blinked as if struck. "Oh," she said then. Something

175

seemed to turn hard within her. She said, a new voice now: "It's gone."

Isabel swallowed. "Gone."

"Gone. You won't get it back."

"You admit it, then. You're a thief. You came here to steal from me. That was your intention all along, wasn't it? That's why you were so intent on—so sure about—yesterday, and Louis, and, oh!" A single laugh came out of Isabel's throat, a harsh croak. "Harmless! A harmless girl. Isn't that right."

Eva, in the kitchen entryway, held herself up by the door's frame.

Isabel said, "Well? What have you to say for yourself?" Her voice cracked. "You have nothing to say."

Eva stared at the diary. She looked—distant, out of it, and Isabel wanted to clap her hands, bring her back. Make her bear witness. She raised her voice, said, "Have you sold it? How much money could that have possibly been—a few spoons, a knife. Pathetic. I'm certain it was worth the trouble."

Eva said, tar rolled in gravel: "You are blind."

"I was, yes. I was, when it came to you. No more. No—" She touched the back of her hand to her lips, swallowed it down. She did not look at Eva. She said, "Leave."

The kitchen was silent.

Isabel said, "Leave this house. Go get your suitcase, leave."

Eva did not move. Her eyes were hard on the table—on the diary. She was breathing hard. She took a step, then rushed forward, was reaching for the diary and Isabel quickly closed the book and rose to her feet and moved away.

Eva paused. "Give it back," she said.

"No."

Through clenched teeth: "Give it—"

"I will call the police." Isabel held the book closer to her chest. "If you do not leave. I will call the police."

Eva's face was set in a grimace, eyes wet, nostrils flared, jaw tight. When she first came down she still had the look of sleep-warmed skin. Bile rose up Isabel's stomach, and she turned away from Eva, closed her eyes.

"Leave."

She heard Eva's retreat, did not see it. In her absence, she got out of her chair so quickly that it toppled back. She went to the sink and retched. Nothing came out. Her hands shook, her face was clammy with sweat. The activity upstairs was quick and violent. Isabel put the diary in the pocket of her robe and went to the front door, opened it, stood there waiting.

Eva's suitcase was too big for her to carry down the stairs by herself. It was a furious, clambering way down; embarrassing and clumsy. Eva was flushed from her forehead down her collar. She had put on her red hat again, and from under it her roots were showing badly: several fingers' length of coarse, dark-dark hair.

Isabel watched her struggle. The last few steps the suitcase slipped from Eva's grip and fell down the rest of the way. It had been hastily closed—only the strapped buckles, not the zip—and the thing banged open when it hit the ground. Clothes spilled out. Eva turned a deeper shade of red. She hurried to stuff everything back, one knee to the ground.

Isabel took a step, took two. She stood by the clutter. She bent down and picked up one of the things that had rolled away a short distance.

A broken piece of ceramic. Blue flowers along the inch of a rim—the back of a hare's leg where the plate had—

Eva looked up at her, eyes black, shiny-wet. Isabel could see her heartbeat under her skin, in her neck.

Isabel said, "*Out* of my house."

Eva glanced at the shard, looked like she was about to say something, something desperate and begging, and Isabel would not let her. "I swear. I swear I will call the—"

Eva stuffed everything back in the suitcase. She wiped her arm over her eyes as she closed it, again and again, between every movement—wiped at her eyes. She was silent. Isabel took a step back as Eva rose to her feet, marched toward the door.

One foot out, she paused. Turned. Said, "You were never supposed to have it." She said, "It was never yours."

Isabel closed the door behind her. Locked it, then went to the kitchen and locked those doors as well. She wasn't breathing right: she was breathing as if there was a rattle in her lungs, an animal in her throat, a terrible sound on every inhale, every exhale. She went to the living room and climbed onto the couch to look out the window. Eva was walking down the gravel path, suitcase in hand. Her pace was quick. She didn't stop, didn't put down the heavy weight, not once. She got smaller and smaller. The back of her shirt wasn't pushed into her trousers right, and a white lip of cloth draped out over the waist.

Isabel stared at that lip until Eva was a blur of a person, a vague movement in the distance. And then she was onto the road and walked toward the stand of trees, and was gone.

Louis arrived in the early evening. He woke her up. She was on the couch still. In her house robe still. She had fallen asleep. Her face was paper-dry, her nose stuffed. He stood at an awkward distance from her, unsure of what to do. She sat up and pulled her robe closed tighter, tried to pull her hair together with a twist alone.

Louis said, "Are you ill?"

"She left," Isabel said. "She is not here. She left."

"Oh," Louis said. And then sighed expansively and sat down in the armchair. "God," he said, and laughed a little. "What a relief!"

Isabel went upstairs. Louis, before he left, said he would call her a doctor. He shouted up the stairs: the doctor would come by tomorrow. He shouted up the stairs: will they have dinner soon? He shouted up the stairs: it had been a while since they had dinner. He said: "It'd be a nice chance to meet Mary." He said, "You'll love her."

She was, in fact, ill. The doctor had come by and confirmed: ill, a summer cold, a fever. She spent several days throwing up and then shaking in her bed while Neelke sulked downstairs and occasionally brought her food: a clear soup, dry bread. It tasted of nothing. Neelke's small hand when she pressed a wet cloth to Isabel's forehead felt like nothing.

She was slow to recover. She'd wake up sweaty in the night, half in and half out of fevered dreams about mouths, about a soft body pressed to hers. She'd wake up and be sure there was a sound at the door—a knock, a startle. But the room was always empty, and the house was always empty. There was no one at the door.

Harsh winds whistled July's end and into August. Louis brought the new girl home for dinner. He had called Isabel about it, and Isabel had not quite heard what he'd said, was too bleary and tired to follow his rambling: something about wanting Mary to see where he'd come from, something about an eye on the future. Isabel coughed over the line and missed some words. Louis then made a joke about promising to not leave Mary behind at the house. After the call Isabel wanted to go for a walk, announced to Neelke she wanted to go for a walk, and Neelke helped her into her coat and Isabel swayed and Neelke said: "It will be good to get out of the house. Fresh air." She sounded doubtful. Isabel stood in the hallway with a head full of cotton. She had kissed Eva against that wall. She had kissed Eva in that doorway. The memories were heavy, empty things low in her gut and only angered her: that her own doorway could be taken away from her, that a childhood and a youth and a life lived through that doorway could disappear in favor of a single person. The blouse Eva had worn that day, the way she had done her hair.

Isabel walked to the end of the drive and around the stand of trees and then had to stop. She leaned against a tree. She pushed the heels of her hands to her eyes and breathed.

Hendrik did not join them. Over the phone he'd said, "Oh, I'm bored of it, Isa, how many more girls must we entertain this year? They come, they go, we never hear from them again. No thank you." There was a rustling on the line, and then he said, a little distracted: "How *did* he break it off with Eva, anyway? Poor thing. She was too clever for him, anyway."

Isabel had made a sound. She hadn't meant to. Hendrik said, "Isabel?" and Isabel said, "I'm going to lie down, I have a headache," and Hendrik said: "Are you still sick? Hasn't it been a while?"

Mary was a reedy girl, sunken cheeks, a big red mouth. Her hair was done up neatly. Her dress was pretty. She didn't speak Dutch, only English and French. She kept a purse to her midriff and didn't touch anything in the house. She didn't seem to look at anything directly on, only glanced. About the painting in the living room she said, "Oh, lovely, the dunes," and Louis said, in his broken English, "Of course you have good taste," and didn't correct her at all.

She wasn't at all like Eva. It should have been a relief but it wasn't. Louis still looked at her like he wanted to go to his knees for her, like he wanted to tilt his chin and open his mouth for her. Isabel knew that look now. Knew how it looked on her own face, too, so similar to his. And the evening kept on, and Mary sat in the chair where Eva once sat. She held on to Louis's arm, the way Eva once had.

No one had been there to see it. No one had known it was happening. Isabel, tired and woozy with a leftover fever, wondered whether it ever happened at all. Neelke had prepared a nice dinner for the three of them: potatoes, greens, meat. Mary asked, "Did you make this?" and Isabel replied in Dutch: "No." Louis said, "She has someone who helps around the house," and Mary said, "Oh, that's nice," and Isabel could no longer eat. Louis said, "You don't look very well. Are you still sick? It's been a while now, Isabel."

When she went to the bathroom she overheard them having a low-voiced conversation. Louis saying, "Do you like it?" and Mary saying, "The food?" and Louis saying, "No, the house, the house," and Mary saying, "Oh! Oh, it's very nice." She said, "But she lives here all alone? All the time?"

She misremembered Isabel's name when they left, called her Isadora. Louis laughed at this, kissed his Mary on the cheek, and asked her again as they walked down the driveway: "Did you like the house?" to which she said: "It's so far away from everything."

"Isn't it?" he said, like he'd now decided that was a good thing, and that Mary was good, in turn, for having recognized it.

She called Hendrik. Hendrik said, "How was it, tell me everything!" and Isabel couldn't. She was quiet on the line. She breathed heavily. "Isabel?" Hendrik said. "Isabel?"

She hung up. He called her again, she did not pick up. In bed that night, her stomach turned in terrible knots, nauseous and tight. Something creaked about from under the floorboards—a mouse or a bug or simply the pull of heat cooling at night. Isabel reached under her pillow and took out Eva's book. She turned on the reading lamp. She wanted to see the list again. She wanted to be reminded, she wanted to be angry again, she wanted to let her heart do anything other than devour itself, shrink and shrink and shrink. She opened it and there was no list. An unfamiliar name on an otherwise empty page. She felt fever-confused, blurry, and then turned the book over—opened the back, and there: the list. The list was at the back, not the front.

She paged through it quickly and saw: the first half of the booklet full, entries upon entries. Eva's handwriting, curt and to the point, each entry quick, none more than half a page, most just a few sentences. Days, days, months.

Isabel went back to the beginning. Her hands were clammy and unsteady. She read the name once, read it again. Passed a hand over it, as if trying to see whether it would change, as if the ink was a trick—an illusion, a game.

It wasn't. Isabel stumbled out of bed and opened a window. She stuck her head out and breathed. A breeze passed, ran through her with a shiver. Her nightdress clung to her spine, to the sweat down her back.

If found, said the single line on the opening page, *return to:*
And then a name, unknown and known at once:
Eva de Haas.

PART III

PART III

12

January 5, 1960

She's been gone ten years today. New diary. When she passed it snowed badly. It took very long for the rabbi to arrive. Tante Malcha got nervous and opened all the windows for the spirit to leave and Mum's body turned blue in the bed. It was so cold. In the picture I have of her it's summer and she's in the garden. Anyway it's not snowing today, it's weirdly warm for this time of year. I took the tram to Malcha and took off my scarf. It was too hot.

January 10, 1960

Basje hurt her ankle going down the stairs so we were missing a girl at the line today. We had to package at twice the speed. Terrible. Barely had time for a smoke during break! My second and third finger on right hand were swollen before but now better. Writing hurts, will not say much. Geertje wrote back, found no trail, will put in touch w someone. Sometimes I

January 21, 1960

Infection better now—fingers no longer size of sausages! Missed week at factory. They will take me back, Jan owes me. Called with Geertje's guy today. Just like the last one: ƒ150 up front. Fuck them up the ass. Sometimes I think: I will go to the old house myself. I will take the train and I will go to the house. I will knock on the door and they will open the door. I will walk inside and I will not leave. What will they do? Call the police? So the police will come. I will say: try, drag me out. I will say: show me the papers. I will say, show me the deed. I will scream if they touch me, I swear I will scream.

February 3, 1960

Rice	39ct.	ƒ9.80 -	
Beans	89ct.	ƒ4.45	
Bongo coffee	1.69	ƒ4.08 ???	
Matches	39ct	5.35 -	Marianne? .45
Eggs (12)	1.09	1.00 - (Ruben)	?? Fish
─────────		0.22 - (Basje)	* let landlord (זמרוו) know
		ƒ4.45	0.05 - (LM)
		─────	tl. 05202-6 P? Ank. yl.
		ƒ4.08	

February 10, 1960

Walked by an open window and smelled polishing oil and re-membered hiding under Mum's desk while she was writing let-ters. Her leg hairs through her pantyhose. Before we left she had me clear out my room and fold my clothes into a suitcase and put all my toys into a box. She had packed her good shoes. That's what we thought we could take with us in case of an emergency: a box of toys! Good shoes and a suitcase of dresses! I used to think about that box a lot, the way you think about the bit of the sandwich you dropped on the floor long after you've eaten the rest of it. I used to wonder whether anyone found my toys, and if they would send them back to me.

February 20, 1960

Mark, the donkey, came by this evening. The stove is broken. He said his cousin has an old one he can bring here. Okay, I said. I let him put his hand under my shirt. He wanted under my bra. No, I said, and he said: Have you never done this before? I put on big eyes and acted so scared. Never, I said, and shook in his hands. Be gentle, Mark! Take it easy on a virgin like me! Donkey. He will bring by the stove tomorrow.

Hand healing slowly. Long shift at factory. Basje taught the girls to blow rings. The trick: push your tongue out when you blow. Ha!

March 4, 1960

I'm thinking, What did they keep? What did they sell? I don't know if it's worse if they kept everything. Malcha told me she knew a woman who came back from the camps and then went to the family who was safekeeping her things. They told her that they had sold everything. Then one day she walked by their house and looked inside and saw they were eating from her plates, and using her silverware, and the meal had been cooked in her oven dish. I asked Malcha what she did then, and Malcha said the woman did nothing. That she walked on. I said, why didn't she knock? Why didn't she say, I see you didn't sell my things, give them back now. Malcha said they didn't lie because they were embarrassed. They lied because they were never going to give them back.

A bit of sun today! Such a small square of sun in the yard. Basje and I crowded into the square and had to hold on to each other like men on a sinking ship. She teetered and I screamed and said, No don't fall don't leave me! And she laughed so much she snorted and then Jan shouted at us to stop fucking around so we had to go inside. No more sun when I walked back home. Sad. New stove. Good.

March 16, 1960

2:30. Night. Nightmares nightmares nightmares nightmares nightmares nightmares nightmares nightmares

Soft sheep. A plate of buttered carrots. A big hug where someone holds you tight and long. Music & dancing to music. The smell of someone else's coffee through a window. Slippers by the door. Dry sheets. Smiles! Smiles! Slow kiss. The bottom of a foot. The bottom of a foot. The bottom of a foot of someone you love. The bottom of a foot of someone you love when they're lying on the couch and their legs are up over the armrest and they're not wearing socks and it's summer and you pass by and you see the naked bottom of their foot and you drag a finger down the middle and they

March 30, 1960

Went out to town with Shula & Basje & Lola. Good time. Small bar, no one was dancing, but we started dancing, and people joined. Sweat so much! Very drunk, not great. Shula stayed here, roads too slippery for biking back. We talked and talked and talked. It was so cold! I put four blankets on her and she was still shaking. She kept saying, You're so lucky! You have all of this to yourself, you're so lucky! And I look around and I see a room the size of a box that is a kitchen and a bedroom and a living room and the shower is a curtain and there is a mushroom that is growing from the rotten windowsill. I asked her about coming back. She said she was very young when they came back, that she probably did not remember things correctly, and I thought: Someone has told her to say this, when people asked. Someone told her to always wear long sleeves over her wrists. Anyway she is my age so she must have been around twelve. You remember your life at twelve. I didn't say this. Her cousin once told me that Shula was the youngest kid to come back from the camps, which is probably not true, I don't know. She was only there at the very end. Her family got their home back after the war but had to pay outstanding taxes so had to sell it in '47. They all live in an apartment in Slotermeer now, all 6 of them. 2 rooms. I said, Don't you ever want to go to your old home and go inside and scream and tell these people to get out get out get out? She said, No, we sold it. I said, So what? She said, It's not ours anymore, we sold it. I said I disagreed with her: if you have to sell something because you've been tricked into poverty, then that's not an honest thing. If you haven't given it away out of free will, it is still yours, I said. She was too drunk to have this conversation. She started crying very loudly and I stared at the window mushroom until she fell asleep. In the morning we went to Café Goededag for breakfast. I ate three buns! Cheese was good. Mmmm

April 11, 1960

April! April! Does whatever it wants! Snow today. Poor baby flowers, poor baby birds, poor baby toes of mine. Frozen blue on the way to work, brrr! It's Erev Pesach.

April 15, 1960

Seder with Auntie Malcha. Mostly we got drunk before the end of the plagues. Frogs! Blood! Drink drink drink. She has an old Haggadah from when they were kids and in the back there is a little drawing of a sheep that Mum drew when she was eight years old. Baby Mum, I can hardly imagine it. Sausage little fingers, baby. She was a baby once. It's hard to think. Soft little baby in a blanket with tiny nails and tiny toes.

May 3, 1960

Danced with a man last night. What was his name? I don't remember. He put his hands on the small of my back. I thought, touch me! I thought, touch me touch me touch me! And then he tried to kiss me and I thought I would be sick. Could not recall ever wanting to be touched by anyone, anyone ever. I pulled away and he would not let go and I shouted at him and gave him a big fright. How strange can the body be. I do not know it, I never know what it wants. Does anyone know their body truly? I wonder.

May 30, 1960

Busy. Basje's wedding next week. Short on funds. Not turning on lights, but nearly summer, okay.

June 10, 1960

Wedding! Was lovely. Cried.

July 13, 1960

Went to visit one of Mum's cousins up north. Took the train and there were so many fields. Saw two hares jumping out of grass. Remembered the time with the hare. Could not stop thinking of the moment Papa realized the animal was out of control. His face—horror. Uncle Shimon ran after the thing like he could catch it and he couldn't. I started laughing in the train and could not stop. A woman in the compartment got up and left. I really could not stop laughing. I don't think I was breathing at all. I smoked a cigarette to calm down & it helped. Mum's cousin Rita was nice/sad. She had written to me & so I knew she was missing her left leg but I still startled when she got up from her chair. She wanted to look through photo albums together. We looked through photo albums together. She asked me if I knew who the people in the pictures were and I said no. Before I left she said that she had seen my father two days before they killed him and that he looked proud even though everyone's feet were ankle-deep in shit, and that she wanted me to know that, that he looked proud. I don't know why I need to know that. I don't like thinking about it.

August 5, 1960

Stormed out, lost job, fuck them up the ass. Have decided to try out at the Bijenkorf! A fancy place, a department store, I can do that. I will dye my hair blond, I will put on a voice, they will not know. I can be just like any girl working at the department store. Maybe I will move out of this damp cave hole of a house maybe I will find something better I can be just like

October 1, 1960

Yom Kippur. On a Saturday this year. Stayed inside and smoked a whole packet. Wanted to fast but had a cucumber at four. Will God punish me now? Haha

October 12, 1960

Had my first week with De Leeuw. Smell like pickles & brine. Will possibly always smell like pickles and brine always from now on. I shower and it doesn't go away. I doused myself in perfume and it only got worse. I will resign myself to it: I am now pickle girl. Got job through Shula who got me in touch with a cousin who still had a favor with the son of the owners. Nice people. Not quite Bijenkorf. Not quite department store. It's getting colder. Today I smelled autumn in the air.

October 30, 1960

Birthday. Dreamt of Papa. Not nice.

November 11, 1960

Shula came over with a friend, Miriam, who was very unlikable. Would not stop talking. Did not take off shoes. She did tell one interesting story. She'd heard of a girl from the Prinsegracht who pretended to be a maid and got the family who now lived in her family's home to hire her. She lived there for a half year pretending to be a maid and piece by piece took back things that had been left behind. First a fork, then a napkin, then a painting, then a necklace. By the time they figured it out she'd made a run for it. I listened to this story and it was like my blood was on fire inside of my body. I thought: I am going to do that. I didn't say it, I just thought it, and Shula just looked at me for a long time like she could see it in my face and said it was a fantasy and things like this never happen anyway. Then Miriam said no one would hire me as a maid anyway, because I couldn't keep a home and everyone would recognize a Jew face and that I smelled like pickle brine. Miriam's face is worse than mine but I didn't say that. I didn't say a word. I went to the window and smoked in silence until they didn't know what else to do and then they left. Good riddance. No, not Shula, I like her, poor thing.

December 2, 1960

The snow has started and will not stop. Basje is pregnant. She said she could dye my hair in their new kitchen, she has a big sink now and a window that can open all the way.

December 15, 1960

Craving rhubarb. With cream and sugar from the oven, mmmm. Mum in her straw hat in the vegetable garden cutting rhubarb. I close my eyes and I see it I see it. The fight they had where Papa said he was going to cut down the firs because they blocked the sun and Mum who loved the firs saying, Oh you're God now? You're God now and you get to decide where the shadow falls and where it doesn't?

December 25, 1960

Little baby Jesus everywhere. They have no problem letting Jews into their homes as long as they're carved from wood, do they.

January 5, 1961

She's been gone eleven years today. Woke up with what I thought was a bad hunger and then as the day went on I realized it wasn't hunger. Really want to hold something that she held. Asked Malcha if I could look through the boxes for Mum's old diaries and Malcha said I could but that there probably wasn't anything there, and that a lot got thrown out or burnt in '42. Remembered the time she gave me a booklet to write in when I was a kid. I said I would keep a diary and then never did. Didn't want her to nag me about it so I gave the notebook to some girlfriend and pretended it got lost. She found out and got so angry. Well. Look at me now, Mama!

January 21, 1961

More snow. Remembering the house when it snowed. The sound of snow falling from the branches like a muffled word. *Hmph!* The sun in the mornings and the shadows of the trees on the curtain. It was dark & evening the time we drove there in '46. We parked by the front of the house and so I couldn't see anything except that the lights were on inside. Do I remember what the family who lived there looked like? No. I think I looked inside but maybe what I remember is made up. A few kids, younger than me, at the table and a big dinner. It was a cold night, I wanted to run away when that woman answered the door but I just stood there. Do I remember what they said to each other? They were shouting, and Mum said something about being let in, about it being our house, and the woman said she'd call the police if we didn't leave. Mum shouted: "Call the police! Let them come! Call them!" And then I cried. The woman closed the door and Mum banged on the windows for a long time. The police didn't come. The ride back home was freezing. It was the year the window in the car fell into the door and we could not fix it. I kept sobbing and Mum got angry and told me to stop whining. She was smoking, no gloves. She was missing a few teeth and the rest were yellow. Some illness from the camps which some doctor told us about later but I forget the name of the illness. She held on for a few more miserable years and then died freezing in a small bed waiting for me to find her in the morning.

February 8, 1961

God—

I went to pick up my shoes at the shoemaker (sole) and I ran into an old neighbor. I didn't recognize her at first. I was unlocking my bike and she stood across the street, an old goyish lady in a big winter coat and hair like feathers. She was staring at me. She stared in a way that I knew she would want to talk to me. I did not want that. She came to me just as I wanted to bike away and held my arm and said that I was Esther's girl. "Aren't you? Aren't you Esther's girl? You are, I know it." I couldn't say anything. It was like someone had put a stone in my mouth and now I could not speak. Who says my mother's name other than Malcha? No one says her name to me these days. She insisted on speaking to me. She wanted me to come have tea at a café at the corner. I thought, Oh, she has someone waiting there who will get me and send me to the Germans. That's what I thought! And then I thought: that can't happen anymore. Isn't that strange, how that works? You can think something that used to be true but isn't true anymore but still believe it in your bones. I did sit down with her at the café. I didn't want to stay long, I hated it. She talked a lot. First she asked about Mum and Dad and I didn't want to say it, she understood what that meant and didn't ask about them anymore. And then she wanted to say things about how she always liked our family, and that the other neighbors didn't but she did. She said one time when I was three she had come over for lunch and that Mum was very nice to her. She kept saying she didn't know what would happen. She wanted me to say that I believed her that she didn't know. Eventually I said I believed her. What does it matter to me? I just wanted her to stop talking and I wanted to leave. She said that she later heard it was another neighbor who sent the boots on us in '42. I don't care I don't care I don't care I don't care

When I went to leave she held on to my arm and said that I looked just like my mother, and that my mother was also such a pretty Jewess. I said please let me go. She said do you forgive me, tell me you forgive me. I said I forgive you so that she would let go. She did let go. Before I left I turned to her and I said, Who lives there now? And she said that a family without a father used to live there but the mother died a few years ago and that the two sons had since moved out. Only the daughter lives there now on her own. I said what are their names. And she told me their family name is Den Brave. They moved in during the hunger winter, from here, from Amsterdam. A son called Louis and another one called Hendrik and the daughter is called Isabel.

February 9, 1961

There was a girl called Isabel at the last address when I was still hiding up in Friesland. She was older than me. Hair so blond it looked white. One time the family wanted me to stay upstairs because there were Boots around and the parents sent her to bring me food and she held the plate like, Come get it then, and when I reached for the plate she dropped it to the floor and the food went everywhere and it made so much noise. She told her parents that I did it, that I dropped the plate. Every time I hear the name Isabel I think about that. Now an Isabel lives in my house. I'm sure this means something. What does it mean? I'm sure it means something.

February 27, 1961

Met this guy at the bar and we went to his place and he lived in this beautiful apartment on one of the canals. Ceilings so high! Everything was so clean. I wanted to know how much everything cost. I went around and asked him, How much was this couch? How much was this chair? How much was this mirror? And he said he didn't know and kissed my neck etc. etc. He didn't know! I can't imagine. If you come into my house and ask me how much my chair cost I will tell you.

March 1, 1961

A lady came into the store today with a baby girl called Isabel. She kept saying, Isabel come here! Isabel don't put that in your mouth! I wanted to put my hands over my ears, I don't know. Children are just children, what did they do, she can't help her name. But then she smeared her oily fingers on the glass and I asked the woman if she could tell her to not do that, and the woman said, Oh she's just a kid! I was so angry. So what she's just a kid! I have to clean that!

March 3, 1961

Wondering how Fred is doing. I saw a girl who looked like her today. It wasn't her. When did I last see her? Before Mum found me, '46, something. Missing how hot Fred would get at night. It's cold here. She breathed so loudly in her sleep that it was almost snoring but she never snored. One time she told me every segment of an orange has exactly three seeds. Nonsense. Liar.

What is so funny in telling small lies like facts? So I believed you, is that so stupid of me? Am I the stupid one? Her fingers were the longest fingers I'd ever seen. She was nice to me in that bed though, wasn't she. So nice and so quiet in that bed. Kisses kisses kisses in the bed well what use are kisses in the end I wonder it's still cold here and where are you now so what use is

March 15, 1961

Found one of their names in the newspaper today. I was eating an apple and the piece I was chewing fell out of my mouth. It was a small print about a ship inspection down at the docks and they quoted two engineers and one of them was named "Louis den Brave (31)." It's him isn't it? It has to be him who else could it be. There's nothing to be done with this. It is just a name. What can I do with a name? I can do nothing

March 20, 1961

Lola knows him. Lola *knows* him. *Lola knows him*. We had drinks at Goededag and I started telling her about the old neigh-bor lady, and the three siblings, and Louis den Brave in the news-paper and she said, "Oh I know that guy." And I said, No you don't, go away. She said she did! She insisted she did! He lives in Den Haag and he went with a friend of hers for a while and one time she visited that friend and he took them both out dancing. Lola said he's a spender and a sweet talker and the worst kind of both and that he dumped her friend very suddenly just a few weeks later. That her friend was pretty broken up about this, that Lola had her on the phone crying a few times. I said it made sense that he was a fucker. And then that thing happened again where I started laughing and couldn't stop laughing and Lola got worried. I smoked a cigarette and that helped. So then I asked her where he lives. She wouldn't tell me. I asked her what bar he took them to. She said she'd tell me if I promised not to go there and to not bother him. I promised I would not bother him and so she told me the name of the bar. It's Monday today. I will take the train on Friday.

March 25, 1961

He is more handsome than I imagined but otherwise he is exactly as I imagined.

March 26, 1961

I saw him and I thought, Do I remember him? Is that the face I remember seeing through the window, sitting at the dinner table.

He didn't look like anyone to me. Mum was banging on the windows saying get out get out and his mother looked my mother in the face and said, This is not your house, and she closed the door in her face. And still he just looks like a man. Like any man looks like any man.

March 28, 1961

I wonder if I ask him about the hearth in the kitchen will he have anything to say about it. Will he say, That is my favorite place in the house. That is where it gets warmest and where I can sit on a chair and hold the bare soles of my feet to the fire. I wonder if I ask him about the creak in the hallway and the firs and my mother's spoons will he know which spoons I mean will he have used them will he know

March 30, 1961

Basje is huge now, all belly. She bleached my hair in the kitchen sink. That stuff is a chemical weapon I swear. It's been two days and all I can smell is ammonia. My scalp burnt something awful and now it itches. Every time I see myself in the mirror I'm not sure what I'm seeing. It's not especially pretty and not especially ugly. Very yellow, very strange. Heading back to Den Haag on Saturday. I am borrowing one of Basje's old dresses and her good lipstick.

April 2, 1961

It was terribly easy. I danced with one of his friends and while I danced with this friend all I did was look at him from across the room and look at him and look at him. Isn't that it? Most people just want to be seen. I let him buy me a drink and gave him my name and then said I forgot his name several times even though he kept reminding me. I asked him to tell me about boats. He said, "You mean ships," and I said oh I'm so stupid about these things, I don't know anything, tell me about boats. He said: ships, you mean ships. I said: ships, whatever you want. He asked to see me again. I said oh but I barely know you. He said, Don't you want to get to know me? I said, Who knows, maybe.

Pesach. Chag Sameach.

April 6, 1961

We went out to lunch. He likes to order for you and then he likes to watch you eat it. We took a walk along the boulevard. It was gray and windy the waves were high. My hat flew off and he caught it for me. I held it over my face, and he said, "What are you doing?" So I explained that I was keeping the water from my face so my makeup wouldn't run and he laughed like this was a very funny thing to say. He said I was a strange girl and that he liked me. He asked to walk me home and I said that I'm staying with a friend in Amsterdam because I was looking for an apartment. I knew what he was going to say and then he said it: "You can always stay with me." Oh? I said. Oh? Where do you live? He explained where he lived. I said, "Is that the only place where you live? Where else do you live?" And then he laughed again like I had said something very strange.

April 15, 1961

Have been bad with work & fired. Went home with Louis last night. A damp apartment, shared kitchen & bathroom. Housemate wasn't home. He was all hands and a lot of mouth. Gnawed more than kissed. It was over quickly. In bed at some point he said, "I love how you have so much body" and I said what do you mean I have so much body? And he said "oh you know what I mean" in this sweet voice with his hands all over me. He isn't bad I've definitely had worse for worse causes. I asked him to tell me about his family. He said there isn't much to tell. I said tell me their names, what do they do, where do they live. He wanted to know why I wanted to know. I said, "I want to know about your life and where you came from." He said that his parents were dead. That his brother Hendrik also lives in Den Haag and that he was an accountant. His sister Isabel lives in the east in their old family home. I asked, Alone? He said, "She has someone who helps with the house come by every other day." I said that that still meant she lived alone. He said, "Then I guess she lives alone." I asked if he ever thought of moving back, such a big family home, there must be space. He went quiet for a while and then he said that actually it was his. I said, "What do you mean?" He said, "The house. My uncle holds the deed but it goes to me." I said, It *goes* to you? And he said that when he wants to start a family the house is his. When he marries. When he wants to have kids. My heart was beating so hard I was sure he could feel it. I was lying half on top of him, naked, he should have felt my heart going *thud thud thud!* But he didn't. I said, "Is that something you want? To get married and have children?" And he put his hands around me tightly and said "Oh, when the right girl comes along" and then kissed me like he was trying to make me feel special.

April 17, 1961

I could make him marry me. I think it would be easy. I don't think it'll take me long. I'm writing this and I am seeing the words on the paper and my head is saying, this is crazy, this is a crazy idea, what are you saying you crazy girl. But then I think, haven't people married for bad reasons always? I could've met him at a bar without knowing who he was or where he came from. I could've met him just as easily and he would've still fallen for me, because he is that kind of man. He has security and he has a good future and who doesn't want security and a good future? There are worse men. It is an accident that he has something of mine. It is an accident that he can give it back to me. This could've happened any other way, too.

April 18, 1961

Saw a woman at the market today with a number that was two numbers off Mum's number. I wanted to talk to her. What could I have said to her? There was nothing to say. One time Mum told me that she and the other Dutch people were the last ones to leave the camps. That the Red Cross came for the French and the Swiss and everyone and that the Americans kept saying, Oh you need to wait for someone to come get you to bring you back. And that some people just went because who was going to stop them? But some of them stayed and slept in the same bunks and some of them died in those days. Later they heard it took a long time because no one was coming. The Dutch didn't send anyone to bring back their Jews. She told me she knew a father and a daughter who survived but the mother didn't and they didn't want to wait so they went with the Swiss Red Cross and ended up in Switzerland. They had a really nice time recovering there, nice beds and food and the dad was a dentist. He helped anyone who needed something fixed. They were there for a few years and then, when they came back here, they get this bill for something like thousands of gilders, thousands. The Swiss government had sent a bill to the Dutch government and the Dutch government said: pay up! They didn't have the money of course. They were sent to the old factories in Eindhoven that they used like a big barn to send all the left-over Jews. I was in one of those for a while. Mum said that when she arrived at Amsterdam central in that summer of '45 in that dirty uniform the lady at the returnees reception table said that she should count herself lucky to have been in those camps, that at least she'd been fed in those camps. The whole of the Netherlands had suffered a great hunger, that's what the lady told her. Mum didn't know where I was, if I was alive or not, if they'd got me and sent me to some camp. She asked the lady at the desk if anyone with my name had come by. The lady said she didn't know and that Mum needed to move along. Mum said she started screaming and pulling at the lady and that some goyim who worked there dragged her away and made her stay outside the station and that was the first time she saw Amsterdam again.

April 22, 1961

Yesterday Louis said, "I can tell you one thing about my mum. Her favorite animal in the world was a hare." I thought I was going to die. He said, She had these plates, no one was allowed to touch them. We used to eat off those plates every day, and then that birthday party and the wild hare and one of them broke, and Mum wasn't even that upset. Life happens, she said. We took almost nothing when we left. Mum kept saying, Don't worry we'll come back we'll come back so soon, and it was a lie. I think now to how they found that house with everything still in it, Papa's book still left open on the page where he stopped, and I am sick I am sick to my stomach. Whose stuff did they think that was? They must have known I can't imagine they didn't know. Who doesn't know a thing like that? They must've known.

April 23, 1961

He will marry me and if he won't marry me I will make him take me to that house and I will stuff everything into a big bag and I don't care I will run all the way back to Amsterdam I don't care I'll do it.

April 30, 1961

Out of money & behind on rent. Took out a loan with little Daantje like I've always been told not to. I told Louis my friend wants me out of her apartment and he said I can come live with him. So easy! Come live with me! Should've seen these people in '42. The first address we hid at, Mum and Pap and I, the people asked for ƒ1000 for the month and we stayed in a stinky small attic room with straw so we wouldn't make any sound and Mum would have these whispered conversations with Pap saying, We can't afford this for much longer and Pap said, How much longer can it go on? We'll be back home in a month.

But then they couldn't afford the next address for all three of us and just sent me ahead. ƒ300 a month for a 12-year-old, what a bargain! A cot in a pantry up in Groningen. A mother with a bird face and a dad who worked at a mill and was missing two fingers. They told everyone I was a cousin from the west. Their son told me I smelled like poop. Six months I was there, and then one day soldiers came by and then ƒ300 wasn't enough and they sent me away and I—I thought, if Mum and Pap will come find me they'll come here, and if I'm not there they'll never find me. I screamed! I screamed the whole way! It didn't help. Into the back of some farmer's truck. Friesland, a cold winter. ƒ500 up front. That was the last of the money. Drenthe, nice people, two weeks, they had some dogs, and the dogs didn't like me. Too much sound. I left that place on my own. Got my first period in a shed somewhere, God, hay rolled up in a ripped hem from my skirt—stuffed into my underwear, had no idea what I was doing, how long was I supposed to bleed? A day, two days, weeks? I didn't know a thing. I wanted Mum. I slept under a meat hook for that whole summer. A grandma at the next farm knew I was stealing from her kitchen and pretended she didn't see me. Bless her, the single good person left on this earth.

May 1, 1961

It's a gorgeous May day. The sun is so soft and everything is in bloom and the air smells like an exclamation mark for something that's about to happen. Louis is at work. Met his housemate. Maurice, who I know, who is Geytele's cousin whose friend got me that second hiding address in Drenthe in '43. He didn't recognize me. It's been over fifteen years and I am blond now. I am scared if he looks at me for too long he will recognize me, so I will stay in the room or I will go outside. I think I'll get Louis to marry me. Have taken diary with me, have decided I am not worried: Louis does not notice me much or the things I have or the things I do. He wants me! Obviously. He does not notice me.

May 2, 1961

That's what I imagine. That's what I imagine a big love is like. Sometimes I think about Dad and the time he wanted to show me how to play checkers and I said no, boring game. I want to scream at myself. Now you'll never know how he plays checkers or how he explains the rules and these are things you'll never ever ever know. That's what happens when people die. They take themselves with them and you never ever find out anything new about them ever.

I think that big love is like that but no one's dead or dying. And then I think: it's much better to just like a person a lot. Who makes good decisions when they're in love? I know no one.

May 4, 1961

I thought I was in love with Martijn. He was a good kisser, and he kept the bed so warm, and God when I talked he looked at me like I was the smartest person in the whole world. And when I fed him he said, Mmmmmmm! As if he hadn't tasted anything better in his whole life. But then he left and I was angry for two days and then I thought, Oh, it's nice to have time to myself again. And when Basje told me he was sleeping with Janneke I thought, Good luck Janneke, so I don't think that was love after all.

May 12, 1961

Louis wants to take me to a family dinner next week to meet his brother and sister.

May 16, 1961

The days are warming but the nights are still cold. Today I remembered when that lady decided keeping me in the basement was too dangerous and sent me out at night and that was also May and that was also such a cold night. I found a barn and hid in the hay under the meat hook. They bombed somewhere nearby I didn't sleep a wink. Louis does this thing in his sleep where he doesn't hold me but just puts a very soft hand on my hip. I hate it, it drives me crazy. I want to shout, Either you hold me or you don't touch me at all!! What is this hand, it's nothing!! I roll away.

May 21, 1961

Dinner with his siblings last night. I was so nervous. I thought I would look at them and they would know who I was somehow. I thought I would see them and recognize them in a way that I maybe didn't recognize Louis, like maybe I've remembered their faces where I didn't remember his. I didn't. They were strangers to me. I hoped she (his sister) would be a nice person and I had a plan where I would say how much I wanted to get away to the country and she would invite us for a weekend but none of that happened. She is awful. She is sour and mean and she looked at me like Louis had dragged me into the house under the sole of his shoe. She kept looking at me like she was trying to—I don't know. She kept looking at me. She and Hendrik came here after for drinks, oh it was awful! But I didn't show, I smiled and I smiled and I said, Oh it was so nice to meet you Isabel! So lovely! We hope to see you soon!

Her face, I swear. Not even honey could sweeten that vinegar.

June 1, 1961

A miracle. Louis got called to substitute for a colleague, work trip, something or the other. He will be gone a month. I said, I can't stay here alone with Maurice. He said, Can you invite a friend to stay with you? I said, Can't I stay with your sister? He said, Isabel? I said, Isabel. We are driving out in 10 mins. My suitcase is half-empty. I will fill up the rest.

June 2, 1961

I'm here. I'm here. I'm here. I'm here. I'm here. I'm here. It smells the same. The walls. The things. The firs and the garden. The painting of the Veluwe Uncle Avrum brought that one time all wrapped in brown paper and oh they barely changed anything. These people—they—! The curtains are new. This bed is new. I can't stop touching everything, everything. Mum's room. I now touch things that she once touched. Her secretary—still here. The initials I carved into the drawer. Who do they think that is? Who do they think that is? Have they ever wondered? They have never wondered. These people do not wonder. I am here. I am here. I'm here I'm here I'm here.

June 3, 1961

Will anyone recognize me? Will the neighbors? Will the postman? Will the farmer on the other side of the dike? What will they do? Strangely I am not afraid and I am not worried. I woke up and the sun came through the window through the firs and the shadows on the curtains. I can just hear her, it's like she's downstairs: Oh you're God now and you get to decide where the shadow falls? I was born in this room. Mum could not get to the hospital, I was born in this room, and these walls were witness, and this desk, and these windows too. The house wants me here even if no one else does.

June 6, 1961

She thinks I'm after her brother's money. Ha. I have woken up in the night and I have taken a spoon. Tomorrow I will go to town and I will mail the spoon to Malcha and it will be mine again. No matter what happens at least I will have that spoon.

June 7, 1961

She's taken care of Mum's garden. It looks nice. I saw her cutting the rhubarb today. She did it the same way I remembered, with the basket and the scissors. I stood there and tried to think, You thief, you're a thief. It's hard to think that at someone cutting rhubarb in the hot sun. Then she told me to roll up my trousers before I got on the bike and I did. I mailed the spoon to Malcha.

June 8, 1961

She has made the strangest trap of this house. She has drawn herself a circle and she lives inside that circle and anyone who comes in or leaves must answer to her rules, which she barks at you, like some prison officer. Madness. I barely move. She will not look away. I wake up and she is there. I turn and she is there. She will not speak to me. I left the house the other day and her anger almost felt like worry, she is making me go mad alongside her. I ask her, What are the joys in your life! What are the things you love or hate or want to do! She looks at me like she's guarding the Queen's jewelry. Like every word she gives me is some precious thing that I will abuse.

There's a maid (Neelke) who comes and helps with the house. Poor thing.

June 9, 1961

Went looking for Father's letter opener & she walked in and I said, I dropped an earring. I nearly ripped my ear off, taking it out quick quick. I thought my heart would beat out of my chest. She—I don't know. She stood very close. Sometimes I think she knows. Sometimes I want to push her and see what she does. Sometimes I think she's at my door at night. I wonder if I stay away again, if that will get her angry again. Maybe I should just leave altogether. Maybe this was the worst idea I've ever had. I've never met a woman so tall and she's not even that tall at all.

June 10, 1961

Dreamt she was at my bedside watching me sleep & woke up and she wasn't there. Can't fall back asleep. She keeps this place so neat. Today she took out every piece of Mother's hare china and rolled it in water with a hand soft like to a baby's neck. She's found a shard of the old broken plate in the garden and now keeps it on the mantel like some treasure. She's all alone here.

For years she has sat at the kitchen table all alone and taken my mother's things into her hands and cleaned them.

June 12, 1961

Louis called today. Hearing him was a bucket of ice water. I think I've been dreaming or asleep since I got here. I can't explain. I'm here. I can't explain

June 13, 1961

If this was any other house I would leave. I would run from here. If I had no other purpose I'd be gone. I am going to go insane, she is going to drive me insane. *A drink*, I had a single drink with the *maid*, and she—what am I to her? What do I owe her? I'm the one who's owed, it's me, and she talks to me about her life, and she grabs me and I still have the bruise of her hand on my arm. Oh I have drunk too much I think . . .

June 14, 1961

I wonder if she remembers the time we almost met. After the war when I was sixteen and on that side of the door and she was only just a few years younger on this side of the door. Mum knocked and knocked and they wouldn't let us in. Sometimes I can feel her eyes on me like it's on my skin. I think she thinks I don't notice. She looks at me like she wants to embrace me, hold me, and then I look back at her and she says the nastiest things. I want to see what happens if I crawl into the attic and hide and she can't find me. Will she lose her mind? Will she turn the house upside down looking for me? I think she will. I want to see what would happen if I walked up to her and put all of my face in her face and she can finally have what she wants which is she doesn't have to look anywhere where I'm not.

June 15, 1961

God help me. I can still feel her mouth.

June 16, 1961

Hendrik here now. She said—oh, she said, I think I have a fever. I said you don't have a fever. But I feel it too now. My head is hot. I won't sleep. I am sick. I am sick. I want her here. I want her in this bed, God, what have I done. I don't know—Oh, what have we done. What a mess. No more, no, no more, it is done.

June 18, 1961

God let her not know herself. God let her have mistaken in herself. God let her like him more than anything. God let her be confused and God let her not know touch and not know the one kiss from the other and confused and God let her like him more than me. God take it away from me God take her away God please God please take her from me.

June 21, 1961

I think she wants to eat me. I think she would inhale me if she could. I think she'd crawl herself inside of me if she thought that's where she'd find something that I've kept hidden from her. God help me. Would I let her? I would let her. God help me she looks at me. God help me I don't want her to look away.

June 22, 1961

Have I ever been a body before? I don't know. I think I'm a body now. Last night she woke me up from a terror and held me like a straitjacket. I could feel I had skin where she touched and where I had bone and where I was human. God what sense does this make, none none, no sense, no sense at all. She wakes up before I do and gets breakfast ready so I can have it when I am awake and it makes me want to cry. People have done this before, it is not special, and still I want to cry. I should run God I should run why am I here

- mother's teaspoons (12)
- bread knife (wood handle)
- yellow eggcups (2)
- rings (? If there)
- paper weight
- tiles (decorative, hares)
- letter opener
- picture frames (the small ones from mother's bedroom)
- napkin rings
- engraved cake knife
- small bread knife

215

- yellow illustrated book (? Title?)
- candle holders (Sjabbat)
- small blue oven dish
- big blue oven dish
- vase (marble, mantel)
- hares plates (5)
- hares soup bowls (6)
- hares big bowl
- hares sugar pot
- hares milk jug
- menorah (if there)
- blue thimble
- pencil box
- bookends (4)
- Haasje

13

IT WAS SUMMER'S END. GRAY-BOTTOMED CLOUDS and a three-day drizzle. Isabel lay on her back under the secretary desk and put her fingers to the etched initials: E.D.H.

Eva had been born in this room. Her small hand was the hand that held a knife that carved this wood.

Isabel tried to tend to the garden because autumn was on its way. The dirt clung to her hands. She didn't dare dig into the earth, kept thinking she felt pinpricks from below—but there were none. No shards, no remains, no new secrets to rise from the ground.

Knowledge came at her in flashes only, truth glimpsed from between a lattice, there and then gone: a hare let loose at a party, a box of toys in the attic, a child's crayon drawing of a horse on the back of a cupboard door. The rhubarb. The trees. Every day she woke up and every day the house unfolded around her like a dark hand. She leaned into rooms and the rooms leaned away. She tried to stand tall and found it too heavy a thing; her posture worsened. She took the piece of broken china from the mantelpiece and hid it: in the drawer, the cupboard, in a box, in with the vegetables in the pantry. And every time she regretted it quickly, went back for it with a fast-beating heart that did not slow until the thing was back where she had first placed it: elevated, watching.

She could not look at it. She woke up from her nightmares—pricking needles and bombs and the thumping on the door and— She was shivering and tangled in her sheets, wrestling, crying out—

"Are you," she started, stopped. It was midday, and Neelke was putting on the kettle. Isabel was at the kitchen table in her nightgown. In her house robe. She was addressing the window, not the girl. She said, "Are you much like your mother?"

Neelke said, "Sorry?" And Isabel did not repeat herself. Neelke had heard. She answered eventually, while pouring out the tea. "No," she said. They had their tea. There was no conversation after that.

Isabel wanted to know what Eva had looked like as a child. Short, she imagined. Cheeks like balls of dough.

There had once been a Jewish tailor in town. He had a shop with big windows and he'd sit by those big windows with his sewing machine and people could look in, see him at work, bent over. Isabel and her brothers liked looking in when they passed the tailor, and their mother would not allow it—would rush them past and say, *Don't, don't look inside, children, come now.* Isabel wondered now at how she could've known that the man was Jewish, and in the moment of wondering she immediately knew, recalled it all at once: a time when mother took one of her skirts to the tailor for adjustments, and then had returned with the skirt and had found a spot of dirt on the hem; the story of her returning to the tailor, driving all the way back, demanding he cover the costs of cleaning. The story of how he refused to, how he insisted she must've dirtied the thing herself when getting into the car. The end of that story, the way it was delivered: "That *Jew.*"

On the morning of the anniversary of her mother's passing, Isabel did as she's always done: she took one plate of good china from the cabinet, off which to eat her breakfast. It was early, and dark outside. Under the dim overhead light, Isabel touched the blues, the whites. The outline of a hare's leg, a tail, an ear.

Eva had watched her hold these things, her own mother's things, had watched Isabel handle them, clean them, call them *hers* and Eva had said—she had said: *You do that with such care.*

Isabel could not eat her breakfast. The plate was on the table, empty. Isabel laid her head in the cradle of her arms. The feeling, when it came, was not new—had been worn familiar in the weeks since Eva had left: the sudden wanting to do away with herself. The thought—*too heavy, it's too heavy*—a desire for someone to take it away from her. The plates, the walls, the weight of her hair, her own damned hands—to let someone else have them. Be done with it.

And then, as always, this emotion was followed quickly by a shudder, a tightening: sit up straight. A voice, perhaps her mother's, perhaps her own: *dramatics.* The worst of verdicts, the worst behaviors—dramatics.

She went hungry that day. Tried to right her posture. She left the plate on the table, where it stayed, untouched, for the rest of the week.

Rains came quick, a mouth opening and closing. It had rained on the drive over, and the streets smelled of wet stone. Uncle Karel lived in a canal-facing town house, a tall building with a triangle of a staircase leading up from both ends. He had a garden out the back with a narrow strip of land and a plum tree with half a head: the branches had grown over the neighbor's fence had been cut back to their border line.

Karel insisted they sit outside. It would stay dry, he said, and the afternoon was so nice and cool—a gift, he said, after the summer they just had. Isabel agreed with a hum and kept on touching her bare neck, as if to pull down the line of her hair—as if uneasy about the hem of a skirt. Uncle hadn't commented on it yet. When he opened the door he'd taken her in and had paused a moment, then said, "So!" and nothing else.

The tea was steaming on the garden table. Uncle had taken out the biscuit tin and had put two single biscuits on a small plate—one for her, one for him—and closed the tin again, put the tin away. When he sat down, he did so directly opposite her. He put his elbows on the armrests. He laced his hands over his belly and gave a few smacking mouth sounds to indicate: *I'm waiting. Talk.*

Isabel had requested this meeting. She called him, she demanded he make time. She had refused to say why. And when he asked that she give him an idea of what was the matter at hand—of how worried he should be—it was Isabel who went quiet on the line, a quiver of a breath. Hand gripping the phone.

The tea was bitter, steeped too long. The leaves were reused from this morning. Isabel scalded her tongue drinking too quickly.

Karel said, "Your hair."

Isabel touched it again. She had cut it off in a fit in the night. A hairdresser had later made of it what she could, but there had not been much to work with—it was choppy and uneven. Now it sat in a thick bob under her ears, at the hinge of her jaw. She caught sight of herself in mirrors these days and would quickly look away.

She said, "My hair. Yes." She wondered whether her uncle saw anything else, other than the hair. She felt he must. She felt she was not who she once was. She felt that this should be visible from a great distance.

"Is this what you wanted to see me about?" he asked. "A new haircut?"

Isabel stopped touching her hair. She held the cup and asked him how he was. He said he was well, and then named several items that were considerably more expensive now than they were last year this time, and then went quiet.

Birds in the prune tree. Isabel held a nail to a chip in the rim of the cup and said, "The house . . ."

"Something has broken," he concluded. "You have come to ask for—support. Of course, Isabel. Come now, what kind of family is this, what do you think—"

"No," she said. "Nothing is broken."

He looked at her a moment.

She said, "You bought the house."

"What house?"

"Our house. During the war."

"I did," he said. It was slow. He considered a moment, added: "For you. You and your brothers. Your mother."

"Was it . . ." She smoothed her hands over her skirt, over her knees. "It was empty," she said it like it wasn't a question, which it was.

Karel reached for his biscuit. "What an odd thing to say Isabel. What are you wanting to know? What an odd thing to ask. It was a house, the four of you moved in, of course it was empty. Wouldn't you have noticed if someone else was living there? What a question." He ate as he spoke and crumbs collected in the weave of his sweater vest.

"Were there things in the house?" she asked. "Furniture, I mean. Plates." A beat. "Spoons and—and the like."

He seemed to notice her now. A slowing of movement, a slowing of his gaze. He finished his biscuit in a purposeful way, thoughtful. He said, "You mean to ask if I came by the house in a dishonest way."

Isabel didn't answer. She sat up somewhat straighter. She fought the urge to swallow.

"Have you read something in the news, Isabel? Is that it? Has someone told you a fantastical story of robbers and thieves and the war? What nonsense. You, of all people, to believe these—"

"No one told me anything. I—" She swallowed. Cleared her throat, said, "I had a memory. I remembered—when we moved in, the house, how it was . . . full of things."

Karel brushed the crumbs from his chest. He took his time doing so. "You were very young," he told her. It was a judgment. "These things are not as they seem when you're a child, Isabel. And now you are no longer a child. Yes, a family lived there. But they left. They did not pay their mortgage, they did not pay their taxes. This happens, it happens every day, people make gambles they cannot keep, people pack up and leave and they don't take their—their plates and their spoons. Goodness! Do you understand? It happens every day. There is nothing untoward here, Isabel. It's the law."

Isabel had a curling thing in the lowest part of her belly. It rose to her lungs, took her by her throat: an argument. She was going to have to form words soon. She was sweating under the cool midday sun, half in the shade of town house roofs.

Karel said, "We bought the house, Isabel. It is our property. We did not *cheat* our way into it. There is a deed, there is—" He slowed himself. He took a loud slurp of his tea, continued: "The house was empty. What do you think happens to empty houses? In times of hunger, of war? Who wants to see empty houses when there's people on the streets? Would you rather I not have given you a home? Would you rather you stayed in Amsterdam, starved, bombed, God knows what—" He cut himself off again. He looked off to the side for a while. He had a mole in the middle of his cheek, same as Mother had had. His hair was thin and combed over, skin soft over his jaw. He had always seemed old to Isabel, long before he was truly old.

"What does it matter," he said, still looking to the side, "that someone has lived there before? They're gone. They did not come back for it. Every house has a history. What house doesn't have a history?"

"How do you know?" Isabel asked.

"Hm?"

"That—they're gone. That they didn't come back."

"How do you know someone has returned, do you think?"

Isabel looked at him. Under the table, she held the skin on the back of her hand in a tight pinch.

Her uncle said, "They knock."

Something must have shown on Isabel's face. Karel made an exasperated sound, gave her a quick smile, said, "Isabel, what is this game? Would they won't they, *meisje*: reasonable people would contact the council, it wouldn't be an unsurpassable hurdle. You call, you send a letter, you—*act*. And besides." He reached for a biscuit—realized in movement that he'd already eaten his share. Leaned back again. "There were outstanding payments. The bank took it back. Parate execution—a standard procedure. You know what I think, *meisje*?"

He called her *meisje* in moments like this. In moments where he wanted her to remember who he was, who she was. *Little girl. Darling girl.*

She said: "What?"

"If they wanted the house, they would've come back for it. If they cared about it, they would've come back for it. No. They're gone. They're gone or they don't care. So many are gone. You don't know, Isabel. You were so young."

An image came to Isabel: Eva, a child. Cheeks like dough. Alone in a field, alone in an attic. Mothers with numbers on their arms. *Young*, he said.

"I want the house," she said.

Karel said, "Pardon?"

"I want the house. I want the house to be mine. I live there. I care about it, I keep it in order, I want—" It got caught in her throat. She licked her lips. "I want to grow old there." She said, "Give it to me."

"Sweetheart." The word was said expansively—too slow. Uncle Karel gave her concern with a frown. "The house is promised to Louis."

Isabel let go of the back of her hand. She flexed her fingers, put both her hands on the tabletop. She kept them there, said, "I know. But what if Louis doesn't want it? He has no use for it." She tried not to move, to look strong, to look determined: "What if Louis wants me to have it?"

"Isabel . . ."

"Can you change that? If we all agree on it?" She licked her lips again. "Can it go to me?"

"Have you and Louis had a falling-out?" Karel asked. "Is that—Isabel. Is that what's the matter?"

"Not at all."

"I know the two of you haven't been—as close as you once were. I know that you and Hendrik—"

"No," she said. "Louis and I are well. We—" She took a tight breath: "We've actually grown closer recently. I really . . ."

Birds in the prune tree. A thin weave of clouds over the sun, and everything went a muted shade, a bright and muted shade. "I was wrong about him," Isabel said.

Karel's frown changed in nature. "Were you?"

"Hm," she said. "Perhaps we should both visit you soon. Perhaps that would be nice." She pushed the plate with the one biscuit a little end toward him. "You can have mine," she said.

"Oh!" He wanted to reach, hesitated, said, "If you're sure?"

Isabel said, "Yes. It's yours."

"Thank you," he said, and ate the biscuit.

"I'll ask Louis," Isabel said. "About visiting you."

Karel gave her a look but did not push. There were crumbs on his sweater vest again. He brushed them off again. In another garden, fenced off, some children screamed out something in joy. The birds startled out of the prune tree. Isabel and Karel turned to watch them in unison: their flurry of wings, their turn about the sky, the search for a new place to settle down.

Napkin rings. Picture frames, the small ones, from mother's bedroom. The big blue oven dish. A vase of marble. Five plates, good china. The ones with the hares. Six soup bowls. A salad bowl. The sugar pot, the milk jug, the menorah. Isabel found that one in the wine cellar: wrapped in a cloth, within a cloth, within a suitcase. The silver had gone gray, brown.

She polished it. It took hours.

Four bookends: a ballerina on each end, leaning in.

Haasje. The stuffed animal had a worn belly. Isabel placed it in the dip of a bowl, and the bowl held it like a bed. The beads-for-eyes stared up, blank, until Isabel turned off the kitchen lights. She left the room and closed each door between her and the kitchen—as if the thing might get up and return to her in the night.

Nothing ever changed about Tante Rian's home. Isabel hadn't been in a while and nothing had changed: not the dust on the shelves, not the placement of the vases, not the dredge of old coffee in the coffee maker—brown filter paper curling at the edges.

Rian had a lot to say about Isabel's hair. She tutted and called her foolish and reassured herself that it'd grow back and then had a lot to say about how Isabel hasn't been by for some months. She also had a lot to say about how no one else has come to see her in a while, how she was being forgotten, and how different it used to be when Isabel's mother was still alive. When Isabel was young. "You used to adore me," she said, half to herself, wobbling over to the kitchen. The house smelled like boxed air. "You and your brothers all! Tante Rian this, Tante Rian that. You brought me drawings you made. I still have them, you know. All of them I kept. Do you believe me? Do you want to see?"

"I remember," Isabel said.

Then Rian had a lot to say about the oven dish, the one she had or hadn't been gifted before the war. She had run into the old neighbor at the market earlier that week. The woman had brought up the dish, and Rian had ignored it, just "pretended I didn't hear her, just as if I didn't hear her at all, I just bought my cheese. That's what I did. Thank you, sir, I said to the cheese man. And when I got home I said to myself, Rian, well done. Well done. You didn't let her get the better of you, well done."

Isabel joined her in the kitchen. It was narrow, barely fit two people. It was built into the side of the house some ten years ago. The old kitchen, the maids' kitchen, had been remade into a downstairs bedroom: Rian couldn't go up the stairs anymore. She hadn't been up the second floor since the forties.

Isabel watched Rian reach up for two cups. Her fingers were swollen at the knuckles. Isabel started, "So she—" Then stopped. Then asked, "She gave you that dish, you said?"

"Yes, yes," Rian said. She poured out the coffee.

"Gave it in what—in what capacity?"

Rian didn't seem to understand the question. "What?" she said. "Gave, gave it, she gave it to me to keep."

"To keep." Isabel accepted the coffee. It was lukewarm. The

pot had been made before she'd arrived. "Where did she go that you had to keep it?"

Rian looked at her now. Looked up with watery eyes. They were small and the color of rust. She had put makeup on, as she always did when Isabel visited: rouge, a faded lip. It made her reaction look startled, flushed. Her cup made a sound on its saucer. "Go?" she said. "Where did anyone go, Isabel. It was war, it was hunger. We were starving, we were living on rations. Do you know how much we had to eat each day? Two slices of bread, one glass of milk, no meat—barely! People came to the door to beg and I had nothing to give. No one had anything to give. What time did I have to pay attention to anyone else? People left, people came, people ran away or hid away, I don't know. I did not keep track of where people go. But I kept that dish for her, you know. Because she was a friend. She wasn't here and I *kept* it for her."

"So was it a gift?" Isabel asked. "Or were you keeping it?"

Rian turned away from her. She walked back to the living room, said, "You're playing with words now. What does it matter, gifting, keeping? She gave it to me. It was a terrible time. She was gone for *years*. Oh!" It came out an exclamation. "Oh, I don't want to talk about it!"

Isabel, half in and out of the kitchen, wanted to say: *You bring it up every time I'm here.* She didn't. She still had the saucer in hand, the cup by its ear. Her breakfast sat sour and high in her stomach. Rian had her back to Isabel. She was arranging a plant on the windowsill, turning it—turning the faded leaves to the light. Isabel had upset her.

After a while, Isabel said, "I'll warm the pastries." She had brought pastries.

"Yes," Rian agreed, and continued to fiddle with the plant.

The pastries smelled fresh, sat prettily in their paper bags, had egg-washed coats of shine. Isabel stood there a moment. It was a bright day, sunny, but the light no longer felt like summer. She wore her hat. She had a jacket on in the car. A shiver ran through her now, so sudden and so strong her teeth chattered.

She held herself. Outside: a pear tree, arms wide, a circle of rotting fruit on the ground. Isabel opened a cupboard and considered Rian's oven dishes. She had five: two of clear glass, two of decorated white glass, one ceramic. She could not guess which one was the kept dish. Rian did not cook for herself. She had a woman who came and cooked, meals that were kept in the icebox and heated, reheated.

They ate their pastries in silence. When Rian spoke again, it was to say: "A nice cup." She meant her coffee. She drank the last of it.

Isabel said, "Yes." She said, "Yes, lovely." She didn't say much else of it for the rest of her visit. She went home and avoided making eye contact with the door or with the hearth or with the box of things. She opened the cutlery drawer and it rattled. She wrapped half of everything in a cloth and made a package out of it. She took all that was fragile and rolled old newspapers around each item. She knocked her palm on a nail sticking out of the side of the box and bled onto the inky paper, and only later—when she washed her hands—did she notice the wound: a red line, irritated.

The water ran pink. She pulled at the skin around it. It didn't hurt. Hendrik asked about it when she came by to visit two days later. Their suitcases were packed in the hallway: they were set to leave for Paris by morning. They sat on Hendrik's balcony and the day smelled like brine. Hendrik insisted they sit outside because he and Sebastian hadn't made use of the balcony all season and now they must make up for it, even if it was too cold. Sebastian was quiet and withdrawn, not quite there. Isabel did not know what the latest news was about his mother's health. She couldn't imagine it was positive.

Hendrik took her hand and said, "Oh, what did you do? That looks bad, it looks quite inflamed," and Isabel said, "It's nothing, it doesn't hurt," and Hendrik looked at her, and looked at her, and said, "You know, I just can't get used to the hair."

Isabel said, "Then don't look at it."

He laughed. He lit up a smoke, offered her one. She rarely smoked, only ever at Hendrik's insistence. She disliked the smell, the tacky film of taste it left behind. She accepted the cigarette now. Hendrik said, "You know you never did tell me what ended up happening with Louis and Eva and everything. Were you there for it?"

Isabel lit her own cigarette. "There for what?"

"Him breaking it off? Did he do it at the house immediately? Or did he pick her up and—"

"She left," she said. Her eyes were dry. "He called in advance and . . . she left."

Hendrik made a sound: a scoff, a laugh, in between. Sebastian looked up briefly. He looked at Hendrik, and at Isabel, and seemed to see something—infer something. Isabel turned from it, smoked deeply. She closed her eyes as though against the bright sky.

Hendrik said, "Well, at least you have your home back. That must be nice."

Isabel said nothing. They were having a glass of port, and Isabel's stomach was empty, and the heat of it spread quickly: to her head, to her limbs. Her hands remained cold. She kept them under the quilt. The wind had picked up.

Then Hendrik reached out and pulled a strand of her hair.

229

Her head bobbed toward the tug. He said, quietly, "So will you tell me what this was about, then?"

She batted him away. "Leave it," she said.

"Very unlike you."

"What's *like* me," she said, and patted her hair down. Touched her neck. It was cold. "There's no such thing. *Like* me. Surely if I do it then it's *like* me." The cigarette had made her nauseous. She put it in the ashtray, still red-tipped.

Hendrik looked at her. Sebastian went inside. He touched Hendrik's shoulder on passing.

"What," she said.

"You're acting strange."

She didn't want to be observed by him and instead considered the roof of the building opposite. "So Paris, tomorrow."

"Yes."

"So dutiful."

"Isabel."

"You know," she said. "You know you used to have night terrors, as a child. All the time. You were so scared. Every night," she told him. "I held you. You cried and I held you."

He tried to laugh at this and couldn't. Instead, he put the knuckle of his thumb to his eyebrow and smoked, and almost spoke and didn't, and so it was up to Isabel to say the next thing.

"You left us," she said. The port was rising in her blood. "Mum and me. But mostly me. You left me—on my own."

It was his turn now to look away from her—look at the roofs. "You had Mother."

"I wanted you."

"Oh, Isabel, you know I couldn't—I couldn't be there. I couldn't . . ."

Isabel took a long sip. They'd never spoken of this. She was not who she once was, and she couldn't imagine it was for the better. Her edges were jagged and her chest cracked open and she said, "I know." She said, "I know Mother was . . . unyielding. She worried."

Hendrik huffed. "I don't think she worried."

"I lived with her after you left. I saw her every day. She'd wait for your letters like—like you were a soldier at war. She'd write to Uncle Karel nearly every day asking about you. She'd—"

"Don't you hear it as you say it? Soldier at war! What war? The war wasn't mine, it was hers. I hadn't died, there were no battles. I was here, I was always here, she could've come to me, spoken to me, she—" He stopped himself. Took a moment and said, a grain to his voice: "It's easier for you. To see her affection. She never had any reason to hold it back from you. God." He breathed a laugh. "You're so much like her."

Isabel nodded. "You think I'm soulless," she said. "That I don't know—"

"Of course I don't think you're—"

"I do know. I do know what it means to want. To—to only want—" She'd raised her voice and was sorry for it now. It started raining. Hendrik looked at her, startled, and she wanted to tell him—wanted to be done with it, make it someone else's burden. No one knew of her heart and no one knew of her grief and it was torture.

She closed her mouth and the rain came louder. They went inside, and Sebastian, who was reading at the kitchen table, pretended not to have heard everything. He said, "All right?" and Hendrik said, "No, no, it's raining, damn it."

When she left, she wished them both a safe trip—wished it tersely, wanted to mean it more than she did. Wanted to be softer than she was. Hendrik was quick with his hug, still sore over their falling-out, but still said: "You can come visit. You should. I've told you."

"Hm," she said, and her throat was tight, and the hallway blurry. She went down the stairs. Sebastian came after her then, quickly, and stopped her right as she was out the door—a hand to her arm. He seemed to want to say something. He opened his mouth, closed it. He was in his socks.

"What?" she said.

"You resent him. For coming with me."

"No."

"You don't approve."

"I—" He was still holding on to her. She was tired. She didn't want to cry in front of Sebastian. "You're lucky to have him, that's all. You should know that. That it's lucky, to have some-one with you. Please let me go."

He let her go. She knew there was something about that word, and how she said it—*lucky*. He stood on the bottom rung of the stairs, a little taller like this. They were both in the shadow, in the dark. "You seem to think you have so little in the world." She could see the twist of his mouth. "But you have so much. Much more than most of us."

She took a breath to argue and found that nothing came out: that her throat had closed up, that only a sound like a sob would leave her. She'd not heard him like this before—harsh. Almost reprimanding.

"He has regrets, you know," Sebastian added. "You could be kinder with him."

"He *left*," Isabel said. The word was wet.

"I know. But he regrets it. So do you, I imagine. It is what it is. It's done. Tomorrow we leave, what can you do. I am scared, what can I do."

He breathed in the dark of the hallway. Then she left, almost left, turned—reached out. His hand met hers halfway, a quick squeeze. His palm was warm. The house smelled like the two of them—Hendrik and Sebastian, the soap they used, the cologne they used, and Hendrik's habit of always opening one window and also a note of something else. Something that happens between bodies, close together, four walls and a roof.

Isabel took the train back home. She was rocked on the tracks. Her belly was hollow. There was a light on in the kitchen as she approached the house. A warm orange, and someone moving inside: the blur of a silhouette; shoulders, hair up in a tail. Isabel was arrested by it—stopped, heart tripping, a dull headache turning sharp. Her body had decided what was happening before the rest of her caught up. She walked, then ran, then pushed through the kitchen door. It overlapped, the scene of it: smell memory of something cooked, of the evening, of the fire in the hearth, the radio on, and a woman's body leaning over the table—a cloth in hand, cleaning the surface.

Neelke startled. Recovered, said hello. She seemed unsure of what to do next. Isabel had come in midbreath, midrun. Her pulse was in her teeth still. Neelke looked lovely in the low light, looked young and flushed and tired. Isabel recalled the evening she had come home and found Eva and Neelke here, here exactly, a bottle of wine and Eva laughing and touching Neelke's hair. They were having a conversation about how Neelke might cut it. Isabel had got so angry. She had sent Neelke away. Eva had called her a tyrant. Isabel had grabbed her, had grabbed her arm—had been reluctant to let go.

"I didn't—" Neelke started, stopped. She held the cloth in two hands before her. "I meant—to be done. I ran late."

Isabel didn't reply. She went to her. It was a dazed moment. Neelke shifted, stood differently—stood to attention. Stiff. Her blouse was red, tiny purple flowers, and was missing one little button: between her chest and her navel. She was wearing a white shirt underneath. Isabel, close and blurry-eyed and dizzy, held Neelke's face in her hands. It was such a small face. Her skin was soft, and warm. Eva would tilt up open-mouthed when held like this.

The fire crackled. Neelke breathed fast and audible. Isabel looked at her, and looked at her. She let her go. She sat down at the table and ran a hand over her face and dug her nails into her cheekbones.

Neelke said nothing. She moved quietly and washed the cloth. Wrung it out, hung it over the oven door. She made to leave. She was in her coat, at the door, when Isabel spoke up.

"Neelke—" she said. It came out like gravel. Neelke had been so quiet the week Isabel had fallen ill. She had occasionally sat by the bed as Isabel slowly ate her soup. She had asked about Eva once and had received no answer, and had not asked again. "Do you—" Isabel cleared her throat. "Are you alone? Do you have someone?"

Neelke didn't seem to catch the question at first. She worked a breath, confused, then said: "A boyfriend?" Her voice was so small.

Isabel looked at her. "A boyfriend."

Neelke blushed quickly. Her jacket was a dark green. "I do," she said.

"You do."

"Bas. Bas van der Laan." His full name, as if making sure he's real.

"Is he nice to you?"

"He—Yes."

Isabel took a breath. "You will not be here forever," she said.

Neelke looked out of her depth. Isabel said, "I'm not firing you. I'm only saying. You will go one day."

"I don't," Neelke said. "I don't know what—"

"It's all right. Go."

Neelke stood, hesitant, one hand on the door handle. She had made the kitchen a lovely place. Isabel could cry at it: at how a room could be made, and left behind, and turn terrible by way of absence. How a space could miss a person. How a person could stop—

"Good night," Isabel said.

Neelke waited several seconds, then left. Isabel listened to the new silence: the fire, the hum of the pipes. The vitrine was empty. The light from the fire reflected in the glass, and behind it—nothing. A shard, a single piece, and nothing.

Isabel had known Johan would show up eventually and then he did. Isabel would not let him in. He stood outside by his car parked on the gravel, his hands in his pockets and talking loudly at the house. There was a waver to his stance, and Isabel could imagine it: he'd been drinking with his friends in the city—then passed by Isabel's on his way back to his mother's. Isabel stood in the doorway, half inside, the door open just enough to answer him through it. If he came closer she would shut it.

"So you're not coming outside," he said. He sounded angry about it, or maybe he was being sarcastic, or was hurt. "You're afraid of me now?"

"It's not a good time, Johan," she said.

"I haven't seen you in a while," was his answer. "Your kitchen girl said you were sick."

Isabel tightened her hold on the door handle. "I was."

He made a sound. "You look fine to me now."

"I'm better. Yes."

He laughed. It wasn't a nice laugh. He leaned back against his car. He wasn't leaving quickly, not easily. He looked up from under the fall of his hair. "I thought we had a nice time," he said. "Didn't we have a nice time, Isabel?"

"You should leave," Isabel said, and Johan said, "Wait wait wait—" and made as though to go up to the door, and Isabel made to close the door—and he stopped. One foot up the step. The door was now only open a crack. Johan scoffed, took a step back, said louder than before:

"This hair doesn't suit you at all. Very unflattering."

"Why are you here?"

"Why am I—" He cut himself off with another laugh. He was moving, pacing. He had the energy of a poked animal—something that looked like annoyance but felt like danger. "Do you think you have options, Isabel?" he said, louder than before. "Do you think they're lining up? At your age? With your—" He sucked his teeth. "Tread carefully. I might leave. I might not come back."

"Yes," Isabel said, heart beating fast.

"Yes? Yes what?"

"Don't come back." She wanted to say it more clearly. It came out soft, and she didn't know whether he heard it at first, but he did: turning to the door with a sharpness, a wide-pupil eye. She saw only a sliver of him, was peering at him through the door crack.

He was silent. Then, "You wasted my time. You played with me."

"Please leave."

"Is that so?" He came to the door. She could smell the alcohol. "I don't think I will," he said, and Isabel closed the door quickly and he was there in a few strides—was banging on the wood. His shape was blurry through the glass panel. Isabel locked the door with fumbling hands and the sound of the key seemed to anger him more: rattling the handle, shouting to be let in. He called her arrogant, and a bitch, and asked her to come out, and said he only wanted to talk, and then put on a sweet voice again. Then—quiet.

Isabel was rooted to the spot for a moment. She couldn't see him anymore. She thought he was going to the car at first, and then realized—and ran. To the kitchen. She got there just in time, just as he was rounding the house and coming up to the back door. She locked the door and yelped, startled, when he tried to rattle that door, too. She stepped away.

"Why don't you send out that girlfriend of yours instead?" he called through the window, his hand an oily stain on the glass. He looked a terror like this, hair mussed, face red. He said, "She was much nicer than you. Nicer to look at, too. Send her out, I want to say something to her. Send her out. Send her—"

Isabel went to the living room and closed all the curtains and stood in the middle of the room. Johan stood outside for a while. He shouted some more terrible things. Isabel turned on the radio as loud as it went, and then covered her ears, shut her eyes tightly.

It was a long time before she opened her eyes, uncovered her ears. The noise had stopped. On the radio, a song: it was a bop, a lyric that went, *I'd bounce to you, I'd bounce bounce bounce!*

Isabel pushed aside the curtains to peek. It had passed the dark turn of evening, and the pale twilight was only a very far strip. Johan's car was gone. Johan was gone.

That night, Isabel did not fall asleep in her own bed. She did not change out of her clothes. She lay herself down in her mother's bed and did not think of it as Mother's bed. She got under the sheets and held the pillow tightly to her face.

She dreamt of dark homes with the lights off and people banging on windows and doors wanting to get in. She was very young and Eva was very young, and she was outside, crying. Someone's voice was loud and whispered at the same time, and Isabel crawled under a table. Eva called her name. Isabel covered her ears. She startled awake, choked by the top button of her dress.

She couldn't get it to open. She couldn't get it off. She pulled, and pulled, and the dress tore and she shimmied out of it—gasping, gagging.

Autumn had barely entered, barely taken off its coat, but the air smelled like winter already. Outside the café people bustled by and pulled clouds of breath behind them. Coats and hats and umbrellas held like walking sticks; the streets were slippery with last night's cold snap, and across the street a vendor blew on his gloveless hands.

Louis was silent for a long time. He'd been late, and then when he arrived he gave Isabel a quick kiss on the head and announced that he would not be able to stay long—had other things to do, had a long list of errands, had his girl waiting back at home—and so Isabel said what she had come to say. He sat down, and she said what she had come to say: what she wanted, and what he must do to give it to her.

"Isabel . . ." he said now, and Isabel looked back to him. He said her name like an admonishment. "Isabel," again. "What's this? Are you—insecure? Uncertain?"

She did not follow. "Insecure?"

"That you will not find a man? Isabel, you will. If you try a little, I'm sure you will. Dress nicely, give a few compliments, it's really—Look in the paper. There's always men looking for women in the paper. I'm sure you'll find someone nice, Isabel, and when you marry your man he won't want to—" A waiter came by for Louis's order. He ordered a coffee, sat back in his chair. Wiped the sweat from his upper lip. He'd been rushing and still looked hot from his commute. He said, "What man wants to move into his wife's home? No, no. He'll want to start a life for the two of you. He'll want to buy, build, not—"

"I will not marry," said Isabel.

"Isabel. Come now, what's—"

"I will never marry. I'm telling you."

"Don't say that," he said. "You don't know that." His coffee arrived. He used pincers to put in the sugar cubes: three. He said, "You just need to get out more. Don't you have—friends? To take you out? Of course you're never going to meet anyone cooped up in that depressing—"

"Hendrik," Isabel said, "will never marry."

He stopped stirring his coffee. His eyes were sunken, milky gray. They were her eyes, too. He said, "Hendrik . . . Isabel. Hendrik . . ."

"I will never marry," she said.

"That's not the same. You know that's not the same. You know why he . . ." Louis glanced around. He did that when Hendrik's life came up: as if someone might hear and come to some conclusion, and he would have to explain something. Get in some kind of trouble.

Isabel said it again: "Louis. I will *never* marry. Hendrik will never marry and I will never marry. Do you understand?" She reached out quickly—unplanned, desperate, placed her hand over Louis's where it rested on the table. She gripped it, hard. "Do you understand?"

Louis stared. His eyes were restless, back and forth. A flush rose: over his jaw, his neck. He swallowed. He looked at where her hand covered his, then back to her.

She said, "Give me the house."

He opened his mouth, closed it.

Isabel leaned in. She wanted to bare her teeth. *"Please,"* she said.

Louis did not respond. Eventually, he pulled his hand from under hers—held it in his own hand as if she'd hurt him. As if she'd squeezed too tightly. Isabel sat back, breathless, hot under her collar, under her arms.

Louis exhaled, slow and long. He looked out the window. A couple walked by: she was short, a fur coat. He was tall, noticeably tall, and had to lean down a little to hear her talk; she pushed herself flush against him. Smiled up at him. Her lipstick was on her teeth.

"Louis," Isabel said.

Louis put a hand to his forehead, closed his eyes. He had their father's hair: thick and upright. Mother used to tell a story that Louis, four years old, had cried a full evening because he could not be a dog—could not turn into a dog. He had somehow got it in his head that people could turn into the thing they wanted: dogs, birds, airplanes.

"Louis," she said again.

"Yes, just—" He took a breath. "A minute. Give me a minute." The coffee steamed between them. Louis said, "I need just a minute."

14

JANUARY LOWERED ITSELF OVER AMSTERDAM AND
would not rise again. The clouds stayed close to building tops
and yesterday's snow would not be willed away, it turned to
sludge and turned to ice in the drains. Isabel stood and shook.
She could not cross the street. She held her purse with two hands
and said, "No, no," to herself, walked away, walked back. She
made to step onto the road, and then a tram whooshed by in a
rush—honking, wheels throwing up a wall of water, ice. Isabel
scrambled back and held a hand over her heart.

Traffic slowed. Isabel crossed the road.

It was a slim building, a storefront with fogged-up windows.
And below it the basement apartment had one small pane peeking out at street level and a lowered staircase behind a railing.
The lights were on down there. People walked by, and continued
to walk by, and Isabel had to move or get out of the way altogether.

The stairs to the basement were slippery. She rang the bell
and heard it as loudly outside as it sounded inside. She retreated
several steps, did not breathe.

Eva opened the door. She was wearing two jumpers, one over
the other. A pair of tights and socks. A scarf around her shoulders like a shawl. Her face was a blotchy red from the cold. Isabel's chest clenched like a vise and did not let up. Eva looked

tired and confused and then on seeing Isabel—evened out. A blank sheet. She had let the bleached hair grow out, or had dyed it back, or had cut it off and let it return as it wanted: brown, frizzing around her ears. It made her look shorter somehow. Her hair, and how she stood there, with Isabel looking down at her from halfway up the basement stairs.

"Ah," Eva said, and swallowed. "You found me."

Isabel could not reply. Eva's voice was as familiar to her as her own. She stared. Behind her the crowd did not let up, footsteps in the snow, bikes, trolleys, a loud tram pushing through it all.

"Have you come to call the police on me?" Eva asked. She had begun to shiver. "Are they on their way? Have you come to watch the show?"

"No," Isabel said. "No, I . . ." And then, "Eva," only to feel out the shape of her name. To look at her and say her name. She had agreed with herself, before coming, what she was allowed, what she was not allowed. It made no difference now she was here, she already knew. Her mouth would not be her own. It would say what it wanted.

Eva said, "Who was it?"

"Who was . . . ?"

"Who told you where to find me."

"Eva," Isabel said. "I only want—"

"*Who*," Eva said, and Isabel held her purse close, held the shape of the book within it and said, "I went to—the store. De Leeuw. Someone there knew where you'd—"

Eva turned sharp. "De Leeuw?" And then a sound like she had a question, cut it off, understood: "You read my diary."

Isabel tried to move quickly but it was cold and she was warm under her coat and her hands did not go as she wanted them to go. She fumbled. She got the book out of the purse. She held it out to Eva. She said, "I realized too late. I only—I wanted, I mean to—"

Eva took it from her and walked inside and left the door open and spoke as she went, "Well, I suppose you've come for your stuff, then. You won't get them. You can fight me if you'd like. Should we fight? I might be able to take you. Should we try? Might as well. You can call the police after all, I don't care much, you can fight me if you'd like."

The apartment was a matchbox, a doll's house. Isabel had to duck to get through the doorway. A kitchen by the window, a table by the back door. A corner for a bed. The sheets were mussed. A red gauze had been draped over a lampshade. The space smelled like Eva. Like her, and like cigarettes, and like oil fried with the windows closed.

There was something of a garden out back: a single square meter of concrete. A dead plant in a snow-filled pot. A jar for cigarette butts. Eva, wrapped in knits, opened the back door and leaned against the post: lit a cigarette, blew out the smoke. She'd tossed the diary onto the table.

Isabel stood lost in the middle distance in her coat and muddy heels and said nothing. The house was cold. There was a heater in the corner and it was turned off. Isabel tried to consider Eva, tried to consider her face and her health and found she couldn't, found she had to look away. Found that love was a sickly thing that punished you for each step you took in its direction.

"You cut your hair," Eva said. Then, into the next silence: "God, to look at you," and then she, too, looked away. Spoke to the dead plant outside her door: "It suits you."

It could have been an insult as much as a compliment. Eva smoked half her cigarette, unmoving. Isabel stood and stood. Then she stepped forward: took the packet out of her purse, placed it on the table. Placed it next to the diary.

"Have you brought me a gift now? How kind," she said. She was trying to be mean about it, but it came out strained. Isabel watched her take the packet, watched her unwrap it. She held her smoke between two knuckles, and the plume rose and lingered under the ceiling. Eva had a palmful of brown paper and in its heart: a piece of china. A sharp cutoff, a shard of a thing. Blue flowers along the inch of a rim, the suggestion of a hare's leg where the crockery had broken.

My cousin got a hare, Eva had told her once. *A stormy day at the lake. A terrible idea, of course, to keep a hare inside a house. It jumped around from room to room, into the garden, scared for its life. Gosh. Got up on the table somehow. Smashed a few plates . . .*

Eva's throat worked. She licked her lips, twice, put the thing back on the table.

"So what is this," Eva said. "You're not here to fight? You've come to apologize? You've come to weep at my feet and beg for forgiveness?" She added a laugh. She made to take a drag of her smoke and found it had gone out. She said, "I was born there. Did you know? You do now. You've read it. My father bought the house. He was a principal at a school. He died in the camps. He didn't pay his mortgage because he died in the camps. That's why the house was sold—because he didn't pay his mortgage. Because he died."

"I—" Isabel held back. She pressed her teeth together. She said, "I didn't know. Not a thing. I didn't know a thing."

"I know. I know you didn't. Isn't that funny? No one ever knows anything in this country. No one knows where they live, who did what, who went where. Everything is a mystery. Knowledge is elusive. People disappear in the night and—"

"I'm not speaking in riddles. I truly—I truly didn't know, Eva, I—" Her voice was thick, and Eva heard it, said:

"I apologize! Have I upset you?" Eva clucked her tongue. "So sorry."

There was no speaking of it. Eva was wrapped in thorns. Isabel closed her eyes tightly, opened them again. Said, "Why didn't you—" She stopped. She tried again, and the first words broke: "Why like that. Why Louis. It didn't have to be him, you could've come to the house, I would've—we could've met like that. You could've said, explained, I would've—"

"You forget," she cut in. "You forget, Isabel. I came to you as—as *family* and you despised me on sight. God!" She laughed. "Imagine if I would've come to you as a stranger!"

"I wouldn't have sent you away."

"Wouldn't you? Truly, Isabel? Be truthful. Be truthful about who you were when we met. Don't pretend."

A gust of wind whirled itself into the nook of the basement garden. It made the dusting of snow dance up, around. Eva closed the door, locked it. The sound of the city dampened. Eva's mouth was red and chapped. She looked unwell. Isabel recalled: Kissing Eva in the car outside the house. Biting the heel of her hand. Eva saying, *Let's go.* Isabel saying, *Inside?* And Eva saying: *Sure. Inside. Sure.*

Isabel sat down at the table. Her coat was big and awkward in the small space. She said, "Did you mean it?" She said, "Any of it?"

Eva was still leaned against the door. She had her arms around herself, holding on to the scarf. "Any of what?"

"Louis," Isabel said. "Me."

Eva laughed, a short and cruel sound. "Isabel," she said, as if chastising a dramatic child. Then, "Do you really want to know?"

"Yes."

"Don't just say yes. Think about it."

Isabel looked up at her. She let her heart drop. She said, "Yes."

"No," she said, harsh, on purpose. Then, on a harsh breath, leaving her all at once: "Yes. God, what do you ask me? You've

read it. You know—you know what I . . ." Her eyes were down.
"Louis liked me. I thought—perhaps this is what's meant to happen. Perhaps this is how I get it back. All of it, all of it. Not just
parts, not just crumbs, two spoons and a knife, all of it. The house
would be his, and maybe . . . it could be . . ." She took a breath.
Squared herself. "But that wasn't what was meant to happen at
all, was it. God, I was stupid. I ruined it all. I should've never . .
." She smiled something private and terrible.

"Should've never what?"

Eva looked at her. "You know what."

"Why did you?"

Eva opened her mouth, closed it. A tremor, the dimpling of
her chin. She looked like she might cry. She said louder than
before: "Oh, I don't know, Isabel. You were there, you . . ." She
decided not to finish her sentence. She shook her head, looked at
things around the room: the table, the bed, the ceiling. She was
trying not to look at Isabel. She said to the lampshade covered in
gauze: "You see, when you spend a very long time being—being
quite invisible, really, and quiet, then . . . You see—" A halted
word. "I thought you saw me. For a second there."

Isabel was quiet. A hand was squeezing at her throat.

Eva said, "I was wrong about you, too. You saw nothing."

Isabel's voice came out like an upturned barrel: "No, I—I did,
I do, Eva, I—"

"You saw me? You saw what you wanted to see. A stupid girl.
And then you saw—I don't know. Something you could have.
And then you thought I was a thief and then you did what you
were always going to do. What you've always done to people like
me." She said, "You sent me away."

The back of Isabel's hand was pinched red. She wanted to
argue and she couldn't, wouldn't, was nauseous and the air
did not do what it was meant to do, going in. Coming out. She

wanted to leave, she never wanted to leave, she wanted to sit there and sit there and wait until something broke.

She said: "Come to the house." She said, "Eva. There's—something I want to—" She swallowed. "To give you."

Eva's expression was bewilderment. She started walking. There wasn't much space to walk, and so the steps were halted, awkward: from the door to the foot of her bed to the wall. She said, "I won't—I can't, I won't go back there, I can't, it's—"

Isabel stood. The chair scraped over the floor.

Eva said, "You don't know, what it's—To have and to lose and have and lose over and over—"

It did not take a big gesture to reach for her. She was, in the end, so close. Isabel took her in her arms and Eva pushed and sobbed and Isabel tugged and Eva pulled and then pushed and then held: twisted hands in Isabel's shirt. She fit into Isabel's neck. She fit perfectly. Isabel held her by the back of her head, held her by her ribs, shook and kissed what was near: her cheekbone, her ear, the dear line of her ear.

Eva breathed unevenly. Isabel said, "Eva." Held her closer, said, "Eva, Eva." Said, "I'm so sorry. Eva, can't you see? Can't you see how I—What I'd do for you. How I'd—" She swallowed, felt the bobbing of her own throat against Eva.

Eva calmed. She pulled away enough to look. "How you'd what?"

Isabel wanted to tighten her grip. She didn't. She counted the seconds. She said, "I want to die at the thought of anything hurting you."

Eva was so near. There was smoke on her breath, the coffee, the winter's sleep, and the heat of her skin. She put her forehead to Isabel's chin. "And what if that's you?" she said. "The thing that hurts? What if—it's who you are? What if it's where you come from and—"

247

Isabel turned her face down: to be closer. To feel the words with the heat of her mouth.

Eva whispered, "What will you do then?"

Isabel's hands under the wings of Eva's shoulders. She could not answer. She could touch: Eva's back, her face, the bruised skin under her eye. Eva leaned into it, leaned into her, and then went from her. Turned her back and stepped away—a hand to the table. The space was so small and they were still in touching distance. There was a wall right there. Eva could not walk away.

"Please leave," Eva said.

Isabel grimaced. "Eva."

"Leave," Eva said. The scarf had fallen from her shoulders, and now she was only a tight line of a neck. Three holes in her jumper: two near the collar, one over her spine—in the middle, exactly so. She said, "You have to leave."

The distant sound of the upstairs shop door opening and closing. A young child was being told to calm down in order to be lifted back in its pram. The child would not: it screamed and cried and said, *No no no no no no!*

The house was cold. The back of Isabel's hand hurt. She opened her mouth for words, and no words could come. She stood there for a long while, lost, and then did as she was told. She left.

The house did not greet her. It kept its eyes turned from her, ashamed. She accepted it. She did not turn on the lights. Outside, the snow kept on falling. She took off her coat, lit a fire in the kitchen, and made herself small before it.

And then: one quiet and freezing morning Isabel went for a walk. The trees stood bare and skeletal and beautiful with their fingers all crystal and white. The frost had made everything a crunch, the pastures and the fields and the gravel paths. The canals had frozen over. Isabel tested one with her foot and found it solid, and then stood on it in wonder: a miracle, she thought, to stand so solidly on what could also engulf you.

The sun came up slow and blushing, a misty pink. In the distance, a farm where a few sheep were making do with frozen grass. Two looked up at her. She stood, and waited, and looked back.

She went back home. She banked the fire and let it warm her fingers back to life. The house was as empty as a house could get these days. Neelke had stopped coming. She and Bas had gone to city hall and had married on a drab Monday morning; the registration costs were lower on a Monday. On her last day with Isabel, Neelke had brought with her a list of names, of girls she knew from town who would make for good help; then Isabel had said, "Walk me through your tasks," and Neelke had given her a look that said: *It's you who gives me my tasks.*

Still, she did. They went from the kitchen to the living room, they considered the curtains and the duster and the oil that needed to be applied to the staircase railing. They went through the linens and the name of the washer who did the job in town, they went through the bathroom and the beds and the silver and the windows.

Isabel said, "It's quite a lot, isn't it."

And Neelke, with a frown, said: "It's a house." She said, "There's always a lot to do in a house."

The list was still on the table where Neelke had left it. Isabel had looked at the names and had made a note to contact a few; she had meant to set up an interview and she had not. She would have to, eventually: the dust was collecting more quickly than she knew how to manage, the bathroom had grown into its mildew faster than she expected, and her dinners were always one of two things: cooked too soft or not cooked enough.

Her hands were sore these days.

The day began. She sat in the study and replied to Uncle Karel's solicitor and then to one of Louis's more practical letters, and then sent a word of thanks in response to a postcard from Neelke and Bas: they had gone up to one of the islands for a honeymoon holiday. A picture of a lighthouse. On the back it said, in Neelke's self-conscious school scrawl: *Hearty Greetings, Neelke & Bas*

She went to town and sent out her mail and picked up the linen from the cleaner's. She went by the grocer's, she went by the cheese farmer, she turned onto the Schoutenstraat on her way to her car and came to a standstill. She had seen the synagogue before. She had seen it as she had seen most buildings in Zwolle: as places that were either there for her or not there for her. The post office, broad and surrounded by trees: for her. The bright cafés, the ones where women sat: for her. The church was for her, some stores were for her.

The synagogue, an undefined broad facade between two streets, had not been for her. With its red brick and inlaid windows and a wrought iron fence it sat like a bad taste, a bad memory of something old. She had walked by it before and had quickened her pace. She had tried not to think of it too much, she did not wonder at the people behind its doors—how many of them were left at all. The lettering above the windows looked frightening: she did not know what it meant, what it said. It could mean anything. She could not read it and it could mean anything.

She considered it now again. The frost had touched it as it did all the other houses in the street: fogged up its windows, pulled tight over its doors. Glistened on the brick. To its left, a narrow family home. To its right, another home, this one broader, taller. Attached, it was, to everything that touched it.

The Hebrew scripture was inlaid in what once must have been a gold-painted stone but was now graying, dull. She stepped closer. In Roman letters, the quote announced itself: Isaiah, 56:7. Isabel drove back home. Her Bible she kept in her room, on her shelf. The little hare leaned its little back against it.

Isabel found the quote. *For my house will be called,* she read, finger next to the number seven, *a house of devotion for all.*

She sat on the edge of her bed. She touched the page, and it was thin, and the letters so black against the grain of the paper. She touched the word *house*. She touched the word *devotion*.

She put the Bible away and went downstairs to finish the day: to sweep the rooms and wash this morning's dishes and peel potatoes for dinner. Inside her the words repeated themselves, tumbled around: *my house, my house, my house,* echoed with her hands in a bucket of suds; *devotion devotion devotion,* a loop, drying a single knife. A single fork. A small teaspoon, its twisted neck; its drop of a head.

Night fell quickly. She fed the fire, turned on the radio. She poured herself a glass of wine and sat by the hearth with a half-eaten plate; potatoes, beans. A cut of meat, burnt and tough. She lifted her skirts and lowered her stockings and opened her legs and let them warm by the grate. Her knees were red and bruised easily. They looked to her like hard fruit gone bad. Someone knocked on the door.

The house held its breath. Isabel thought she had not heard it right, that it was the knock of a branch against a window or something that had fallen in the other room. She sat very still and listened.

The knock came again. Thrice in a row.

Isabel pulled up her socks, pushed her skirt in order. She went to the door. The wine had gone to her head too quickly and she felt flushed, unsteady. Again: a knock. It wasn't urgent, wasn't a demand, simply an interval of a thing. *I am here*, it said. *Come to me.*

Through the glass Isabel could see the shape of her, short in a big winter coat, rubbing herself warm on the stair before the door. For a moment Isabel thought that she had made it up; that she had fallen asleep by the fire and was dreaming the walk from the hallway to the door. But the cold was biting here, and her belly too hollow and the dread too sharp to be any sort of fantasy.

She opened the door.

"I walked from the station," Eva said. Her teeth were chattering. She was in a hat but the ends of her hair that peeked out below had frozen. Her shoes weren't winter shoes. She laughed and said, "I didn't—think, God this was a bad idea, oh God I should—"

She made as if to turn, as if to go away, and Isabel reached out and didn't touch her—was careful this time. "No," she said. "No, please—please don't go. Please. Come in. You're—you're freezing, come in."

It was very quiet outside. It was quiet inside, too. Isabel could barely hear the whine of the radio from the kitchen. It started to snow, faint and so soft. It would gain in force tonight. It would blanket the garden. The earth was frozen solid and the snow would stay.

Isabel said, "The fire is on in the kitchen."

The light from inside the house spilled out low and orange. Eva's eyes were shiny.

They went inside. Isabel felt pulled to the left of her body, not quite there—floating. She took Eva's coat. Eva shivered. She was in the same two jumpers, the ones with the holes. The hems of her trousers were wet. Her shoes were wet.

She was a body needing to be held but Isabel was not allowed to hold her. Isabel walked ahead, Eva half a step behind her. She thought: *What if I try to take her hand?* But Isabel was not allowed to take her hand. The kitchen was warm. Isabel went to turn down the radio, went to clear her dinner and put it on the counter, went to get something for Eva, didn't know what. Said, "Please, sit. Do you—want some tea? Or—wine? I have . . ."

Eva stood, stranded, between the fire and the table. She looked around her, sad. A wry smile like she wanted to make fun of something: herself, the room. The shivering hadn't lessened when she sat down. Said, "Wine," a flat word.

Isabel reached for a glass and now knew what it meant to be so distracted by another's presence, distracted with her heart in her throat and in her ears and her very fingertips. Now she knew of that suffering, too. She poured the wine, miserable. She gave Eva the wine and found that her heart had not grown any lighter over the months, had not grown any lighter at the sight of Eva. She loved her. She might always.

Eva did not drink right away. She extended her hands toward the fire. Isabel wondered if she had done so as a child, sitting where she was. Eva could see, from where she sat, across to the dining room: the glass cabinet. Isabel saw the moment she noticed it, and noticed it was empty, and said nothing of it and so Isabel volunteered, gestured at the corner of the room: "I wrapped them up. For you. And—and other things. They're in boxes. If you—if you'd like—"

"Ah. Is that what you wanted me here for?" Eva said. "Is that what you wanted to give me? Boxes?" She turned to Isabel. "Did you want to send me off with boxes?"

It was as though someone pulled Isabel's breath from her lungs: quick and harsh and like a cough. "No," she started, but Eva would not let her answer, added a fast:

"Packed it all away. Very neat, very efficient. Can't imagine

you wanted all of that lying around, now knowing who it belonged to, knowing—"

"That's not true," Isabel said. Eva was not listening. She continued, not looking at Isabel, looking instead at the room, at the
boxes:

"Was it very terrible, lately, sleeping in a bed you knew wasn't
yours? Eating from plates that weren't yours? I imagine it was.
Oh, I imagine you hated it, or—no, maybe you did not care at all.
Maybe you didn't feel a thing. Maybe you slept like a babe, slept
right through the night, how peaceful! God, why am I here? I
shouldn't—I shouldn't have—"

"I'm glad you came," Isabel said.

"Glad!"

"No—" Isabel saw now, there was nothing for her to say. "Yes,
I—have missed you. I wanted to say, how I—regret—"

But Eva was not listening. She was riling herself up, speaking
over Isabel, speaking faster, saying, "You remember—do you? Do
you remember? When we stood right there, right there, Mum
and I—" She meant the window, she meant outside, the pathway
to the house. "Did you hear that? Did you remember that? She
begged. She begged for her house back and where—" She looked
at Isabel now. "Where were you?"

The room had gone blurry, a wet film. It was not a true question: they both knew where Isabel had been. Still, Isabel answered, a quiet "I was—young. I was—"

"And what was I?" Eva said. "What was I, do you imagine?"

"I know," Isabel said, and she did—knew it in her bones, in
her marrow, had been haunted by it for weeks, months. Eva, a
teen wrapped in her own arms, outside by the bush, waiting as
her mother screamed to be let in, to have her house back. Eva before the war, a child, collecting her things in a box, colored pen-
cils and a doll with long hair and a little stuffed animal of a hare.

"Do you?" Eva said. "What do you know?" She worked a word in her mouth—almost speaking, then all at once the rambling fire left her. She sat back in her chair, a tremble in her—held the back of her hand to her eyes. The fire crackled. A log broke and fell, and the flame rose dramatically—then quieted. Isabel said, "Eva."

"Eva, Eva, she says. What is it, what do you want, what could you possibly want from me now, God, haven't I given—haven't I—"

"Ask me again."

She faltered. It came out on a breath: "What?"

"Ask me again."

"Ask you what?"

"What I'd do. Ask me again."

Eva's mouth was parted. She had not drunk the wine though it looked like she had; a dark inside of a lip. A shine. A flush was coming up now, up her neck, her cheeks; the heat coming back into her body.

Isabel went to her. Isabel went to her knees. Isabel held Eva by her shins and put her face to Eva's sodden hems. She wanted to stay. She wanted to be allowed to stay. She didn't know how long the moment lasted. The radio was a soft blur and the fire a warm brick at her back and all she knew was the hard press of Eva's legs. She had sat like this as a child, under tables with her hands over her head, as per instruction when the bombs fell. She was afraid then. She was afraid now, too.

"Isabel," Eva said. It was quiet, and softer. She sounded lost. She put a cold hand to Isabel's hair, shakily, pushed at her, said, "Isa. Isabel, come now. Isabel. Get up, no."

Isabel looked up. She did not move away. Eva hesitated, then touched her face. Her cheek. "What terrible ideas you have," she said. "What a terrible thing to ask me to return here."

255

Isabel put her face to Eva's palm and hid there. She said, "The house."

Eva's touch stilled. Isabel did not look at her. She remained in hiding. She said, "I have arranged it. It will go to me. It's done, and I want . . . You should live here. In your house."

"Isabel."

"It's mine. And it's yours. If you want it."

Eva rested a finger at the corner of Isabel's eye. She rested it there until Isabel looked at her. The room was blurry at first. Eva was blurry. And then Isabel blinked and everything sharpened: Eva's sad tilt of a mouth, the way she sat, as if she was in pain—a wound to her waist. She held Isabel like one might hold a dear pet at their feet: cradled in a palm.

"Yours," Eva repeated.

"No," Isabel said. "I only—I wanted, it could be—"

"Mine. If I want it."

Isabel felt she had said it wrong, again. That she had meant the one thing and said the other thing without understanding the difference.

"What does that mean?" Eva asked. "Yours or mine? What are you saying?"

"I'm sorry. I don't . . ."

"Do you mean to trick me?" Eva was so close. Her voice was so small. "That to have the house, I must have you, too?"

Isabel shook *no*. Went up on her knees, said, "No," said, "No, no."

"So I can have the house?" She, too, was shivering. "And you will leave if I ask? You will give me the house?"

"I don't—" Isabel's hands fisted into the fabric of Eva's skirt. "I can only . . . It will go to me, when he passes, that is all I can do. I can—I cannot leave, I have nowhere else, but you can have anything. All of it. Or not, if you don't want it, or me, if you will.

Will you?" Said, "Have me? Will you have me?" She said, "Have me. Have me."

"Have you," she repeated, quiet-sounding, bewildered. "And you?"

"I—"

"You'll have me? Send me away again? I can't—"

"I won't," Isabel said.

"You will."

"No," Isabel said, and took Eva's hand and pressed it—over her chest, pressed it flat, held it there. She wanted to say, *It is done*. She wanted to convey, translate it, how there was nothing else for her now. She didn't know how to, and so she stayed like that: pressing Eva's hand harder against herself.

A wobbly laugh left Eva. "Is that the promise you give me?" she said. "Is that the guarantee I have?"

Isabel closed her eyes so would not have to see whatever came next. She did not think she could witness it.

"This fleeting thing? This changeable thing?"

"Yes."

"Look at me."

Isabel looked at her. Eva kissed her. It was a hard press of lips over teeth, it was angry. Eva was still weeping. "I'll never leave," she said. "Do you understand? You leave before I do. If I stay, if I'm yours then you can never—"

The chair scraped and Eva was on her knees, too, and Isabel held Eva under the fall of her hair and they swayed. Isabel spoke, muffled and lost between their mouths, said Eva's name and asked to be had and said, "Love, my love, my love." And, "Let me," she said. "Let me. My love. Let me try."

257

Morning rose in the quiet chord of winter's pink. The snow had silenced the world: the two evergreens in silhouette, the vegetable garden only a relief of a fence. *Remembering the house when it snowed*, Eva had written in her diary. *The sound of snow falling from the branches like a muffled word. Hmph! The sun in the mornings and the shadows of the trees on the curtain.*

Isabel knew the scene like from a dream; knew it from childhood, knew it from every winter she had spent in the house. And now she knew it through Eva's eyes, too, an echo of the same story. A new key for an old tune.

Isabel stood by the window and looked out. Eva's touch was a soft one, first, two fingers to the dip of her spine in hello: *I'm here*, it said, *don't startle*. Isabel did not startle. She knew Eva was there, knew she had approached. She would never not know. She would never leave a room again and not leave half of her behind.

She turned her face to the side and Eva stepped in closer, her body warm to Isabel's back—hands sleep-soft over Isabel's belly. Eva had to go to her toes to kiss the hinge of Isabel's jaw. Isabel could only see the blur of her hair from here; the slope of her nose, the rise of her cheek. It was not enough. Isabel turned in her arms to have more of her.

Eva tilted her face up. Isabel bent toward her, bent to what was offered—a gift.

כִּי בֵיתִי בֵּית תְּפִלָּה
יִקָּרֵא לְכָל הָעַמִּים

Isaiah 56:7

Acknowledgments

In 2021, my grandfather passed away very suddenly, and then my grandmother—two days later, across the world—not so suddenly. It was a terror of a week. In a car on the way to one of the funerals the idea for this book came to me like a shudder. It felt, still feels, like a parting gift. Opa, the kindest of us all. Safta, the brightest. From my deepest, thank you.

To the brilliant Anna Stein: you called my book rare, which I then told my therapist, who made me write the word on a post-it and stick it to my mirror. How embarrassing, it's still up there, I read it every day. Thank you for changing my life. To my UK agent, Karolina Sutton, whom I adore: what a dream to be chosen by you. To Lauren Wein, my US editor: I can't imagine kinder or more capable hands. Sorry for the beats, thank you for absolutely everything. Isabel Wall, my UK editor: you have achieved an impressive feat, that is—making me believe that everything is going to be all right. More than that, that it's going to be great. How clever are you? To everyone at Viking and Avid Reader, for their faith. Especially: Jofie Ferrari-Adler and Amy Guay. Big thanks to Jessica Chin and Jane Elias for copyediting. God bless copyeditors, who would we be without you. A massive round of applause to the team that has sent this book all around the world and also answered my endless barrage of emails: Claire Nozieres, Zoe Willis, Julie Flanagan, and Will Watkins.

To my Dutch literary home, Uitgeverij Chaos, that I once

helped built and to which I now get to return. To Sayonara, who I met for the first time at nineteen at a laser-game party, and then again, ten years later, at a bookstore. The second time bound us for life. My eternal cheerleader, thank you, just try and get rid of me now. And Thalia, my rock: it wasn't real until I got you on the phone. You said, 'It's happening', and only then it was happening. You make things feel true. To Daniël, Marscha, Frank, Isabel, and Bowi: what a gift you are.

I owe the greatest debt to all those who read this book in its various stages of completion and weighed in: Yumi, my very first reader; you sat on this couch and I sat on the floor and I told you, 'And then Eva says: "It's not yours to give."' And you showed me your goosebumps. I will never forget that moment. To Alice Winn: I owe you several life-debts. How did I find you! What are the odds! Thank you for St. Augustine and the pears. People won't stop talking about the pears, they're a great hit. You're a genius but I'm trying to be cool about it. To Mikaella Clements: oh, you know why. You made this book come alive; thank you for Hendrik and Sebastian, thank you for being sure of this when I wasn't. To Rebecca Kantor, for your good heart and your sharp eye—if only we lived in the same city! To Onjuli Datta: you were the first to say, 'it's done, just send it', and it was terrifying and thrilling. I don't think you know how much I look up to you, and it meant the world! To Steven and Michelle, for your generosity and time and expertise. To Amarantha, my love, my best girl, may you have this one. To Anna, I still see you through the kitchen window, reading, basking in the sun. Estrella, for Ezra, for all that came before this. To Siobhon: there's no reader like you. May I pass everything I ever write through you first? And Francis, oh Francis: you fixed things I didn't know needed fixing. To Emory, too, for everything I didn't get to read in the group chat. To Blue, z"l: I think you would've liked this one.

To Simone Atangana Bekono: for letting me pick your mind for gems, for letting me have an absolute meltdown on your couch. To Daphne Huisden, the only person who thought this book was hilarious. To Marga Minco, z"l, whose short story, "Het Adres", inspired the bones of this novel. To the awe-inspiring Michal Citroen for her extensive research into how post-war Netherlands treated Jewish people who returned from the camps (*U word door niemand verwacht*). To everyone who let me write in their homes, who fed me, who let me weep near or in their arms: Silvana, Ankie, Riva. Thank you! You have done a very good deed indeed. To Kimberley and Laura: you're my people, there's nothing else to it, I love you so much. You knew I'd get here long before I did. To everyone that summer in Limburg: thank you for making Isabel's house a real place.

To all of my students, young and old: you've brought me so much joy. Thank you for letting me talk books at you.

To Longleaf Review, who in 2020—March, just as the lockdown started—organized an online writing workshop 'on silence'. One assignment read, 'write a scene around a major elephant in the room'. I opened a document, titled it, 'siblings go out for dinner', wrote the opening sentence, 'no one knew where Louis had dug up this girl', and then forgot about it for a full year. Isn't that a good reminder? Maybe that note you just scribbled down will end up being the heart of a story.

And of course, to my family, whom I love so much, for whom I barely have the words. Ima, papa: sorry for the time when I was nine and you tried to get me into reading and I said I couldn't because 'the letters were so small and boring'. I just wanted to play outside, but I get it now. I am humbled by how much you believe in me. Tamar and Shira: the first interesting thing I ever did was be your sister. I am bursting with pride for you. Anything meaningful this book has to say about siblings and dogs comes from us. Thank you all for not talking to me about chapter 9, you're very respectful people.

Also: thanks, Utrecht-Maastricht morning train, you were quiet and you let me write; thank you, Utrecht-Berlin train, for the diary chapter; thank you to my landlord, for not fixing the leak for so long that a mushroom grew from my window sill—very inspiring.

About the Author

Yael van der Wouden is a writer and teacher. Her essay on Dutch identity and Jewishness, "On (Not) Reading Anne Frank", has received a notable mention in *The Best American Essays* 2018. She currently resides in the Netherlands, where she lectures in creative writing and comparative literature. *The Safekeep* is her first novel.